# A CHARIOTEER'S PROMISE

## ROMAN HEARTS SERIES BOOK TWO

### TANYA BIRD

*For Shannon*

*Have you seen the chariots pour from the barrier,*
    *rushing to attack the flat, competing headlong,*
*when young men's hopes are roused, and fear throbs,*
*draining each exultant heart? On they go with*
    *writhing whips,*
*bending forward to loosen the rein, the red-hot axle*
    *turns:*
*Now low, now lifted high, they seem to be carried*
*through the void, and leap into the air:*
*no delay, no rest: a cloud of yellow dust rises,*
*and they're wet with foam, and the breath of those*
    *pursuing:*
*so strong the desire for glory, so dear is victory.*

— PUBLIUS VERGILIUS MARO

# CHAPTER 1

May 4, 207 AD

*Y*ears of invisibility had taught Dulcia patience. No one paid attention to the quiet girl standing at the back of the queue with her eyes down. She was used to waiting while others pushed in front and would say nothing when they shouted over the top of her.

'And a dozen pears,' she said to the merchant, pointing to the fruit at the far end of the stall.

He nodded and loaded them into her basket two at a time. When he was done, he grabbed a handful of dried figs and threw those in also.

'For the walk home,' he said, winking as he handed her the basket.

It was around her sixteenth birthday when everything changed. About the time her hips widened and her breasts finally arrived.

Dulcia smiled at the man. He could afford to be generous

with his wife absent. It was the middle of the afternoon, and she was likely at home with the children.

She dropped the coins into his hand. 'Thank you. That is very kind.'

He kept hold of the basket. 'It's heavy. Will you be all right with it?'

She had been carrying baskets to and from the market since she was five years old. Did he really think in her nineteenth year it would suddenly be too heavy for her? 'I will be absolutely fine, thank you.' She gave the basket a gentle tug, pulling it from his grasp.

Turning away from the stall, she searched for her older sister amid the busy crowd, spotting her a few stalls down. Mila gave her a tired smile. She was the same vision of strength and beauty Dulcia had admired her whole life.

'Done?' Mila called over the noise.

Dulcia nodded and wandered over to where her niece stood scolding the twins running in circles around her. Giving up on words, Asha blocked Caius with her hip while Mila caught Atilius by the arm.

'I need cinnamon,' Dulcia said, bending to kiss the top of her nephew's head, 'but I figured you might know a spice man.' She tried to take Caius's hand, but he wriggled free of her grip. Three was a busy age.

Mila handed her basket to Asha and caught Caius with the expert grip of a mother. 'If you come by the apartment, you can take what you need.'

Dulcia reached for the figs in the basket and held them up so the boys could see them. They froze, eyes fixed on the dried fruit in her hand.

'Careful, they will tackle you to the ground,' Mila said, a smile in her tone.

'No they will not. They will hug me appreciatively, or I will hand them all to Asha to eat.'

Her niece giggled, enjoying being a part of the joke.

Two sets of arms wrapped her thighs, squeezing so tightly she almost lost her balance. 'Much better.' She dropped her basket to the ground so she could hug the chubby little boys, then handed out the fruit.

Mila ran her fingers through Caius's hair as he chewed, cheeks bulging. 'I hope Germana did not need those for a recipe.'

Dulcia rose and picked up her basket. 'They were a gift from the merchant.'

'Oh really?' Her tone was coy.

'The *married* merchant.'

Mila ushered the children towards the street. 'Best stay away from the married ones.' She looked both ways before stepping out. 'What happened to the apprentice brazier who was following you about the city a few months back?'

'Slight exaggeration.'

'Mother told me he waited outside the house for you.'

'Once. He did that one time.'

Mila glanced sideways at her sister. 'What was the matter with him?'

Dulcia shrugged and swapped the basket to the other hand. 'He had an odd smell about him.'

Mila rolled her eyes. 'I met him, and he smelled just fine.'

'Sometimes he spat when he spoke.'

Mila laughed. 'And the one before that?'

'Too old.'

'Too old?'

'He was a widower.'

'A very *young* widower, according to my sources.'

Dulcia pressed her lips together. 'I would have been better suited to a life of celibacy.'

'I do not doubt it, but you are not destined to be a vestal virgin, despite the company you keep.' Mila was referring to the priestess Licinia. The pair had formed an unlikely friendship over the years. 'Pity a priestess cannot come from a slave mother. I am certain Rufus would have volunteered you.' Mila called out to the boys to slow down as they darted between passers-by. 'Of course, I am secretly relieved. The vestals are nothing but scapegoats living in constant fear.'

Dulcia stepped out of the way of a group of women caught up in their conversation. 'Here it comes—'

'Independent and wealthy. No need of a husband.'

'I feel as though we have had this conversation—many times.'

'And yet they are at the mercy of the very men who grant them their *independence*.'

Before Dulcia could argue, she spotted Felix and Albaus coming towards them. A giant and a dwarf stood out in any crowd. She found herself looking past them, but Nero was not there. A bad feeling enveloped her.

The twins ran ahead, and Albaus bent down, catching one in each arm.

'Good catch,' Mila said once they had caught up.

'Is Nero at the stables?' It was the first question from Dulcia's lips, and she knew immediately by their shared expression that he was not. Looking between them, she waited for a response.

'Not quite,' Felix finally replied, wearing a guilty look Dulcia had come to recognise.

She drew a calming breath. 'Fighting, then?'

Silence.

'Why does he continue to fight? Did Nerva not give him a job that pays for everything he needs?' It was one of the perks of having a half-brother with money and influence; they could occasionally ask for favours. She focused again on her sister. 'You should put a stop to it.'

Mila laughed. 'You want *me* to stop him? I helped train him.' She took one of her wriggling sons from Albaus and handed him the basket. 'He is a grown man. He stopped listening to me some time ago.'

4

Felix began backing away from the group, and Dulcia's eyes narrowed on him. 'Where are you going?'

'I have business in Caelimontium.'

She rolled her eyes. 'I am coming with you.'

'Nero will not like you being there,' Mila called.

'Well, I too have grown up.'

'Yes, but you still listen to me *some* of the time.'

Felix did not move. He was looking at Mila, as though waiting for her approval.

'I do not need my sister's permission,' Dulcia said, grabbing his arm. 'Let us go.'

Mila waved her off. 'Fine, but take Albaus with you. You will need someone to carry you home when you faint.'

'You offend me,' Felix said, looking down at his diminutive but muscled frame. 'I have carried many swooning women in my lifetime.' He paused. 'Well, some of the larger ones I dragged along the ground until help arrived.' Sighing, he looked up at Dulcia. 'He really does prefer you to stay away from the arena.'

'Funny that. I have made the same request of him, many times. Let us go so I might remind him of the fact.'

'It will not do any good,' Mila called to her back, taking her other son from Albaus.

But Dulcia was no longer listening.

THE SMALL ARENA was located a few blocks from *Ludus Matutinus*. It was predominantly used for the execution of criminals, but Gallus Minidius sponsored various types of games, his wealth generated predominantly from the men who gambled on the fights.

Dulcia knew they were close when the smell hit her, a smell that would only get worse as the weather heated up. She covered her mouth as she followed Felix and Albaus towards the pit, stepping between men who shouted all kinds of profanities.

Beyond them she could hear the scrape and clash of wood and steel that was all too familiar to her. It was the sound of her youth, the sound of Mila and Nerva sparring while she hid away in the kitchen, humming to block out the noise.

'Stay close,' Felix called over his shoulder, looking far too at home.

She winced at the sound of someone hitting the ground. Cheers erupted around her as she slipped through the small gap to see who it was. She spotted Nero standing over his opponent, panting. His bare chest glistened with sweat, blood painting one arm. *Blood.* She held on to Albaus for a moment to steady herself.

Felix glanced at her. 'Do not faint.'

'I am fine,' she shouted over the noise of the crowd. It was too late to stop Nero, so she had no choice but to watch instead.

Nero could not have possibly heard her, yet his head snapped in her direction, as though sensing her arrival. His grey eyes locked on hers, then widened slightly. The muscles in his jaw ticked, the way they did when he was angry. Taking advantage of the distraction, his opponent swung a leg out, taking Nero's feet from under him. The crowd erupted as Nero landed on his back, the shield falling from his hand on impact. The other man was back on his feet in his next breath, towering over Nero, who failed to raise his sword in time. A shield came crashing down on his arm.

Dulcia knew it hurt him by the way his face contorted. He was holding in a scream. She turned her head, a hand instinctively going over her eyes.

A few moments passed. Slowly. She held her breath. Finally there was applause mixed with some disappointed grumbles, depending on which way the men had bet.

'It is over,' Felix said, patting her arm.

She lowered her hand and turned in time to watch Nero push himself up into a seated position. A drizzle of blood ran down his left eye, and he wiped it with his hand. As soon as people began to move, she went to him, crouching down, looking him over. She struggled to contain the panic. There was a small cut above his eye, and she instinctively reached for it, ignoring the dizziness that accompanied the action.

'I'm fine,' he said, pulling back from her hand.

She exhaled. 'You are bleeding.'

He rested his arms on his knees, looking at her. 'What are you doing here?'

Dulcia spotted Felix talking with Gallus Minidius, chatting away while Nero bled out on the dirt. 'I was hoping to change your mind.'

He wiped at the blood again. 'I was about to win.'

She swallowed. 'Should you lie down for a bit?'

'Absolutely not,' Felix called, finally joining them. 'He has embarrassed himself quite enough for one day. Up you get.' He gave Nero's leg a kick, and Dulcia turned to glare at him.

Men were exchanging coin around them, Nero seemingly invisible now that the fight was over. Gods, she hated the sport.

'Let me help you up,' Dulcia said.

He looked down at the hand she was offering, one corner of his mouth lifting. 'You don't actually think you could lift me, do you?'

She withdrew her arm and stood, watching as he sprang to his feet as though nothing had happened. He bent to collect the sword and shield, then straightened to face Felix. 'You shouldn't have brought her here.'

'Who am *I* to stop a determined young woman?'

Nero touched his forehead and winced, then looked at Dulcia. 'You hate this place. Why did you come?'

'I already told you. We were hoping to talk some sense into you.'

A man walked over and dropped a few denarii into Felix's extended hand. The dwarf counted the coins before pocketing them. When he looked up, everyone was staring at him.

'You bet on the fight?' Dulcia asked, unable to keep the disapproval from her tone.

Nero threw his hands up. 'You bet *against* me?'

Felix shrugged. 'I bet to win, not boost your ego.'

Dulcia cleared her throat. 'I take back my earlier remark. It seems we had very different reasons for coming here.' She saw a smile flicker on Nero's face as she instinctively reached for the cut once more. 'You might need stitches.'

Nero gently pushed her hand down 'Let me clean up a bit. Then I'll walk you home.'

'I am quite capable of walking myself home.'

'Don't be ridiculous. I'll walk you.'

Nero gestured for her to start moving, but before she had a chance, Albaus arrived with a bag of Nero's clothes. The others looked at each other, wondering where he had disappeared to that whole time. The man was the most social mute in Rome.

Dulcia found herself averting her gaze as Nero slipped his tunic on. It felt inappropriate to watch his muscles shift as he lifted his arms. She never used to notice, but his growing physique naturally drew the eye. Though as she looked around at the others, she realised it might just be her eye.

She stared down at her feet as he slipped on his sandals and belted his tunic. Once dressed, he stuffed his swords into the bag. Displaying them on the street would only invite trouble.

He turned to Felix. 'I'll meet you at the tavern.'

Felix clapped him on the back. 'Always the gentleman.'

THEY STROLLED through the streets of Rome, Nero enjoying the slower pace that was typical of that time of day. Shopfronts were closing, their occupants standing outside, making dinner plans and exchanging gossip.

Dulcia walked beside Nero, her bare arm occasionally brushing his. He was still sweating after the fight, but she did not seem bothered by the state of him. She had even insisted on washing the cut above his eye, despite her aversion to blood.

His height and broad shoulders protected her from the harsh western sun. It was a long walk, and he could tell from her dry lips that she was thirsty. He found a juice cart near the forum, and they stood in the shade for a moment, watching people come and go.

'Better?' he asked, taking her empty cup.

'Better.'

He handed the cups to the merchant and gestured for her to go ahead of him.

As they were leaving, a soldier came towards them, his gaze sweeping the full length of Dulcia as he approached.

'Good day, Dulcia.'

Probably one of Nerva's friends. *Eyes up*, Nero wanted to say.

'Good day, Commander,' she replied.

Her reply was so quiet that Nero doubted the *commander* had even heard her response. She had come a long way from the shy girl he had befriended upon his return to Rome, but she still had a tendency to shut down with most people.

Nero could not help a glance over his shoulder at the uniformed man, and found him turned, leering at Dulcia. When he realised he had been caught staring, he faced forwards.

'Friend of yours?' Nero asked, keeping his tone casual.

'Third legion.' She looked up at him. 'Why do you ask?'

He shook his head. 'No reason.'

Three years he had been back in the city, and he found himself growing more protective of her with each passing day. Of course, their friendship had been inevitable. Aside from the easy company they provided one another, they were practically family. Mila was like a sister to him, so it was only natural that he should form a strong bond with her younger sibling.

'You are very quiet this afternoon.' Her arm brushed his once more as she moved closer to talk. 'Are you mad that I ruined your fight?'

He touched a hand to her back, guiding her around a group of old men stopped in the middle of the street. 'I'm not mad. Though I could've done with the coin.'

'Is Nerva not paying you?'

Her sarcasm was always delivered with such sweetness that most people missed it. Not him. 'He's paying me.'

She shook her head.

'What?'

'Men.'

'*Men?*'

She stepped around a puddle of water, bumping him lightly. 'You are always chasing more. Why not be happy with what you have?'

'Because more is better, and every sensible man knows you should have a second source of income, a backup plan.'

She brushed hair from her eye. 'It is called family. That is your backup plan.'

'Rely on others' generosity? *That's* your advice?' He checked behind them, then the windows above.

'Stop,' she said.

'Stop what?'

'Waiting for the sky to fall on us.' She nudged him. 'Enjoy the walk instead of preparing for certain death.'

She was right. He was waiting for the heavens to come down on them. It was a habit formed in his early years when he lived on the streets, when the only name he went by was Rat. There was always someone coming for him in those days—usually because he had stolen something.

They reached the bottom of the hill that led to the Papias house. Dulcia lived there with her mother and her father's legitimate family. The two sisters were the worst-kept secret in Rome. Even the lady of the house, Aquila Papias, had given up trying to deny their blood relation. Rufus's ongoing affair with Dulcia's mother was the second worst-kept secret in Rome.

The pair climbed the hill in silence, stopping a few doors down. He turned to look at her properly. She was staring at the bloodstain on his tunic. Hooking a finger beneath her chin, he forced her gaze up.

'If you faint, I'll have to leave you on the doorstep, because they won't let me inside.'

Her eyes creased at the corners. 'I had better not give them another reason to be rid of me.'

His hand fell away. 'What do you mean *another* reason?'

She focused on the blood spot once more, twisting the bronze band on her middle finger, the one he had won in a fight two years earlier and gifted her.

'I heard Aquila telling my mother it was time I married.'

His eyebrows rose in surprise. '*Aquila* wishes you married?'

'She wishes me out of the house. Marriage solves that problem, I suppose.' She pressed her lips together before continuing. 'There is no reason for me to remain unmarried. Even Licinia has pointed out the fact a number of times.'

He rested his free hand on his hip to stop it from balling into a fist. In his other was her basket. 'You're taking marriage advice from a priestess?'

'She serves Vesta. What better person is there to take advice from?'

He shrugged, his gaze sweeping the street once more. 'A

person who knows you.'

She laughed, putting all her brilliant teeth on display. 'Like you?' A hand went to her stomach. 'Why did I not think of that?'

'My advice—'

'Do tell.'

'Is wait. There's no rush.'

She let out a noisy breath. 'I cannot share a room with my mother forever.' Her eyes searched his, still light from laughter.

'You also can't marry the first man who asks.'

She tilted her head. 'But he will not be the first.' The light vanished. 'He will be the third.'

His hand slipped from his hip as he stared at her, waiting for her to tell him she was joking. 'The *third*?' Another long pause. 'Why have you never mentioned this before?'

She looked away. 'You want to hear about a man I am *not* going to marry?'

'*Two* men.'

'Both of whom I am not going to marry.' There was a hint of exasperation in her tone.

He felt something that could only be jealousy based on how hard it hit his gut. 'So… you just told them no?'

'Rufus told them no.' She was watching his face carefully. 'The decision is his.'

'Thank the gods he saw sense.'

'He seems to think I can do better.'

'He's right.'

There was amusement in her eyes. 'You never even met them.'

'And yet I already know you can do better.' He searched the streets again. What in heaven's name was he looking for? Potential suitors preparing to leap out and ask for Dulcia's hand, perhaps.

He took a step back from her and ran a finger down his

nose. 'You should go inside.'

She nodded but did not move. 'Thank you for walking me home.'

He met her gaze once more. 'I don't have a choice. You're easy prey.'

There was that hint of a smile again. She closed the distance between them, her hand going to his forehead and her brow creasing with worry. Gentle fingers brushed either side of the wound. He did not push her away that time.

'It's just a scratch,' he reassured her. He was waiting for her to turn and rush up the steps, like she always did.

She took the basket from him. 'Will you be at the *Trigarium* tomorrow? I could visit there after I pray.'

He looked past her to the house. 'By yourself?'

She suppressed another smile. 'Yes, as is my right as a freed person.'

He shook his head, realising he was not going to win that argument. His first instinct was to say no, because the chari-oteers and grooms had a tendency to look at her like she was a prime cut of pork. But she enjoyed seeing the horses, and if he said no, he would not see her at all. 'We can go down to the river when I'm done.'

The light returned to her eyes. 'We are too old to climb trees.'

'That's something an old married woman would say.'

She could not stop the smile that time. 'I trust you will behave yourself tonight. No fighting.'

'No time. A quick drink at the tavern, and then it's home to work on my poetry.'

Her gaze fell to his grin, then away. His dislike of poetry, and her love of it, was a constant source of amusement between them.

'Good day, Nero.'

He watched her leave, the basket swinging in her hand. 'Good day.'

*D*ulcia snatched her palla off the bed and pulled back the curtain. She gasped when she almost collided with her mother. Tertia reached out to steady her.

'Where are you going in such a rush?'

'I told you last night. Prayer, then to the Trigarium.'

Her mother's face creased with disapproval. 'To see Nero?'

Dulcia tried to step around her. She was late thanks to Aquila changing the evening menu, resulting in a second trip to the market. Then she had been forced to endure Germana's foul mood as she slammed ingredients on the bench and ranted to herself. The woman really should have retired, but Aquila did not want to go through the hassle of replacing her. Apparently Dulcia was not a viable option, despite having cooked for the family since she was seven years old. 'I am allowed to socialise,' she reminded her mother. 'My work is done.'

Tertia kept hold of her arms. 'I encourage you to socialise, but do you not have other friends?'

Dulcia stopped trying to squirm free. 'I do not need other friends. I like the ones I have.'

'A priestess and a groom?' Tertia exhaled. Aquila had been working her hard also, and she looked exhausted. 'What about appropriate friends?'

She tried again to break free of her mother's grip, that time succeeding. 'I have to go. I am late.'

Her mother's gaze fell to the carrots she was carrying. 'Please tell me that is not your offering to Vesta.'

Dulcia looked down, then back at her mother. 'An offering for the horses.'

Tertia rubbed her forehead, then waved her daughter off. 'Be back before dinner or Aquila will make life unbearable for both of us.'

Dulcia was already walking off, rolling her feet in a way that made her footsteps soundless. She paused at the atrium to ensure it was not occupied, then hurried off in the direction of the front door.

'Dulcia, is that you?'

Aquila's voice stopped her. She groaned inwardly before turning, her expression neutral, trying to cover the carrots with her palla as she did so. 'Yes, Era?'

Her domina's painted face was hard-set, her mouth pinched.

'I need you to run some errands for me.' She touched a hand to her freshly done hair. 'Do I need to write you a list, or do you think, just once, you can keep everything in that simple head of yours?'

Dulcia's eyes went to her feet. Aquila had a way of making her feel like the awkward slave girl of her youth. It would always be that way. Her domina did not care if there was a piece of paper that stated she was free. Her house, her rules. And Dulcia's endless humiliation. 'I will remember, Era.'

Aquila drew a long breath, then released it. 'You know, these tasks are too important to rely on your memory. I suppose I shall have to write it down after all.' She went to turn, then stopped when she spotted the end of a carrot poking out of Dulcia's palla. 'What is that?'

*Here we go.* 'Carrots, Era.'

Aquila's eyes trailed up to meet hers. 'Yes, I see that. What are they for?'

Any attempt to lie would only be punished. 'I had planned to take them as a treat to Nerva's horses.'

If she thought Aquila's mouth could not tighten any further, she was wrong.

'To *my son's* horses?'

That was her way of laying claim to the man Dulcia dared to call brother out of earshot.

'Yes, Era.'

Aquila jutted her chin. 'You can put those back in the kitchen. The only places you will be visiting this afternoon are the ones on my list. Understood?'

Dulcia bowed her head. 'Yes, Era.'

Both Nero and the horses would have to wait.

THE FOLLOWING AFTERNOON, Dulcia finally made it out of the house. First, she took some bread to the Temple of Vesta, lingering on the steps until Licinia was able to come see her. The priestess dusted her offering with *mola salsa*, a special flour made by the vestal virgins for that purpose, then sat on the steps.

The girls had met at age thirteen, a few months after Mila had left to go to India. Dulcia had visited every temple in the city, trying to fill the void of her sister's absence with prayer. She had spotted Licinia feeding a stray dog by the fountain, where the vestals collected water, and had been immediately intrigued by the young girl in white robes. Licinia had looked up from the animal, and Dulcia had seen her own loneliness mirrored back at her. It was by no means a conventional friendship, but a few stolen moments here and there had sustained them for years.

'Are you going to watch the horses?' Licinia asked.

Dulcia nodded. 'I was supposed to go yesterday, but Aquila was determined to keep me busy.'

Licinia appeared to mull that over for a moment. 'She continues to have difficulty adjusting to your freedom.'

'Yes, it has been a tough few years for her.'

Her sarcasm was not lost on Licinia, who smiled down at her lap. 'You are a constant reminder of her husband's sins. Perhaps it is time to leave the household.'

'And go where?'

Licinia looked up and watched the passers-by for a moment before replying. 'You could find a husband.'

Dulcia shook her head. 'It appears to be a popular topic at the moment. I was just discussing it with Nero a few days back.'

'You were speaking to Nero about *marriage*?' There was a coyness in the priestess's tone.

'He was not offering, if that is what you are getting at.'

Licinia sighed. While she would never admit it, she was a romantic at heart. 'He is probably too afraid of rejection.'

Dulcia laughed. 'Nero is afraid of nothing. He has not asked because he sees me only as a friend or a sister.'

'Do you actually believe that?'

'He is family.'

'He is besotted.'

Dulcia's cheeks coloured. 'I think the fire in the temple needs stoking.'

Licinia suppressed a smile and stood. 'Let us pray Vesta shares your sense of humour.' She adjusted her robes. 'Are you not going to thank me for my counsel?'

'Is that what that was?'

The priestess glanced behind them, ensuring no one was listening. Clearing her throat, she tried to muster a more neutral expression. 'Ask Nero what he feels. Perhaps he needs encouragement.'

Just the thought of that conversation made Dulcia's stomach knot. 'And get laughed at?' She bowed her head for the sake of anyone watching them. 'Thank you for your *counsel.*'

Licinia's eyes shone at her. 'May Vesta watch over you.'

Turning, Dulcia hurried off down the steps.

～

NERO CHECKED that the horses were behind the line drawn in the dirt. When he beat Manius Liberia, he did not want to be accused of cheating.

He glanced across at the spoiled pleb, posing as a nobleman atop his chariot. Four ridiculously expensive horses, all paid for with his father's coin earned off the backs of slaves. Manius always put Nero on edge. Maybe it was because he always seemed to arrive at the same time as Dulcia. He liked to make a show of himself whenever she was around, and she was too polite to insult the man by letting her disinterest show. But Nero saw through her frozen smile and well-rehearsed manners; she was as bored as any other listening to the man talk about himself.

'Ready to lose?' Manius called.

Nero shook his head at the pompous fool. There was no questioning Manius's skill as a charioteer, but Nero had proven enough times that he was just as good.

A groom stepped forwards and raised his arm. 'On my signal,' he shouted.

Down went his arm.

Nero's chariot was first over the line. He hissed at the horses, barely touching Amator with his whip, while Manius flogged his lead stallion as though he were running the last lap at the Circus Maximus.

They had agreed to one lap, four horses, and a rather appealing prize pool from where Nero stood. It was insignificant for a man like Manius, who did not race for coin but for his ego.

Nero was disadvantaged being on the outside, thanks to an unfortunate coin toss. He would need to get in front after the turn. Wide was safest, but he would be unlikely to make up the distance if he did that.

'Ha!' he shouted, slapping the reins on the rumps of the horses. When Manius went to take the turn, Nero went for the narrow gap on the inside, leaning all his body weight to the left to prevent the chariot from tipping. The risk paid off, and he came out of the turn in front.

'You are mad!' Manius shouted behind him.

It was not the first time someone had told him that.

Hooves pounded the dirt, and wind roared in his ears. For just a moment, he forgot about the insignificance of the race, instead envisioning thousands of spectators either side of the track. He imagined the feeling of crossing the finish line first, the rewards that would rain down on him. Not only the coin, but also the respect. People might finally see him as something more than a rodent.

The flash of Manius's horses in his periphery brought reality crashing back. It was a timely reminder that his entire wage for the month would be gone if he did not cross that finish line first. It would be nothing for Manius to lose, but utterly humiliating for Nero to explain to the household why he needed to borrow money—again.

'Ha!' He ran the whip over Amator's back. It was all his lead stallion needed, surging forwards with renewed energy, knowing exactly what his driver needed from him.

Nero blinked against the dust as Manius closed some of the distance between them.

'Ha! Ha!' Nero shouted, putting a bit of muscle behind the whip.

He thanked the gods when he crossed the finish line half a length in front of his opponent. As the horses slowed, he prayed they would not pull up lame and give away his misadventures to Nerva Papias. The general had entrusted the care of his racing horses to him on the word of his sisters.

When he finally turned the chariot around, he was met with a very unimpressed Manius. 'Better luck next time.'

The charioteer nodded and turned to the groom holding the coin. 'Pay him. I will make it back tenfold at a real race.'

Nero did not mind the dig, because his opponent's clenched jaw and fierce eyes told another story entirely.

'Nero.'

He turned, searching for Dulcia amid the horses. She stepped out from behind a passing mare, a smile lighting her face when she saw him. He should have been unaffected by the sight of her by now, but his temperature always ran a little hotter when she was around. Even with her simple braid and faded stola, she looked like she belonged on a pedestal with an altar at her feet.

He had been worried when she had not shown up the day before, but after asking around, he learned Aquila had her running errands all over the city. That woman sure loved to remind Dulcia of her place in the household.

Jumping down from the chariot, Nero walked around to hold Amator's bridle while he waited for her to reach him. 'They missed you yesterday,' he said when she got there. It was easier to speak for the horses than himself.

Her hand went to the stallion's neck. 'Did they? Well, it is a good thing I brought apology carrots, then.' She walked around Nero, breaking the vegetables in half and sharing them out among the horses. When she was done, she looked over at Manius, who had stopped to watch her. 'Did I see you racing?'

'I don't know if I'd call it racing.'

The groom chose that exact moment to walk over and

hand him his winnings. He had no choice but to pocket it, aware of Dulcia's eyes on him.

'What would you call it?' she asked.

He cleared his throat. 'Had to make back what I lost the other day.' Worst excuse ever.

Dulcia crossed her arms in front of her. 'Spoken like a true gambler.'

He took in her amused expression, his gaze falling to her lips for a moment. The sound of approaching footsteps made him look away. He knew by the gait that it was Manius. 'I have to tend the horses, but then we can take a walk.'

Dulcia gave Amator another pat. 'I am yours for the rest of the afternoon.'

'Good' was his only reply.

Her choice of words threw him. Before he could add to his response, Manius joined them, his presence immediately dominating the space. Dulcia took a step back, her shoulder brushing the horse.

'Good day, Manius.'

'Now it is. You look as lovely as ever.'

She seemed to shrink in his presence, despite only being half a head shorter than the man. 'Thank you. Generous given that I have been stuffing fish all morning.'

Nero shifted his weight. He had no idea where to look in moments like those.

'I am rather fond of seafood, as you know,' Manius replied.

Nero turned, busying himself with the horses. They were sharing food preferences with each other now.

'Yes, I recall you telling me.'

He glanced at Dulcia, noting her body language. She was uncomfortable. 'Don't your horses need tending?' He could not stop the question spilling out of him. Even Dulcia looked at him in surprise.

'I have men for that,' Manius said, his tone smug.

That was true. When your father owned every marble quarry in the region, you could afford an entire team of grooms to take care of the work.

'How is your father?' Manius asked her.

Dulcia swallowed. 'He is well, thank you.'

Manius nodded as though approving of her answer. 'Excellent.'

Nero fought the urge to roll his eyes. It was no secret that Manius was campaigning for a place in the senate. Rufus Papias was a rather handy acquaintance for someone seeking a way in.

'I should get the horses to the stables,' Nero said, gesturing for Dulcia to follow.

When she went to move, Manius put a hand on her arm to stop her. 'Surely you are not going to make the lady accompany you to the stables?'

Nero's eyes narrowed on the hand holding her arm. He sniffed.

'I do not mind, really,' Dulcia said, taking a small step towards Nero. Manius's hand fell away, and Nero could breathe again.

'Nonsense,' Manius insisted. 'I will wait with you until he has finished his work.'

Every muscle in Nero's body went rigid. If the big peacock insisted on parading his feathers, Nero would tear them out. But the moment he went to move, Dulcia's hand landed on his arm, and he stilled. The lightest touch held him in place as though it possessed magic.

'That sounds like a sensible idea,' she said. 'I will watch the horses train until you return, and then we can go.'

He dragged his gaze to meet hers, noting the gentle plea in her eyes. Dulcia was a peacekeeper. She did not like confrontation and hated to disappoint people—and it drove him mad. She never said no to anyone, and often did things she did not want to just to keep everyone else happy. Heaven forbid her father heard anything other than glowing reports of her.

He played along for her benefit only. 'I won't be long,' he said, surprised he was able to get the words out. There was relief in her eyes.

'Let us find somewhere to sit,' Manius said, fingers grazing her back as he guided her away. 'If it is horses you wish to see, I will show you some of the best in Rome.'

Dulcia gave Nero a reassuring smile. That only made him angrier. She was probably recoiling inside at the man's touch, and yet she felt the need to assure him all was well.

'I won't be long,' he called, but she had already been swept away. He took a calming breath as he turned, tugging on Amator's bridle. 'Let's go.'

# CHAPTER 3

'All right, I give up,' Dulcia said. 'Why are you holding hoops and sticks?'

Nero had collected them from the stadia on his way to get her. He might not have been able to offer her a tour of his elaborate collection of horses, but he knew other ways to make her smile. 'I thought we could race.'

'What?' she laughed, looking around. 'In view of everyone?'

He rolled his eyes. 'We can go down to the water if you're going to get all shy on me.' Taking her by the hand, he led her down the slope to the Tiber. They ran most of the way, stopping at the tree-covered path adjacent to the slow-flowing river. He stared out at the murky water for a moment, then turned to her. She was flushed and breathing hard after trying to keep up with him. While she was now a woman in every sense of the word, he knew she was still a child at heart. It was one of the reasons he loved spending time with her.

Letting go of her hand, he passed her one of the hoops and a stick. 'Here.'

Dulcia took it and looked around. A pair of lovers strolled

on the path ahead, but they were only paying attention to each other.

'Don't worry, we'll go the other way so we don't run anyone down,' he said, reading her mind. He readied his hoop.

'Why do you assume I know what to do?' Though even as she asked the question, she had her hoop balanced and the stick in the optimal position.

'Because I remember you telling me that you played with Nerva when you were little.'

She looked up at him. 'You remember that?'

'Yes.' He remembered everything she told him. 'Ready?'

She stared off down the path. 'I am at a big disadvantage. You are faster than me.'

'But you're better at doing multiple things at once.'

That earned a smile from her. 'All right, go,' she said, hoop already rolling away in a straight line.

'You are also the biggest cheat I know,' he called, taking off after her.

She laughed over her shoulder. 'Not my fault you are slow off the mark.'

He bit back a grin and concentrated on his wobbling hoop. Once he had it under control, he picked up speed. 'First to the bridge.'

She squealed as her hoop went off course for a moment. Nero glanced across, preparing to grab it if it suddenly turned for the river. There was no chance of him going in to get it.

'I believe I am going to win,' she teased, moving farther ahead. 'Perhaps we should have put some coin on it.'

'You don't have any coin, remember?'

'Exactly.'

He was too busy watching her to put in the effort required to win. She was laughing, forgetting herself—just the way he liked her. He kept on her though, all the way to the bridge.

When she reached it first, her hand slapped the stone, marking her victory. She turned to him, panting. 'Please tell me you did not let me win.'

He stopped next to her and collapsed against the bridge. 'You're the true victor.' Letting his hoop and stick fall to the ground, he slid down the wall onto the dirt, and she sank down next to him.

'Let me catch my breath and we can race again,' she said.

He drew his knees up and linked his hands in front of them. 'One more race. Then I better get you home.'

She rested her cheek on her knees, looking at him. 'I do not want to go home.'

His eyes went to her. 'Aquila's keeping her hands off you, isn't she?'

'She prefers venomous words nowadays.'

He blinked with relief. If anyone put their hands on her, he would not be able to contain himself. 'It's just noise. Block it out.'

'Easy for you to say. Everyone in your household adores you.'

'Maybe the children.' Nero faced the river again, calmed by the sight. 'Any body of water always reminds me of India —even the murky Tiber.' He released a breath. 'It was a good life.'

She was silent a moment before speaking. 'You could always go back there. If you wanted to.'

He rolled his head to look at her. 'It wouldn't be the same on my own.'

They watched one another for a moment.

'Then take someone with you,' she said. 'Marry and travel there with your wife.'

He tilted his head, trying to tell if she was serious or not. 'And who shall I marry?'

Now it was her turn to look at the water. 'Do not pretend you have no prospects. I have heard Felix mention Cassia from the tavern a number of times.'

She sounded jealous, and it pleased him immensely. 'Cassia and I have fun. She is no more interested in marrying me than I am her.' He flicked a small stone at her foot. 'Besides, what would you do without me?'

'I would be forced to find someone else to climb trees and race hoops with.'

Nero thought. 'Licinia, perhaps?' Her head fell back as she laughed, and he watched in awe. 'All right, enough playing matchmaker. Are you ready to lose?'

She turned her smiling face to him. 'No.'

He took in her brazen expression. 'Too bad. You only get to win once.'

NERO KNEW Dulcia had to be home in time to help with dinner, and he insisted on walking her the entire way. Everyone they passed seemed to be in a hurry, while they strolled, not wanting the afternoon to come to an end.

They went along the outskirts of Subura in order to avoid the chaos. Nero stopped to say hello to a butcher he knew. The man was cleaning a pig in the alleyway, a stream of bloody water pooling on the street. When they left, Nero guided Dulcia around it. They moved from the alleyway to a main street, and when cavalry approached, he moved her to the other side of him.

'Goodness, I am getting dizzy from you throwing me about,' she said. 'Remember, I survived on the streets just fine before I knew you.'

She said that, yet whenever there was a fight, someone shouting, or a drunk stumbling in their direction, she always shifted so close to him that he felt the warmth of her body.

'When are you going to come by and see the children?' It was easier to change topics than try to explain his actions.

'Soon, hopefully. I miss them.'

She was expected to be on call at the Papias household, so Nero had grown used to seeing her in small bursts. But he hated not knowing when they would see each other next. 'Tomorrow afternoon, perhaps?'

They were nearing the house.

'Maybe. I really cannot predict Aquila at the moment.'

'She can't object to your praying, surely. I could meet you at the temple.'

Her warm eyes assessed him. 'If I can get away, I will wait for you there.'

She was standing really close again, visibly relaxed. His fingers twitched at his sides. They were silent all the way up the hill, but when they reached the house, he stopped and turned to face her. The orange sky did something to her complexion. She looked so beautiful painted by the colours of the setting sun. He thought about telling her, then changed his mind. This was the part where she was supposed to go inside, but she did not move. It was like she was waiting for something, but he did not know what.

He was about to ask when the front door opened. Dulcia flinched at the sound, and he took a small step back from her in case it was Rufus or Aquila. But it was neither. He looked up just as Manius strode out. The charioteer paused on the top step when he saw them. There was no mistaking the flash of annoyance in his eyes before he managed a smile in their direction.

'Dulcia,' he called, descending the steps towards them. 'Twice in one day. Lucky me.'

It was comical that the man had the audacity to act surprised by the encounter when he had shown up on her doorstep.

Dulcia took a step back, as though she had been caught

doing something wrong. Nero resisted the urge to pull her back to him.

'Manius,' she said, unable to hide her genuine surprise. 'I was not expecting to see you here.'

He trotted down the steps, coin jingling in hidden pockets and rings reflecting the sun. 'I was just meeting with your father,' he said, stopping in front of her.

A bad feeling enclosed Nero, squeezing tightly. It was not helped by Manius's smug expression.

'I will let him tell you the good news.'

Nero stood taller, his hands balling into fists.

'I should go inside,' Dulcia said to her feet, her shoulders rounded.

The confident woman who had stood before Nero a moment ago was gone. 'I'll see you tomorrow.' His feet did not move. He could not leave until he knew she was safely inside. Though how safe could she be with Manius roaming freely about the place?

'Good day, Nero, Manius,' she said before turning away and walking slowly up the steps.

Normally she ran. It was all a big display of propriety for the man who seemed to think he had a right to stand there watching her also.

When the door closed, Nero faced Manius.

'So what's the good news?' He hoped the man could not hear his stomach churning.

Manius eyed him coolly. 'Nothing that concerns you.'

'If it concerns Dulcia, it concerns me.'

'How do you figure?'

'She's family.'

Manius's lips twitched. 'I suspect Rufus might see things a little differently.' He clapped Nero on the arm before turning and striding off in the other direction.

Nero stood frozen in front of the house, dread coiling inside of him, squeezing the air from his lungs. Manius was up to something, possibly something Nero was not ready to consider. Or perhaps the charioteer was just toying with him, his pride still recovering from the loss.

That was what he told himself as he headed back down the hill towards the slums.

# CHAPTER 4

'Where have you been?' Tertia asked, smoothing down her daughter's hair. 'Rufus wishes to see you.'

She had been afraid of that. 'See me about what?'

'It is not my place to speak for him. He waits for you in the tablinum.' She gave Dulcia a gentle push in that direction, but her daughter's feet had suddenly grown roots. 'What is the matter?'

Dulcia held her mother's arm. 'Has it something to do with Manius Liberia? I ran into him outside.'

Tertia cupped her daughter's face. 'Please listen to what he has to say before you worry.' Her warm hand fell away. 'I assure you it is good news.'

*Good news for whom?*

Dulcia nodded and walked to the tablinum, where she found the door open and her father seated behind the large table, quill in hand. He looked up at the sound of her soft footsteps.

'Come in,' he said, placing the quill down and straightening. 'There is something I wish to discuss.'

Dulcia wiped her clammy hands on her stola before stepping into the room. Her eyes went to the large painting of a naval ship hanging on the wall to her left, then to the sculpture in the corner, a stone carving of Augustus. She usually only entered the room when cleaning it.

'Manius Liberia came to see me this afternoon,' he began.

She cleared her throat. 'Oh?'

'He wishes to take you as his wife.' Rufus leaned back to watch her reaction.

She wished she had been able to display something other than blind panic in that moment. *Wife*. 'That is…' What was it? An honour? A mistake? A mistake, surely.

'You seem surprised.'

That was one word for it. 'Yes, very. I barely know him, and he is… Manius Liberia.'

Rufus suppressed a smile and stood, walking around the table and sitting on the front of it. Crossing his arms, he looked almost… proud. 'I was equally surprised by his interest, but it seems you caught his attention. He tells me you have been spending time at the Trigarium, a fact I was unaware of.'

'I like to watch the horses.' It was mostly true.

'And that slave boy your sister took in, it seems.' There was disapproval in his tone.

'He is not a slave,' Dulcia replied, her voice suddenly quiet. 'He is free, like me.'

Rufus regarded her for a moment. 'The man was raised in a brothel.'

Dulcia felt the small hairs on her body bristle. 'He was left on the streets with no one to care for him.'

Rufus nodded, clearly not wanting to argue the details. 'I do not judge him. I am just stating the facts.' He paused. 'You are not children anymore, and some might jump to conclusions. Rightly or wrongly, it seems people have connected you with the Papias name. While this opens some doors for you, it also means you will be scrutinised.' He was silent a moment. 'I told Manius you would be honoured to accept his proposal. Your mother has been informed and was also agreeable.'

She felt completely betrayed by that last comment. Her mother had agreed without even so much as asking Dulcia what she thought of the man. 'I can only assume Manius has forgotten I am slaveborn.' It seemed the only likely explanation.

Rufus shook his head. 'Manius would not take a wife without first knowing who she is. He was clear on his choice.'

She suppressed the rising panic and tried to think logically for a moment. Manius was best known for his wealth, and as the blue team's most skilled charioteer. But racing was not a long-term occupation for a sensible man. That was why he had decided on a political career, which had so far amounted to nothing. 'Does Manius's family approve of his choice?'

A nod. 'He would not have come here without his father's approval.' He uncrossed his arms and held the edge of the table. 'You seem hesitant, and I must question why.'

Hesitant? She was terrified, and something else. 'I have spent most of my life as a slave. I am just trying to understand why he chose me.'

'It is a mutually beneficial union. Manius comes from a long line of merchants and businessmen. Successful men, but not a drop of noble blood among them.'

'And you will help him change that?'

'Yes.'

She thought for a moment. 'And what do you get in return?'

'Much-needed funding for public projects, for one.' Rufus pushed off the table and walked back around the other side. 'Many families are preparing to travel south to their villas to wait out the heat. A modest wedding celebration when they return, perhaps. That will give you time to get to know your husband, get used to the idea.'

That was three months at best. Her breathing slowed. Three months until she would marry into one of the wealthiest families in Rome.

She had spent time with Manius that afternoon, while waiting impatiently for Nero to return. The conversation had been stilted and uncomfortable, yet she had sensed his interest by the way he stood too close, his body overbearing and his voice too loud. Then Nero had returned and led her by the hand to a place she could breathe.

Rufus looked up when she did not immediately reply, as though checking if she was still standing there.

'Later in the season, then,' she said, filling the awkward silence. What else was she supposed to say? She backed away towards the door. 'Good evening, Erus.'

The title was dated, as he was no longer her master, but she could not think of a suitable replacement. Employer? Father? If Aquila overheard her referring to their blood connection, she would beat Dulcia with the closest object in reach.

Rufus returned to his work. 'Good evening, Dulcia.'

She practically fell through the door. Once she rounded the corner, she held the wall for balance. The wife of Manius Liberia. What would that life look like? She could not picture it. Was she to travel in a litter? Spend her days weaving and accepting visitors?

Her nails dug into the wall. She would have to say goodbye to her afternoons with Nero—say goodbye to him altogether. Manius would not tolerate her keeping company with a man she did not share blood with. No husband would.

She felt as though she were falling suddenly, and her hand went over her mouth.

'Dulcia' came a whisper. It was her mother, guiding her

away from the room where her father sat, having uprooted her entire life with one statement.

'I do not want to marry him,' Dulcia whispered, grabbing her mother's arm, preparing to beg if necessary.

Soothing hands brushed hair back from her flushed face. 'Shh.' Tertia led her to the bedroom they shared, pulling the curtain across behind them to give the illusion of privacy.

'I barely know him,' Dulcia said, not waiting to be prompted.

Tertia looked only amused. 'Of course not. You have a lifetime for that.'

'It will never work.' She was finding it difficult to draw breath suddenly. 'I have nothing to offer a man like him.'

Tertia pulled Dulcia into her arms and stroked her daughter's hair. 'Shh. You have plenty to offer a man like Manius.'

Dulcia pressed her eyes shut, and Nero's face flashed in her mind, his intense gaze fixed on her.

*Nero.*

# CHAPTER 5

*Vesta, holy mother of hearth and home. Watch over me. Guide me through this marriage, so that I might please my family and husband.*

*My husband.*

The phrase jolted Dulcia every time.

She was kneeling on the steps of the Temple of Vesta, elbows on the ground and a bread offering for the goddess in her hands. Inside the temple, the priestesses tended the flames.

'Dulcia?'

She looked up to see Licinia standing on the top step in her white robes, her hair partially covered. The priestess took in her tear-stained face before going to her. Dulcia straightened and turned to sit on the step, facing east, the same direction as the sacred fire behind her.

'Whatever is the matter?' Licinia asked as she took a seat next to her.

Dulcia wiped her face, feeling ridiculous. She had not even realised she had been crying. 'I am in need of Vesta's guidance and strength.'

The priestess watched her for a moment. 'I know she

hears your heartfelt prayers.' Smiling, she added, 'The priest-esses just heard your sobbing. What is wrong?'

'I am to marry.'

Licinia drew a breath, excitement filling her eyes. 'He did it. He asked your father.'

Dulcia frowned. 'How do you know that?'

'It was only a matter of time.'

She was talking about Nero. The realisation twisted like a knife inside her. 'I am to marry *Manius Liberia*.'

Licinia's eyes widened slightly in surprise. 'Oh. I was unaware the two of you were acquainted.'

'Barely.'

Licinia looked around and cleared her throat. 'Well, Manius comes from a good family. Your mother must be pleased.'

Dulcia blinked back tears. 'Yes she is.'

'And Rufus.'

'Yes.'

Licinia nodded. 'Good.'

They stared at one another, and then Dulcia leaned in. 'Everyone except me.'

Licinia's face filled with pity. 'Because you love another.'

Dulcia's heart thudded against her ribcage, and she gripped her stola. She opened her mouth to object, but nothing came out.

'There you are' came the familiar sound of Nero's voice.

She jumped and turned to see him standing at the bottom of the steps, staring up at her. As she looked at him, she realised Licinia was right. Her heart belonged to another.

NERO COULD TELL something was wrong the moment he spotted her. It was in her rounded back and stooped head. When she looked at him, he could tell she had been crying.

She touched the backs of her hands to her cheeks, trying to remove all evidence of tears.

'Nero.' A smile masked her pain. 'You are early.'

Of course he was early. He had worked at twice the speed he normally did in order to get to her. The lack of sleep had only fuelled his anxiety. Manius's smug face had taunted him since their encounter the day prior. He had come prepared for the worst, but hoped he was wrong. To hear such news from her lips would be something else entirely.

Dulcia rose and Licinia followed, looking between them for a moment.

'Licinia,' Nero said, bowing his head at the priestess.

She nodded in his direction.

Nero's gaze returned to Dulcia. 'Ready to go?' She was having difficulty looking at him, which was not a good sign. He tilted his head to better see her face. 'If you need a moment, I can wait.'

She met his eyes then, her expression bordering on broken.

'I'll be across the street when you're ready,' he said, turning away. 'Take as long as you need.' He crossed the road and fought the urge to pace. Instead, he stood in the shade, watching her gesture as she spoke, her eyes on her feet.

After what seemed like hours, but was probably only a few minutes, she descended the steps and crossed the street to join him.

'What's the matter?' he asked before she had even come to a stop.

She turned to watch Licinia disappear back into the temple, then looked both ways down the street, seemingly everywhere but at him. 'I am to be married.'

He had been expecting that, but the words still landed like a punch to his gut. He stepped back. 'Married.' Not a question, a statement.

'To Manius Liberia.'

As if he needed a family name to know who she was talking about. He had always disliked the man, but now he felt something closer to hate bubbling inside him. 'Congratulations.' The word fell from his mouth before he could stop himself.

Dulcia raised her eyes to him, and he saw disappointment in them.

'Congratulations?'

'His family has a villa in Antium, you know.'

She was looking at him as though he had suddenly grown horns. 'I hear it is lovely there.'

He nodded, and they both turned to watch a mule pass.

'Does Mila know?' he asked.

'Not yet.'

When she looked at him, he saw that the disappointment had dissolved into resentment.

He took another step back. 'Well, you may as well share the happy news.' How he was speaking so calmly he had no idea. Perhaps because deep down he knew she deserved that life. She deserved a wealthy husband, a comfortable life, to travel to Antium for extended stays by the ocean. She deserved everything that man could provide—everything he could not. Only an arse of a man would get in the way of that. 'Let's go.'

Dulcia stared at him for the longest time before eventually turning away. It took Nero a moment to move also. He suddenly wondered if he was up to the task. Could he walk at her side, knowing their days were numbered? That she was no longer his to protect, that she never would be, or worse, never had been? Could he speak through the weight in his chest, the crushing disappointment? For Dulcia he could. He could push it all down, bury it, and walk her to share the news with her sister.

They strolled towards the apartment he shared with his odd assortment of family, barely saying two words the entire journey. Dulcia managed to keep herself a full body length from him the whole walk. Probably best if she wished to avoid a potential scandal.

At some point his childish crush had progressed into something more, something he was only now beginning to understand. He watched their surroundings, trying to think of something to say other than "don't marry him". But nothing came, so he resigned himself to the silence.

When they arrived at the insulae, Dulcia climbed the stairs ahead of him, like usual, and his gaze drifted down to her hips—also like usual.

The apartment was one of the bigger ones in the building. It was back from the noisy street and got plenty of sunlight from the light well. It had three rooms, one which Nero shared with Felix and Albaus, one for Mila, Remus, and the children, and a communal room.

When they reached the first floor, Nero leaned around Dulcia and pushed the door open. The smell of lentil soup and bread greeted them. The children were seated on the floor playing a game, and Mila stood at the table cutting vegetables.

'Dulcia,' she said, putting down the knife and wiping her hands. 'Nero said you might be coming by.'

The children looked up, and the twins scrambled to their feet before running to her. She crouched, almost knocked backwards as she caught them.

'Easy,' Nero said, his hand going to her back in case she fell.

Dulcia kissed the boys' faces, then stood to greet Asha, who was waiting patiently behind her brothers.

'Dulcia has some news,' Nero said.

Mila went to greet her sister. 'Oh?' She looked between them. 'Judging by your serious expressions, it cannot be good news.'

When Nero glanced at Dulcia, he found her glaring at

him. With no interest in hearing the news twice, he turned away. 'I'm going downstairs to wash.' He disappeared into one of the rooms and returned with a towel.

'Do you mind taking the boys with you?'

Of course he did not mind. That was what family did. 'Come on, then.' He patted Asha's head, then winced as the twins ran roaring for the door.

'Behave!' Mila called after them before throwing him an appreciative glance.

He caught Dulcia's eye a final time before she looked away.

~

WHAT HAD SHE EXPECTED? He had done and said what any person would say. *Congratulations.* She wondered what she would have said if the roles had been reversed. *Congratulations, now excuse me while I empty my stomach on the street.*

'Dulcia.'

She jumped at the sound of Mila's impatient voice. What had she asked? 'Sorry, what?'

'I asked you what Mother said.'

Dulcia was struggling to process the news properly herself. She was yet to have any sort of definitive reaction. 'She is thrilled. She said any woman in my position would be falling down with gratitude.'

Mila rolled her eyes. 'Stupid women maybe.'

'You think I should not marry him?' It came out with more hope than she had intended.

Mila sighed. 'I was just saying you are not obligated to fall down with gratitude because one wealthy man took notice of you.' She glanced over at Asha, who was practicing her reading aloud on the floor. 'What is he like, this Manius?'

What was he like? 'Like any man, I suppose.'

Mila touched her sister's face. 'This might come as a

41

shock to you, but they are not all the same. It seems he has not won you over yet.'

'He has always been very nice to me.' She looked to the window.

Mila placed a finger under Dulcia's chin and turned her head so she had no choice but to look at her. 'Nice? He is *nice*?' Her hand fell away, and she smiled. 'What a catch.'

'I barely know him.'

'He seems to know you.'

He did not know her at all. 'This is what Rufus has decided, so I suppose that is that.'

Mila frowned. 'That sounded like a question. Are you asking me?'

'I cannot refuse, can I? Rufus will disown me.'

Mila laughed. 'He would have to *own* you first. Maybe this is the first step.' She moved off her stool and went out onto the narrow balcony, where she stirred the pot of soup on top of the brazier. 'You know you would always be welcome here if that happened.'

'And share a room with the men?' As she spoke the words, an image of a sleeping Nero popped into her mind. She had glimpsed him through the door once when she had arrived early in the morning to collect Mila. A blanket had covered him from the waist down, his torso bare. He had slept on his stomach with his hands stuffed under his pillow, looking too large for the bed.

'There would be no safer place in the city for you to sleep,' Mila replied. 'Those men protect you like they are blood, do they not?'

Dulcia blinked away the image of Nero she had conjured. 'Yes.'

'I must confess,' Mila said, glancing back at her. 'Remus and I were joking just last night that you would end up married to Nero, because he is the only man you actually talk to.'

Dulcia's wounded expression turned to a scowl. 'That is not true. I spoke with Manius just yesterday.'

'Did you?' Mila suppressed a smile. 'Or did you stare at your feet while *he* spoke?'

Dulcia twisted the ring on her finger as she fought the urge to flee the room. She watched as Mila continued to stir the soup. 'He never asked.'

Mila looked over, her head tilted in confusion. 'Who?'

'Nero.'

The spoon stilled. 'Never asked what?'

'Forget about it.' Dulcia shot up, the legs of her stool scraping on the wooden floor. 'I have to go.'

'Wait a moment. To marry you?' Mila hurried back inside. 'Did you want him to ask?'

'It does not matter what I want, does it?'

'Of course it does.' Mila held out her hands. 'Does Nero know you feel this way?'

Dulcia headed for the door, not answering the question.

'I thought you were just friends,' Mila called. 'Get back here. We are not done talking.'

She reached for the door, but it opened before she could grasp the handle. Nero stepped inside. She took a wobbly step back, and he reached out to steady her. His hands felt like they were burning holes in her flesh.

'You're leaving?' he asked, sounding surprised.

She pulled out of his grip. 'Yes.'

'I'll walk—'

'That is not necessary,' she said, stepping around him. 'I can walk myself.' She was through the door and descending the steps before he had a chance to object.

'Dulcia!'

Her sister's voice followed her down the stairs, but she did not stop. The moment she was free of the building, she broke into a run.

# CHAPTER 6

*N*ero slowed the horses to a trot, a walk, and then stopped them in front of Nerva Papias. Mila and Dulcia's half-brother was a *legatus legionis* in the army, a horse enthusiast, and Nero's employer. At just twenty-seven he was young for a general, which did not sit well with some of the men in his charge.

'They are looking good,' Nerva said, walking around to inspect them closer.

Nero secured the reins and stepped down from the chariot while another groom ran forwards to assist with the horses. 'They'll do well next week. With the right charioteer.'

'I have found just the man. He has just returned from Greece, where he made quite a name for himself.'

Nero nodded, a familiar wave of disappointment washing over him. It was always someone else. 'I could do it, you know. And I could win.'

Nerva shook his head. 'Gods, you remind me of Mila.' He stepped back as the horses were led away. 'You lack experience. If you die, I shall be forced to replace you. Worse than that, I will have to live with my sisters' grief. They have grown quite attached to you.'

The sound of approaching horses made them both look up. Manius Liberia stood atop his chariot, looking every bit the pompous fool in his bleached toga. Nero turned away, busying himself. It had been three days since news of Dulcia's engagement had broken, and so far, he had managed to avoid both parties involved.

'Good day to you, General,' Manius said, stopping in front of Nerva and extending his arm.

Nerva stepped up and took hold of it. 'Good day.'

'Your horses are in fine shape.' Manius nodded in their direction. 'You know I always appreciate quality competition.'

Nerva grinned and crossed his arms. 'I have Nero here to thank for that.'

Nero glanced at Manius as he wheeled the chariot to the side of the track.

'He makes a fine stable boy' came Manius's reply.

Nero felt the fine hairs on his body bristle as he pretended not to hear. Three days was not long enough to get a handle on his anger. That man had everything handed to him.

'I hear congratulations are in order,' Nerva said. 'Father told me the good news. I must confess, I was a little surprised.'

'I have been getting that reaction a lot.'

Nerva did a lap around Manius's horses, sussing out his competition. 'I hope you do not mind me asking this, but why Dulcia? You must have women throwing themselves at you.'

Nero could not help but listen for Manius's reply. The fact that the man had to think on the question only fanned the fire inside him.

'She is everything a woman ought to be—modest, humble.'

Nerva laughed. 'Fancy words for shy.'

'She always warms up eventually.' His chest expanded. 'I promise you this, she will want for nothing.'

That should have improved Nero's mood, but he was unable to take any more of the conversation. 'I'll head to the stables,' he called to Nerva.

'I will see you at the apartment later,' Nerva called back. 'Dulcia and I are coming for dinner.' He turned to Manius. 'Perhaps you should join us since you are soon to be family.'

Nero almost tripped on his own foot.

'I am no snob, and accept the invitation with gratitude.'

'It's an insulae full of plebeians,' Nero said, addressing Manius for the first time. 'Not a domus for the wealthy.'

Nerva looked between them, picking up on the hostility. 'Manius does not mind. Nor should he. If he wishes to join the senate, it is better he knows the people he will be speaking for.'

Nero did not stick around to listen to Manius's reply.

There went his dinner. Now he would have to go elsewhere for food.

THERE WAS NOT a chance Nero was going to eat in the apartment with that man. As tempting as it was to check in on Dulcia, he knew he could not sit across from them and watch her play wife. Instead, he went to join Felix and Albaus at their usual drinking spot across the street from Ludus Magnus.

The tavern was packed by the time he arrived, and many of the patrons were already drunk. The air was thick with the smell of cheap wine, the floor sticky underfoot. He weaved between the small tables, spotting his friends near the window. Albaus was playing dice with two men he did not recognise, and Felix sat with a woman twice his height perched on his lap. Nero stopped, wondering if he was in the right mood for the gathering.

'Hello, stranger.'

He turned to see Cassia slinking towards him. As soon as he was within reach, she wrapped her hands around his neck and pulled herself up to kiss his cheek.

'Hello.'

The barmaid smiled up at him. 'Where have you been hiding?'

'Not hiding, just busy.' He gently peeled her hands off his neck.

'At least let the boy get a drink first,' Felix called over the noisy crowd.

Her smile only grew. 'Can't a woman say hello to a man before doing his bidding?' She patted Nero's chest. 'Take a seat, handsome. I'll bring it over.'

'Thanks.' He made his way over to the table as Felix gave the blonde on his lap a tap on the bottom. She wobbled to her feet and wandered off to another table.

'Didn't have to send her away on my account,' Nero said, dropping onto the stool that had been pulled up for him.

Felix assessed him for a moment. 'Why are you not at the dinner party?'

'I could ask the same question of you.'

'Easy.' Felix turned himself front on with the table. 'I hate dinner parties. You, on the other hand, have never missed a dinner opportunity with Dulcia.'

'Don't overthink it. Just not in the mood.'

'I am having difficulty deciphering your expression.' He took a drink from his cup. 'Brooding or guilty? Help me out.'

'Neither.'

Albaus looked up from his dice game.

'Neither,' Nero repeated, raising his hands.

Albaus grunted before returning to his game.

'I see. Avoiding Dulcia,' Felix said.

The tavern had definitely been a bad idea. Just the mention of her name put him on edge. 'Why would I be avoiding her?'

Felix glanced dramatically up at the heavens. 'Hmm, maybe because you have been besotted with the girl for years, and now she is engaged to your nemesis.'

'I think you're drunk.'

'Yes I am. But I am also right.' He waved his cup around. 'This is your own fault, you know.'

Nero rubbed his eyes with his palms. 'What is my fault now?'

'Treat her as a sister, and you are labelled a brother. Treat her as a lover—'

'I see where you're going with this.' Where was that drink? 'She was always going to marry up.'

Felix snorted. 'Would we call it marrying up? The man is just a charioteer.'

'From a wealthy family.'

'A spoiled arse living off his father's coin. I know, because I was him once.'

Felix's sermon was cut short when Cassia arrived with the wine. She placed the cup down in front of Nero and poured.

'Something to eat?'

'Yes,' Felix answered on his behalf. 'Get some food into him before he makes a mess of himself.' He leaned towards the barmaid. 'He is nursing a broken heart.'

Nero shook his head and took a large drink.

'Aww.' Cassia grabbed his face with one hand, squeezing the hollows of his cheeks. 'I'll cheer you up. Just need to wait for me to finish up here.'

'I truly don't deserve you,' Nero replied.

'I will make sure one of us is waiting for you,' Felix said, giving Cassia a coy wink.

'It wasn't an open invitation.' She ruffled the dwarf's hair before walking off, leaving Nero to smile into his drink.

Felix straightened on his stool. 'She is not my type anyway.'

'I heard that,' Cassia called from halfway across the room.

Felix winced while the men laughed around him.

Three hours later, Nero and Felix stumbled out of the tavern. Albaus trailed behind them, appearing sober despite having drunk the same amount. They made their way through the dark city streets, Nero and Felix singing the whole way. Every time someone leaned out of a window above to shout profanities at them, they burst out laughing. This continued most of the way home, until they rounded the corner into an alleyway and collided with another group. The three men responded by shoving them.

'Watch it, *pumilus*,' said one, clipping the dwarf over the head as though he were a child.

Felix caught his arm and twisted it behind the man's back until he cried out. One of his companions made a move in his direction, but Albaus stepped in front of him, a warning in his eyes. That should have been the end of it, but Nero had pent-up anger and too much wine in his belly.

'Who are you calling *pumilus*?' he said, getting in the face of the man who had spoken.

'Back,' Felix said. 'I have this.'

Albaus's large hand landed on Nero's shoulder, but he shrugged it off. 'I think you owe my friend an apology.'

Felix released the man and gestured for him to walk on. 'On your way, while you still can.'

The man remained where he was, glaring at Nero. 'You had best step back.'

'Not until you apologise to my friend.'

Felix looked tiredly up at Albaus. 'This is not going to end well.'

The man took a step towards Nero, his face now an inch away. '*Friend*? What, does he wipe your arse for you?'

It was all Nero needed. In the next beat, his fist collided with the man's face, and it was on. The other men tried to move in, but a simple shake of Albaus's head made them rethink their decision. Felix crossed his arms, preparing to wait out the brawl. He would only get involved if things turned serious.

Slowed by drink, it was not Nero's sharpest fight. He even took a few punches to the face before he finally knocked the man to the ground. Blood poured freely from the man's broken nose.

'Ready to apologise?' Nero asked through blood-covered teeth.

'I believe you have made your point,' Felix said, gesturing to Albaus, who grabbed Nero by the shoulders and dragged him away. The other men immediately rushed forwards to help their friend off the ground.

'You'll keep your mouth shut next time, won't you?' Nero shouted.

Albaus shoved him, and Felix glanced over his shoulder at the mess left behind. 'Let us get him home before the night watch shows up.'

ASHA WAS ENTERTAINING the twins in another room, leaving the adults to eat in peace. The small party was seated on cushions around the low table. Dulcia sat next to Mila, whose head rested on her husband's shoulder. She could tell Remus was not particularly enjoying Manius's company by the way he focused on the food, though he remained polite, for their sake.

Nerva had no problem fitting into their world. Despite

his rank, and their very different upbringings, he had never viewed his sisters as slaves or plebs.

Manius was a different matter. He seemed so awkward sitting on the floor, inspecting the food offered him as though he were searching for fault in it. His expensive toga clashed with everyone's simple attire.

'Would you care for some more carrots?' Dulcia asked him, picking up the plate and holding it out.

He shook his head. 'No thank you.'

Dulcia returned the plate to the table, aware of everyone watching them. She shifted on her cushion.

Remus must have picked up on her discomfort, because he initiated conversation for the first time that evening. 'I've heard rumours that Severus is sending men to Caledonia.' The comment was directed at Nerva, who tore off a piece of bread and dipped it in the fish liquid left on his plate.

'Senecio has asked for assistance, but it is no small undertaking.'

'Surely Severus himself will not go,' Mila said. 'I thought he was plagued by gout.'

Nerva swallowed his food before answering. 'He is a man of war, and he is restless.'

'I will never understand it,' Dulcia said. 'So much bloodshed, and for what?'

'For Rome,' Manius replied, as if it were the only answer needed. 'And you do not have to understand it.'

'Why? Because she is a woman?' Mila asked, her tone flat.

Manius eyed her for a moment. 'No, because she will reap the benefits regardless.'

Remus took his wife's hand, and Nerva cleared his throat.

'The *benefits*?' Dulcia asked.

Manius nodded. 'More food, more slaves...'

Mila frowned. 'More *slaves*?' She looked ready to leap over the food and tackle him to the ground.

Dulcia shot up and began to clear away the mess.

'Leave it,' Mila said, turning to her sister. 'I will clean up later.'

Dulcia continued to load herself up. 'I do not mind, really.'

As she straightened, plates balanced carefully on one arm, the door swung open and Felix stepped inside. He looked around at the small party.

'Oh,' he said, clapping his hands together. 'It seems we are a fraction early.'

Remus narrowed his eyes. 'Early for what?'

Before Felix could reply, Nero stepped through the door, visibly drunk and bloody-faced. He took in the room, his eyes seemingly clearing for a moment when they landed on Dulcia.

'Just need a towel and I'll be out of your way.'

Remus and Mila were on their feet in an instant.

'What happened?' Mila asked.

Felix raised his hands, gesturing for calm. 'A *very* insignificant misunderstanding in an alleyway.'

One of the plates balancing on Dulcia's arm began to slide, and Mila reached out and caught it.

'Let me take those.'

Dulcia did not object that time. She stared at Nero, concern and anger fighting for room inside her.

Manius rose to his feet. 'I should probably head off.' He turned to his hosts. 'Thank you for dinner.' Then, turning to Dulcia, he said, 'Come. I will take you home.'

Dulcia glanced at him. She was used to hearing those words from Nero, not Manius, but he was in no condition to walk her, nor would it be appropriate.

'We will all go,' Nerva said. 'I am staying at the house tonight.'

Relief swam through her.

'I'm going to get cleaned up,' Nero said, backing out through the door.

Felix rubbed his forehead. 'And I am going to bed. That is about as much excitement as I can take for one night.' He strolled off towards the shared room while Dulcia continued to stare at the now-empty front door.

'Excuse me,' she said. 'I will meet you both downstairs in a moment.' She headed for the door, Manius looking unsure if he should follow. Thankfully, he did not.

When she reached the bottom of the stairs, she rounded the corner and made her way to the courtyard. She froze beneath the archway when she spotted Nero stripped down to his loincloth, washing himself. She had seen him that way before, but lit up by moonlight was something else entirely. Bare skin and lean muscle glistened. He stopped scrubbing for a moment and stretched out his fingers, wincing as he did so. She stepped into the courtyard and walked to him.

'Are you injured?'

His head snapped in her direction, searching for her amid the shadows. She could tell the moment he spotted her by the way his shoulders relaxed. 'I'm fine.'

As if he would give any other answer.

She walked over to him and took his hand, turning it over to inspect his swollen knuckles. 'Anything broken?'

He pulled his hand away. 'No.'

Her gaze travelled up to his face. 'What about the rest of you?' She moved to touch him, and he stepped back as though she were holding a venomous snake. Her hand fell to her side. 'What happened?'

He rinsed the cloth, the water in the pail turning red. 'Someone had a go at Felix.'

'And you lost your temper?'

He glanced sideways at her. 'I stood up for him.'

'Felix can take care of himself.'

'I know that.'

She crossed her arms. 'So there is no need for you to beat up strangers who make thoughtless comments.'

He closed his eyes for a moment. 'You really are naive.'

She stiffened, not expecting that from him. Everyone else, but not him. She felt foolish standing there while he took shots at her. 'I should go.' When she started to turn away, he caught her wrist. Her eyes went to the wet hand on her bare arm. She could not have pulled away even if she wanted to.

'I'm sorry,' he whispered. 'You're not naive, just a better person than me. I shouldn't have said that.'

When he let go of her, she drew her arm to her chest, her other hand going protectively over it. 'I just do not want you to get hurt, that is all. You are reckless when you are angry.'

'I'm not angry.'

She searched his eyes. 'I thought perhaps... I *know* you do not think much of Manius.'

'Doesn't matter what I think of him.'

It mattered to her very much. 'I know this is not entirely appropriate for me to say, but I need you in my life.' Her cheeks heated with the confession. 'In case you have not noticed, the only other friends I have are my sister and a vestal virgin who is probably just being kind.'

'It's not because people don't like you, it's because they don't know you. Not like we do.'

'It seems my social skills still need some work.' She looked about the courtyard. 'I suppose I should be grateful Manius is prepared to look past my long list of faults.'

'What faults?' Nero shook his head. '*He's* the one who should be grateful. Any man would be lucky to have you.'

She smiled up at him. 'And that is why I need you. You always know exactly what to say.' Her smile faltered when she noticed the intensity with which he stared at her. She swallowed.

'There you are,' Nerva called from the archway. 'Ready?'

Nero's gaze fell to the pail as he wrung out the cloth once more. 'Good evening, Dulcia.'

It was an effort to turn away from him. 'Good evening.'

# CHAPTER 7

*D*ulcia sat on the steps of the Temple of Vesta, hands curled in her lap as she watched the passers-by. Licinia was beside her, a thoughtful expression on her face. Dulcia was relaying the story of the night prior, right up to the point where she arrived home and was cornered by her mother.

'She wanted me to replay every detail of the dinner, searching my face the entire time, hoping to see her own excitement mirrored back at her.'

'It is natural that she would want to see you happy.'

'Yes.'

'She must be pleased that Manius was prepared to eat with your sister.'

'Lower himself to our level, you mean?'

Licinia bit the inside of her cheek to stop from smiling. 'At least Nero did the sensible thing and stayed away. His attendance would have made for an interesting party.'

Dulcia looked down at her lap. It was the first time she could remember eating with her sister and him not being there. She had spent most of the dinner watching the door. 'He was such a mess when he did arrive home.'

'Give him time. It is a big adjustment, and he is likely hurting.'

'He is just mad. Has barely said two words on the subject.' She let out a breath. 'He does not think much of Manius.'

'I wonder why.' A discreet smile.

'Everything feels ten times more overwhelming when he is not onside. I cannot do this enormous thing and fight with him at the same time.'

Licinia's eyes went across the street, narrowing on something. 'I think you will find he is still very much onside.' She nodded in that direction.

Dulcia turned and found Nero, standing in the shade, watching her. Even at that distance, she could see the bruise on his left eye. His form was so familiar to her now: the shape of his arms, the curve of his shoulders, the way he always stood with his weight on one foot. The angle of his head suggested he was a little unsure about being there.

'It seems my work here is done,' Licinia said, suppressing another smile. She rose and touched a hand to Dulcia's shoulder. 'May Vesta watch over you.'

'Good day,' Dulcia managed to get out, too late to be heard as the priestess was already heading inside.

Pushing herself up, she descended the steps and crossed the street, weaving through the people and animals loaded with sacks and crates moving in both directions. She could not stop the rising excitement in her chest as she neared him. After everything, he had still come for her.

She was slightly breathless when she reached him. 'What are you doing here?'

He glanced west. 'I'm going to climb our tree. Thought you might want to come.'

A smile flickered, but she did her best to match his serious expression. 'We are too old to climb trees, remember?'

His weight shifted to the other foot. 'Says who?'

'Every person over the age of ten.'

He was silent a moment, then nodded. 'All right. I'll let you get home to your weaving, or whatever it is your sort do.' He turned and walked off down the street.

'*My* sort?' She stared after him for a moment, her bottom lip clamped between her teeth. 'Wait!' He immediately stopped and turned, a satisfied expression on his face as he waited for her to catch up. 'I want to climb our tree,' she said, looking up at him.

The light in his eyes made a familiar warmth spread through her.

'You sure? You're a long way past ten.'

She rolled her eyes and walked off ahead of him. 'Let us go before I come to my senses.'

PLANE TREES LINED THE TIBER, but one in particular had a deformed trunk that made it perfect for climbing. They stood at the base of the tree, waiting for the people who had passed them to get farther away.

'All right, up you go,' Nero said, making a stirrup with his hands.

As quick as she could, Dulcia set her foot, and he hoisted her high enough to grab the first branch. She pulled herself up onto it. Nero waited for some more people to pass before using the nooks on the trunk like a ladder and joining her. They stilled as a man passed beneath them, whistling to himself, and then Nero gestured for her to start climbing.

She reached down and gathered the hem of her tunic, tying it in a way that gave her legs more freedom. Nero's gaze fell to her bare calves, then to the ground below. He had seen her legs more times than she could count, but the older they got, the more uncomfortable he appeared.

'It has been a while since I climbed a tree,' she whispered. 'Pray I do not fall.'

That made him look up. 'Do you really think I'd ever let you fall?'

She searched his face for a moment. 'No, of course not.' She tried to focus on the task at hand. Reaching for the branch above her head, she began the long climb to the top. Occasionally her sandal would slip on the smooth bark, and Nero's hand would appear like a step beneath her. Once, he caught her leg, his large hand wrapping her ankle. She looked down, watching his gaze slide up her leg before meetings hers. Neither of them moved for a moment.

'You all right?' he asked, his voice a deep whisper that travelled up her skin.

She nodded. 'Just not very athletic. You must have figured that out by now.'

'Figured it out years ago.' His eyes creased at the corners.

She continued climbing, her heart beating a little harder suddenly, but she managed to reach the top without slipping again. A smile broke across her face as she settled herself on the wide branch that offered a clear view of the river. A moment later, Nero plonked himself next to her, causing their seat to shake. She grabbed hold of him for balance, then made the mistake of looking down. 'I had forgotten how tall this tree is.'

His arm went behind her, holding the branch on the other side. 'But look at that view.'

Turning back to the water, she relaxed and let go of him. Her foot settled on the branch below just as a small rowboat passed beneath them, its occupants unaware that they were being watched. 'When was the last time we came here?'

He thought for a moment. 'A year? You tore your stola, and because you're a terrible liar, you confessed everything to your mother. She forbade you from ever climbing another tree.'

'Well, I'd better not tear anything today, or I should be forced to admit that I broke that promise.'

Some children ran beneath them and they fell silent, watching them until they were out of sight.

'Serious question. At what age *should* we have stopped climbing trees, do you suppose?' she asked, turning to him. He turned also, and she was suddenly aware of how close he was.

'Fifty? Sixty?' When she burst out laughing, his hand went to her waist to steady her. The moment her laughter died, he let go and faced the river. 'Though I'm fairly sure Manius won't approve of his wife climbing trees in forty years' time.'

'Or now, for that matter.' She felt a pang of disappointment as she realised the next few months were all she had left of the childhood she had managed to hold on to. 'You will soon be forced to find someone else to climb trees with. Cassia, perhaps.' She was not sure why she added that last part. Truthfully, she hated thinking about him spending time with other women. Every time the barmaid's name was mentioned, she was left with a heavy feeling in her stomach —one that felt a lot like jealousy.

'I've never climbed trees with anyone else. Just you.'

'Then what do you do with other women?' As soon as the question left her mouth, her cheeks heated, and she was forced to turn away from him. 'Never mind. That was... please do not answer that.'

He laughed. 'I wasn't going to.'

She pressed the back of her hand to her cheek in an attempt to cool herself. Of course, she had to be stuck up a tree with him just inches from her at a moment like that. 'Obviously I know what you do.'

His eyebrows rose. 'You do?'

She cleared her throat. 'What I mean is I have read about such things.'

'You've *read* about it?'

'Poems and such.' Gods, it was hot. She fanned her face with her hand while he grinned at her.

'Now I see where your love of poetry comes from. Why don't you recite one to me?'

She let out an exasperated noise. 'That is not what I meant.'

'So you *don't* read filthy poems?'

She would have shoved him had they not been at least one hundred feet off the ground. 'I was simply saying that you do not need to have experienced the... act of...' She made an awkward circular motion with her hand.

'Stirring soup?'

'Consummation.' Not quite the word she had been searching for, but it was too late to take it back. 'To know what takes place.'

He laughed then. 'Maybe just stop talking.'

'Excellent suggestion.'

An amused Nero continued to stare at her. 'You look a little sunburned.'

That only made her blush further. 'Stop.' Both hands went over her face, and he grabbed hold of her waist to prevent her falling. 'Talk to me about boats,' she said, holding onto the branch once more. His hand left her.

'Before you so subtly change the subject.' He leaned back slightly, assessing her. 'Are you trying to tell me that in the nineteen years you've been alive, your only experiences with the opposite sex have been in the *written form*?'

She did not know where to look. 'That is an entirely inappropriate question.'

'Not even a kiss with one of the stable boys? They must be falling over themselves for the chance.'

She exhaled. 'Everyone in the household knows I am Rufus Papias's daughter. What boy in his right mind, slave or otherwise, would fool around with their dominus's *offspring*?'

'Fair point.'

They both fell silent, watching another boat approach. A bird landed on a nearby branch, then took off when it caught sight of them.

'Tell me about the pyramids,' Dulcia said, eyes on the water.

He glanced at her. 'Again?'

'Again.'

She had never been outside the city walls, while Nero had travelled through Egypt, India and sailed across the Red Sea. She had been twelve when they had left, and not ready to join them, despite the plans she and Mila had made as children, huddled beneath a blanket as the rest of the house slept.

Nero spent the next hour retelling stories she had heard a hundred times. She watched the river as she listened, conjuring pictures in her mind of all the sights, people and places he spoke of. When he finished, she let out a contented sigh, feeling as though she had just returned from the journey herself. She faced him again to find him watching her with a serious expression. Heat rushed to her cheeks as she, once again, became aware of his close proximity and the arm secured behind her. There was nowhere for her to go. Not that she would have moved anyway—she was held in place by his stare.

'What?' she asked, the question coming out breathy.

He glanced at the river before replying. 'I would've liked to have seen your face the first time you saw the pyramids.'

The thought of standing before the pyramids with a smiling Nero made her chest feel light again. 'I would have liked that too.'

He leaned closer, the smallest movement, but she felt the air shift with it. For a moment, he looked as though he might kiss her. She might not have had any experience, but she felt it, or something resembling it. Instead of turning away, as she should have, she tipped her head back ever so slightly.

His gaze travelled down to her mouth, then fell to her hand with the ring on it.

'I can't believe you still wear that thing.'

Whatever had held her in place fizzled into disappointment. It took her a moment to gather herself, to think, to react. She looked down at the thin band. 'Why are you surprised? You gave it to me.'

'Because it's worth nothing.'

She twisted it with her thumb. 'Says who?'

'Every woman in Rome wearing silver and gold jewellery.'

Her eyes met his. 'You once said it looked pretty on me.'

'It does.'

Her mouth lifted in a half smile. 'Then stop being a snob.'

He was looking at her lips again. Still so close. 'I should get you home,' he said, withdrawing from her.

There was that crushing disappointment again. 'Yes.'

Down the tree they climbed, then dropped to the ground.

They walked their usual route through the city, arriving at the Papias household just before dusk. As she turned to Nero to say goodbye, the door opened behind her and Manius strode out. The man seemed to be everywhere suddenly. His expression hardened the moment he registered her companion. She did not dare look back at Nero for fear of what she would see on his face.

'There you are,' Manius said, trotting down the steps and coming to stand with them.

Perhaps it was just Dulcia's imagination, but Nero seemed to grow in height in that moment.

'Good day,' Dulcia said. 'I did not realise you were coming by.'

Manius gave her a small smile, then reached into a pocket to retrieve something. 'I wanted to give you this.' He produced a silver ring, holding it out for her to see. He gestured for her hand.

At first she did not move, only stared at the polished jewellery as though he were gifting her a weapon.

'Your hand,' he prompted.

She saw Nero shift beside her as she reluctantly lifted one arm.

'Insignia of betrothal,' Manius said. 'Now everyone shall know you belong to me.'

Dulcia stared at the ring. It depicted an image of joined hands with Manius's name written underneath, and it looked ridiculous on her slim hand.

'Do you like it?' Manius asked, peering into her face.

She felt sick suddenly. 'Yes. It is...' Heavy? Suffocating? 'Lovely.'

Apparently that was the correct word, because a smile spread across his face. 'The first of many gifts.' He gestured to her other hand. 'A replacement for the bronze piece which is beneath you.'

Replacement? Her eyes went to the thin band, then to Nero. He took a step back from her, as though she were suddenly contaminated by Manius's wealth.

'I have to go,' he said, not looking at her properly.

'Now?' She could see his discomfort, embarrassment perhaps. Of course he had to go.

'I'm meeting Cassia at the tavern,' he added, backing farther away.

'Oh.' Whatever nausea plagued her seemed to double in that moment. Her hand with the bronze ring went to her stomach while the other remained extended. 'Well, have a good evening.'

'And you,' he said, all warmth gone from his tone. He turned his cold gaze to Manius. 'Good day.' Turning, he headed back down the hill.

Dulcia fought the urge to watch him leave, to stare at his broad back. Instead, she faced Manius once more.

'You know, if you need an escort around the city, I can

arrange one for you.' There was an odd expression on his face, despite his pleasant smile.

'I do not need an escort. Nero is just being kind, and perhaps a little overprotective.'

Manius nodded. 'Like a brother.'

'Yes, like a brother.'

Manius clapped his hands together, causing her to jump. 'I have more good news.'

She had hoped they were done with the good news. 'Oh?'

'My mother is hosting a dinner party at the house this evening, and I would very much like you to join us, to meet my family. My sister, in particular, has not stopped pestering me since news of our engagement broke.'

Dulcia cleared her throat, which was painfully dry all of a sudden. 'I will need to check with my—'

'I have already spoken to your father, and he is more than happy for you to dine with me and my family. I will give you time to get ready, then send a litter to collect you.'

She must have missed the part where he asked her if she wanted to go. It was an arrangement between men. Still, she needed to meet his family eventually, and there was no reason to delay. 'I look forward to it.' Her gaze drifted down the hill as she spoke.

He reached up and brushed his thumb along her cheek. 'They are going to love you,' he reassured her. 'Though be sure to wear something nice to make a good first impression.'

She frowned up at him. 'I need fancy clothing for that?'

His gaze travelled down her simple tunic and stola. 'It will definitely help.'

She chose to focus on the part where he had said his family would love her. 'All right.'

He bent to kiss her cheek; it was so quick, she did not have time to react. 'I will see you soon.' Winking, he strode off in the other direction. He did not wait at the bottom of the steps for her to go inside.

She touched her hand to her cheek where his lips had been. 'See you soon.' There was too much distance between them for him to hear.

Her gaze drifted back down the hill, then to the bronze band. Her other hand was weighed down by the world's smallest shackle.

With her chest heavy, she went inside.

# CHAPTER 8

The entire thing was laughable. Sitting in a curtained-off box carried by four men, despite the fact that she had two working legs and sturdy sandals that were perfect for walking. She had a strong urge to tell the men to put her down, that she would meet them there. Thank the gods for the privacy curtains to hide behind.

The house was atop a hill in region thirteen, even larger than the Papias household and just as elaborate. When the front door opened, she was greeted by a slave girl who looked to be around fifteen. The girl made a quick assessment of Dulcia before stepping back and inviting her in. She led her through to the garden where the hosts had set up for the evening.

Dulcia paused behind a pillar, just out of sight, taking in the women's expensive garments and painted faces. Glossy locks of hair spilled down their shoulders, their arms weighed down by gemstones. Her gaze fell to her own cream tunic and lemon stola. She felt very underdressed suddenly.

Her mother had painted her face and helped do her hair in a fashionable style, half up in a bun, though it was not as sleek as those of the other women due to the unruly nature of her hair. Her only jewellery was the silver ring Manius had given her and the bronze band which now hung from a leather thread around her neck, hidden beneath her tunic. She had worked up the courage to take it off, but had faltered when it came time to put it away in a drawer.

'I do not blame you for your hesitation' came a whisper behind her.

Dulcia spun around to find a pretty-faced woman about her age. She had round lips and amber eyes painted blue, matching her sapphire earrings and the gem-infused cuffs on her wrist.

'A rather intimidating group, is it not?' the woman said.

Dulcia struggled to find words. 'I was just... I was just trying to find Manius.'

The woman held back her laughter. 'Of course you were.' She crept forwards and peered around the pillar. 'Argh, Drucia is here. Dreadful woman, and her son is equally as vile. Unfortunately for me, they are rather keen to secure my dowry.'

Dulcia had no idea how she was supposed to respond to that piece of information, so she said nothing.

'I am Junia, by the way. Manius's sister. I am going to hazard a guess that you are Dulcia.'

'Oh.' Heat rushed to her cheeks. *His sister*. And there she was hiding in the garden.

Clearing her throat, she bowed her head. 'It is a pleasure to meet you.'

Junia stepped closer and peered around the pillar at the guests. 'Manius will be in the other group, with the men who talk only of racing and business. They stay away from the women until they are forced together to eat.' She looked back at Dulcia, assessing her. 'I am afraid they are going to eat you alive.'

Dulcia swallowed. 'Manius did warn me about my choice of clothes.'

Junia laughed. 'You cannot win these women over with a nice garment. If my brother told you otherwise, I am afraid you were misled.' The cuffs on her wrist clinked when she brought a hand to her hair, combing the ends with her fingers. 'They can smell a plebeian a mile away.' She gave Dulcia a sympathetic smile. 'Best I am honest.'

She had a kind face and seemed sincere. Dulcia felt a bit braver knowing she would have at least one person to talk to over the course of the evening. She even spent a moment imagining them as sisters, wondering how they might pass time together. Perhaps they could take walks along the Tiber —minus the hoops of course.

'Any tips before I go in?'

Junia adjusted the rings on her fingers. 'Do not lie about anything, not even the smallest detail. They likely already know everything about you, and if there is something they wish to know, they will find out. And if their sources contradict anything you say, they will tear you apart. Stick close to Manius or me. We are your best chance of survival.' She hesitated. 'And best avoid being alone with my father if you can. He can get a little… hands-on when he has been drinking.'

Dulcia blinked. 'I am betrothed to his *son*.'

Junia waved off the statement. 'If *I* am not exempt from my own father, then you are most certainly not. You are just his type—sweet, submissive.' With that, she stepped out from behind the pillar and said, 'Look who just arrived.' She gestured to Dulcia, who had no choice but to follow her out into the open.

The garden fell silent, and everyone turned to stare at her. It was too much. She looked down at her feet.

'There she is,' Manius said, separating from the men at the far end of the garden and walking over to her.

Dulcia forced her gaze up and reminded herself to breathe.

Manius assessed her choice of attire. 'You look lovely.' He offered his arm.

She had no idea if he was being sincere or just polite, but she slipped her arm through his, feeling every pair of eyes on her as she did so. He guided her to the large group of women waiting with their claws extended. Junia walked on the other side of her brother, her head high, looking every bit a noble-woman. There were five couples, ten guests total, not including the three of them.

So much for a family dinner.

She should probably have mentioned that she was not one for crowds. But to what avail?

'Dulcia,' Manius said, 'may I introduce Marcia, Drucia, Hortensia, Fabiola, and my mother, Livia.'

Livia's steel gaze travelled the full length of her before replying. 'So this is your slaveborn *sponsa* we have heard so little about.' Just a few words spoken, yet everything said.

Junia went to stand beside her mother, winking encouragingly at Dulcia.

'It is nice to meet you,' Dulcia said, though her voice barely carried the short distance.

Livia turned to her friends, smiling. 'She is like a little mouse. Squeak, squeak.'

They all laughed except for Junia, and Dulcia's cheeks heated once more.

Manius cleared his throat. 'Mother, you promised to behave.'

'A joke, my love.' Livia turned to Dulcia. 'I trust you have a sense of humour.' When Dulcia did not reply, she added, 'My besotted son assures me you are now a freed woman.'

'Mother,' Junia said, taking a cup of wine from the tray one of the servants wandered around with. 'Dulcia is the daughter of Rufus Papias. I am certain he would not find your jokes funny.'

Dulcia glanced behind her at the exit, forming an escape plan.

'You must forgive my mother,' Manius said, patting the top of her hand. 'She has a tendency to speak before she thinks.'

Livia tutted while the other women continued to watch Dulcia.

'Half slave and half noble,' Junia said. 'That makes you a true daughter of Rome from where I stand.'

Livia stepped back from the circle. 'Then perhaps you should trade places with me, get a better view.'

Junia shook her head, and Drucia squealed with laughter.

'Tell us,' Drucia said, composing herself, 'how did the two of you meet?'

*Here we go*, Dulcia thought. *More fuel for the fire.*

Manius turned to answer the question. 'At the Trigarium. Dulcia often goes there to watch me train.'

Dulcia looked up at him, wondering whether he was lying for their benefit or whether he actually believed that was her reason for going. By the look on his face, the latter. When she faced the group again, she found Livia studying her.

'And your father just lets you traipse about the city?'

Dulcia drew a breath. 'I work in the mornings and evenings. The afternoons are mine to do as I please. I have been going there for years.'

'Years?'

Dulcia clasped her hands in front of her, too tightly. 'Nerva's horses have trained there for a number of years.'

Marcia looked between the other women. 'Nerva Papias?'

'Dulcia's brother,' Junia said.

'*Half*-brother,' Livia corrected. 'I imagine Nerva is rarely there. I am certain he has far more important matters to attend to.'

Junia rolled her eyes. 'He is allowed to visit his horses, Mother.'

Livia seemed to be waiting for a better explanation. Dulcia heeded Junia's warning to not lie about even the smallest detail. 'Nerva's horses are trained by a family friend of mine. He is always happy for me to come along.'

Everyone's eyebrows seemed to rise in unison, even Junia's.

'Family friends who *tend* the horses?' Hortensia asked, her face creased with disapproval. 'What sort of company are the Papiases keeping nowadays?'

Wicked smiles were exchanged between the women.

'Family on my mother's side,' Dulcia explained, though it was a stretch. She could never expect them to accept the notion that family did not have to be blood.

'She is referring to the *slave* side,' Livia said, as if that needed clarifying.

'I understand your sister is married to Remus Latinius,' Junia interjected.

Drucia's mouth fell open. 'The gladiator?'

'He is a spice merchant,' Dulcia said. 'He has not fought in years.'

'A spice merchant and a stable boy,' Livia laughed. 'What interesting family you have.'

Marcia took a sip of wine, then looked between the women. 'Let us not forget the dwarf and the mute who share their house. Oh, and the street rat they took in.'

Dulcia frowned. 'Street rat?'

Manius turned to her. 'I believe Marcia is referring to Nero.' He shook his head. 'Ladies, let us not be unfair. The boy cannot help that he was orphaned, nor that he was raised in a brothel.'

The women exchanged looks of disapproval while anger welled in Dulcia's chest. There was absolutely no reason for Manius to add that last part. It only fuelled them.

She was about to speak up, to defend him, when Junia

stepped forwards and took her other arm. 'Would you like a tour of the house?'

Dulcia could see by her expression that she was trying to save her from the conversation.

'First you must meet my father,' Manius said, patting her hand. 'Come.'

She was swept away from the group, but before they reached the other guests, she stopped walking. Manius turned to her, a brow raised in question.

'Nero spent a few years in that brothel at best before being taken in by Jovian Fadius.' She was surprised by her clipped tone.

Manius glanced about, checking if anyone was listening before responding. 'All right.'

'Then by Remus and Mila, who love him like family.'

He narrowed his gaze on her. 'I cannot change how others view the man.'

'No,' she agreed, 'but how you speak of him shapes how people see him.'

Manius ran a finger down her face, his expression softening. 'I know he is your friend, which is why I do not speak poorly of him.'

She searched his face for an ounce of sincerity but once again found him unreadable. 'Thank you.'

His hand fell away. 'As long as he is respectful of the boundaries I put in place.'

Her eyebrows drew together. 'What boundaries?'

'Do not fear. I understand how you feel about your family.' He bent, brushing his lips over hers as though it were an everyday occurrence between them.

She took a step back, aware of everyone looking. It was the first time she had ever been kissed that way, and she felt nothing but a flush of embarrassment. Her lips were cold, yet she had always imagined a kiss would bring warmth. Then again, she had never imagined kissing Manius.

She looked around at the harsh faces, then down at her feet. Manius took her hand and pulled her to him. The over-powering smell of scented oil filled her nostrils. Leaning close to her ear, he whispered, 'Let us try that again later—without an audience.'

~

CLAUDIUS LIBERIA WAS a quiet man with deep-set eyes. He spoke kindly to Dulcia, but he also seemed to think it appropriate to leer at her like a master did a ripe slave in their household. Manius did not appear to notice, or perhaps he was immune. He seemed to like displaying her on his arm, content with her silence while he did all the talking. They spoke of racing and politics—the two things she cared least for in life. She was thankful when the conversation was brought to a halt by the arrival of food.

They ate in the garden, reclined on lounges. Dulcia sat safely between Manius and Junia, tense and finding no appetite despite the trays of eggs, salted meats, olives, cheese, vegetables, and fruit on display. Wine was poured, and she sipped slowly, despite the constant refilling of her cup. Heaven forbid it sit empty.

'Will you be coming to the Circus Maximus on Friday to watch my brother gloat?' Junia asked.

'She will barely be able to see him gloat from all the way up in those high seats,' Livia said. 'The race experience is quite different for the lower-class.'

Dulcia took a longer drink.

'If she arrives early enough,' Claudius said, 'she can secure a bench seat by the metae.'

'Is that a good viewing spot?' Dulcia asked, making an effort to participate in the conversation. She was hesitant to admit she had never been to the circus. Not due to lack of opportunity, but because she had no interest in watching people die.

'It is the most common spot for collisions and death,' Junia said. 'You will likely be sprayed with blood if you sit there.'

'Yes, but the plebeians love that,' Livia said with a glance in her direction.

'Well, since you are soon to be family,' Manius said, 'why not join us for the day? I am confident Junia will take good care of you.'

'Join *our* family?' Livia asked, visibly surprised. 'You would need to dress the part.'

'Mother,' Junia said, shaking her head.

'What?' Livia looked around at her friends. 'There are standards on the balconies, are there not?'

The other women nodded their agreement.

Manius glanced across at Dulcia. 'With a face like that, there is no need for expensive jewels and feathers.'

It was such a lovely compliment, yet once again Dulcia found nothing on Manius's face to suggest he meant it. 'I do not wish to intrude. If I attend—'

'What do you mean, *if* you attend?' Junia asked, smiling. 'Has my brother not made it compulsory?'

Dulcia watched as her drink was refilled once more.

'I happen to know our Dulcia is not big on the circus or games,' Manius said. 'Too much bloodshed.'

How he knew that, she had no idea.

'What sort of Roman does not care for our traditions?' Livia asked, eyes filled with accusation.

'I prefer other sports,' Dulcia replied. 'Ones that do not end in death.'

Livia scowled at her. 'Such as?'

She picked up her cup to give her hands something to do. 'Harpastum or... hoop racing.'

Everybody laughed, even Manius. Livia smirked into

her drink as though their laughter were her personal victory.

'You forgot knucklebones and checkers,' Claudius said, turning to the other men, who laughed along with him.

Dulcia's cheeks burned as she lifted her cup, emptying it in a few mouthfuls.

'All right, all right,' Junia said, catching her breath. 'I think we have teased the poor girl quite enough.'

Manius reached across and patted her leg, then gestured for one of the servants to refill her cup. A young girl stepped up to pour.

'Thank you,' Dulcia said quietly.

The acknowledgement made the girl look up, their eyes meeting briefly. It was unusual for a guest to acknowledge a slave, and especially to thank them. Dulcia had broken an unspoken rule by making her visible. The distracted girl did not position the ladle over the cup correctly, and a drizzle of wine ran down the side of the cup and onto the floor. She immediately moved to clean it up.

'Stupid girl,' Manius said beneath his breath, shaking his head.

'Sorry, Erus,' she murmured, her eyes down.

'It was my fault,' Dulcia said, bending to help with the mess on the ground.

A firm hand on her arm made her stop. She looked up into Manius's disapproving face.

'Leave it,' he said with a stern expression.

She slowly straightened, and he let go of her arm. All eyes were on her now.

'It must be *so* difficult to break old habits,' Livia whispered rather loudly to the other women. They all exchanged a knowing look.

Dulcia's gaze fell to her lap, and she prayed conversation would resume. But the guests continued to stare at her as though she were an impostor.

'Tell us who you are racing on Friday,' Junia said to Manius, breaking the awkward silence.

～

ONCE EVERYONE HAD EATEN to the point of bursting, the food was taken away, but not the wine. It was getting late, and Dulcia wondered how long she should stay. Restless, she excused herself and went in search of the latrine, if only for a few moments of quiet. On her way back, she loitered in the atrium, wandering between the sculptures and other works of art featured in the room.

'That one was done by a rather exceptional artist.'

She turned to see Claudius behind her. Stepping back from the mosaic image, she said, 'Sorry, I was... it was too lovely to pass without stopping.'

He came to stand beside her. 'A priestess helping those in need is a beautiful thing.'

The picture was of a vestal virgin handing out loaves of bread to sick men.

Dulcia cleared her throat. 'Yes it is.' She turned back to the artwork, but stiffened when she felt fingers in her hair.

'So soft,' Claudius murmured, rubbing the strands between his fingers.

She took another step back, out of reach, recalling Junia's warning. Whatever bad things Livia had to say about Dulcia's family, it seemed her own was no beacon of light to the Roman people. 'I should find Manius.' She hoped her expression said everything she could not.

'There you are,' Manius said, entering the atrium. 'I thought you might have gotten lost.'

Claudius turned to watch his son walk in, his expression easy. 'Dulcia was just admiring some of the art.'

She cleared her throat. 'I was just saying that I should be getting home.'

Manius's eyebrows rose in surprise. 'Already?'

'I have to work in the morning.'

He smiled at her. 'Not for too much longer. Rufus will be reducing your workload moving forwards. Then, once we are wed, you will never have to work again.'

The idea was far from appealing. 'It is only kitchen work, and I enjoy cooking.'

Manius stepped closer, taking hold of her arms. 'I shall find you a more suitable hobby.'

Surely she would be allowed to choose her own interests. Perhaps that thinking had been naive on her part. Manius's tone and expression suggested otherwise.

Looking across at Claudius, she said, 'Thank you for a lovely evening.'

He nodded. 'I shall send for the litter.'

They watched him leave, and then Manius faced her once more, his eyes on her lips, the way Nero's had been earlier that afternoon. But this time, her body did not heat, did not pulse. There was no curiosity, no desire to lean in. He bent and kissed her, and she froze, waiting for a reaction other than a strong urge to pull away. It was the same as earlier—empty, cold.

*Perhaps if I hang in there a little longer...*

*No.* She stepped back, eyes on her feet.

He laughed. Not a cruel laugh, but still a laugh. 'You are too sweet.'

He probably meant it as a compliment, but it only embarrassed her.

When she did not respond, he drew a long breath. 'I have never known a woman like you. You make the vestals look like heathens. Do not fear. I am a patient man.'

She dragged her eyes up to meet his. 'I appreciate that. This is all… a lot.'

'It will not take you long to grow used to this life. Soon you will barely remember your old one.'

A scary thought. She glanced in the direction of the door. 'I should go.' He was waiting for her to look at him, so she did, because that was what grown women did.

'This will be your life soon.' His tone turned serious. 'Tell me you want it.'

It was what her mother wanted. It was what her father wanted. *Father*. The word warmed her bones, still cold from Manius's kiss.

'What sensible woman would say no?' It was more a question for herself than an answer for him.

A wide smile spread across his face. 'I suspect you will be worth the wait.'

Moments later she was escorted outside, loaded into a litter, and sent on her way with another stagnant kiss aimed at her mouth. Thanks to a quick reposition of her head, it landed on her cheek.

The moment she was on the move, Dulcia felt the heat of tears on her cheeks. She brushed them aside, because she had no right to cry, to feel miserable, to feel anything other than grateful. Manius had been kind and patient, but in place of gratitude sat nausea, fear, and something else.

She pulled back the curtain to gauge their distance from the house. About halfway. 'You may let me out here.'

The litter was lowered to the ground. When she stepped down, one of the slaves turned and said, 'We were instructed to take you all the way.'

'It is not far from here. I need some fresh air after all that wine. Thank you,' she said before rushing off.

She thought about going to her sister, lying in her lap and having a good cry, like she had many times. Instead, she made her way to the tavern opposite Ludus Magnus in search of Nero. He would be furious at her walking the streets late at night, but the copious amounts of wine she had consumed in order to survive the evening gave her false confidence.

With her head down, she made her way to the tavern, avoiding any shortcuts that took her down dark alleyways. The safest route was via the busy streets, now alive with carts.

She heard the tavern before she saw it. Drunken noise spilled out into the street, as did drunken people. Just as she went to enter, a man stepped out and vomited on the road between them, his palm pressing the wall for balance. She gave him a wide berth and stepped inside the packed space, looking around for a familiar face. No Felix, no Albaus. No Nero.

'Looking for me, love?' a man called to her.

She turned to look at the grinning man who was missing more teeth than she cared to count. The man with him was laughing as though it were the funniest thing he had ever heard.

'I am looking for Nero,' she shouted over the noise.

Nothing registered on their faces.

'Or Cassia? I believe she is a barmaid here.' Not ideal, but the woman might know of his whereabouts.

The men exchanged a knowing look.

'Another disgruntled wife,' one said with a coy smile.

It took her a moment to register their meaning. 'Oh, no. Nothing like that.'

One of the men looked at her with scepticism before pointing across the room. 'That's her.'

Dulcia followed the extended finger to a pretty brunette perched on a lap, her head thrown back in laughter. She focused on the man, holding her breath. It was not Nero. In fact, he was nowhere to be seen.

She looked around the crowded space a final time, then decided to leave. Even if she had found him with Cassia, what was her plan, walk up and ask to borrow him for a quick chat?

'I can be Nero if you want,' someone said as she turned away.

She did not even glance in their direction. Stepping outside, she saw the sick man from earlier wipe his mouth with the back of his hand before stepping past her and returning inside.

Now to get herself home.

'Dulcia?'

Her head snapped in the other direction, following the sound of Nero's voice down the street. He stepped into the light that spilled from the tavern window, Felix and Albaus flanking him like guard dogs. One glimpse of him and she knew he had been fighting. His face was puffy, his tunic sprayed with blood.

'What are you doing here?' he asked, looking around as though expecting someone to jump out and mug her.

'Looking for you.' Her lip trembled, and she looked away, biting back the tears. It was embarrassing how her emotions ruled her.

Nero stared at her for a moment, no doubt trying to read her. He was good at that. 'You all right?'

Instead of a sensible, grown-up conversation explaining herself, she went to him, arms wrapping his middle like a child. For a moment he just stood there. Then warm, familiar hands landed on her back. He smelled of sweat and sand—a familiar smell that brought immediate comfort.

'I think we might head inside for that drink,' Felix said, glancing back at Albaus, who grunted a reply. 'Good luck,' he added, patting Nero's arm as he passed.

Dulcia let go of him and watched the others enter the tavern. She could not afford to be seen standing outside a drinking house in the arms of a man—especially a man who was not Manius.

'What happened?' Nero asked the moment they were alone, his brows fused together.

She was having difficulty looking at him now. 'Nothing happened.'

He pulled her into his arms again, and his scent wrapped her once more. She closed her eyes at the sensation of his breath on her.

'I swear to the gods, if he hurt you...'

She shook her head. 'No one hurt me.'

His arms tightened around her.

What was she supposed to say? "I was collected in a litter, taken to a beautiful house, served excellent food and fine wine, met Manius's family, kissed, and then told I was worth the wait"? What exactly was her complaint? So what if his mother did not like her and his father was overfamiliar—she was not marrying them. 'I just wanted to see you.' He shifted, and she felt his lips brush her hair. 'Will you walk me home?' she whispered into his coarse tunic.

'Yes.' He exhaled and released her. 'I'll walk you home.'

Keeping an arm around her, he led her away from the tavern. And for a few fleeting moments, everything felt better.

# CHAPTER 9

*R*emus and Mila's import business was in many ways a family endeavour, so it was all hands on deck whenever a shipment arrived at the port. Nero pitched in as often as he was able, fitting it in around his own work. Thankfully Nerva understood that when ships anchored, Nero had to disappear for a few days.

Calm seas meant the Ponto arrived in Pozzuoli on time. The spices were then loaded onto another boat, taking two more days to reach Ostia Antica, where Remus, Albaus, Felix and Nero were waiting. They boarded the boat to inspect the sealed terracotta pots. Satisfied, they carried them one at a time to a smaller boat that would take them up the Tiber to Rome. The process was done with great care, as the cinnamon, incense, ginger and pepper were worth almost as much as the ship that carried them from Barace.

'This is the last one,' Remus said, stepping onto the boat.

'Finally,' Felix complained.

Everyone turned to look at the dwarf as they wiped sweat from their brows. Felix had spent the morning supervising the placement of the containers while the others did the majority of the work.

Albaus grunted, and Remus shook his head.

'Oh, do not look at me like that,' Felix said, settling on a seat. 'You know I must reserve my energy for the seasickness.'

Remus took a seat beside him. 'It's a river. There are no waves.'

'I do not need waves. I am quite capable of crippling nausea on calm waters. We are not all born with fishtails,' he added, directing the comment at Nero, who had stopped listening.

Felix cast a knowing look at Remus. 'He makes your pining look like a good time.'

'I don't pine,' Remus replied.

'Not anymore, but there was once a time when you and Mila did this same dance. Whenever we visited the baths, I used to contemplate drowning you just to put you out of your misery.' Felix leaned back on his elbows just as Nero looked over at them.

'What?'

'Felix was just talking about your fishtail,' Remus said.

'Oh.' Nero's gaze returned to the water.

'Oh, he says.' Felix rolled his eyes at Remus. 'Like he suddenly cares for nothing else, his love of the sea dead alongside all hope. It would make a spectacular play, you know.'

Nero ignored him.

'Maybe once Dulcia marries the senator,' Felix continued, 'he might rediscover his desire to leave the city.'

Nero looked over at that. 'He's not a senator yet. It was you who said he was just another charioteer.'

'Yes,' Felix agreed. 'A very successful and insanely rich charioteer.'

'And his father is just a merchant,' Remus added.

A nod from Felix. 'Yes, a very successful and insanely rich merchant.' He looked at Nero. 'When your family has more wealth than most of the patricians in the city, you can buy any life you choose.'

Remus was watching Nero in a way that made him feel transparent. 'But Dulcia does not care that he is rich. She is not marrying Manius for his wealth.'

'I know that.'

Felix tapped a finger on the side of the boat. 'Then she is an anomaly. Any sensible girl would jump at such an offer.'

'Well, she said yes, didn't she?' Nero was unable to keep the frustration from his tone.

'Her father said yes,' Remus reminded him.

Nero drew a breath. 'She didn't exactly put up a fight.'

Felix snorted. 'You expect a girl who was raised a slave in her father's house, largely ignored her entire life, who is now finally getting the attention she has craved since birth, to turn around and tell him *no*?' He looked between them. 'Anyone else think I spend a concerning amount of time educating you people on the workings of the female mind?'

'Is this about her marrying Manius, or about her marrying at all?' Remus asked, ignoring Felix's remark.

'He's not good enough for her.'

Felix leaned forwards. 'Is there a man in Rome who is?'

'You, perhaps,' Remus said.

Not even him.

When he said nothing, Remus continued. 'You should've said something when you had the chance.'

'I have to agree with Remus on this one,' Felix said. 'Your silence has not done you any favours.'

Even Albaus grunted, seemingly in agreement.

Nero rested his elbows on his knees as the boat pulled away from the wharf. 'I'm not shy, you know. It's just that my feelings are irrelevant. I've nothing to offer a woman like Dulcia.' He had to raise his voice to compete with the flapping of the sail as it was raised.

'I disagree,' Remus said with a shrug.

'I share a room with two men.' Nero's gaze went to the water. 'Besides, she's never said she *doesn't* want to marry Manius. Maybe she does.'

Felix swung his legs leisurely. 'The girl can barely maintain eye contact during conversation. You expect too much of her.'

'If she didn't want to marry him, she'd tell me. She tells me everything.'

Another snort from Felix. 'You have so much to learn about women.'

'I'd be very surprised if Dulcia felt anything for Manius outside of obligation,' Remus said. 'Especially because she knows you don't like him.'

Nero let out a breath. 'Just because I pray most days he'll be thrown from his overdecorated chariot and trampled by his own horses doesn't mean Dulcia shouldn't marry him.'

Felix made a face. 'You would not be the first man to pray for the death of a blue charioteer, but that is oddly specific.'

Nero continued as though he had not spoken. 'She deserves that life.'

Remus frowned across the deck at him, not convinced. 'You're assuming she wants it. I'll bet no one bothered to ask her.'

Nero had to think about that for a moment. Had he asked her? He must have at some point. Of course she was hesitant, probably even afraid. But she was like that with most things, even if she pretended otherwise. Perhaps he should have asked her outright. All he knew for sure was that she shrank back from Manius every time they were together. But that was because he had not won her trust yet, not earned it the way Nero had. He might eventually.

He could not ask her what she wanted, because her answer would come from a place of fear, not logic, and there were only two other alternatives: hiding in the shadows in her father's grand house, or a life of struggle outside of its walls. She deserved more than that.

No, he would remain silent and give her time to adjust to the life he wanted her to have.

'Anyone else feel nauseous?' Felix asked, a hand going to his stomach.

Remus stood and patted his shoulder. 'Remember, eyes on the horizon.'

'Oh, do shut up,' Felix replied, edging closer to the side of the boat.

The others turned their grinning faces to the water.

# CHAPTER 10

*R*ace day was always a mess of nerves and excitement. Everyone involved felt the pressure and knew how easily it could all go so very wrong.

Nero had slept at the stables the night prior to watch over the horses; it was not uncommon for one of the animals to become mysteriously ill or be found dead on race day. He had wandered between the stalls, watching the shadows, listening for noises and bracing for trouble.

The moment the sun rose over the city, the horses began to pace, picking up on the energy around them. They knew what was coming. The grooms had risen early, brushing the horses' coats until they were so glossy they reflected the sun. When the men were done, Nero slipped into Amator's stall and went over him one more time. The stallion shuffled and flicked his head.

'Easy, boy. Don't let the ladies see you nervous.'

A rap on the stall door made him look up. It was Dulcia, her hair in an immaculate crown braid and lips painted a cherry red. Her arms were bare and bronzed from the sun, contrasting her bleached tunic. She held onto the door as she looked Amator over.

'He looks absolutely amazing. I have never seen a more muscled creature.'

Nero's gaze fell to her light blue stola visible above the door, likely belted in that way that made her hips look round and his mouth go dry. He had not seen her since the evening she had come to the tavern looking for him, the evening he had held her so close she had barely been able to draw breath. The scent of her had lingered on him for days.

Stepping back from the stallion, he went to her. 'What are you doing here?'

Her gaze shifted to him. 'Looking for you.' She said it like it was the most natural thing in the world for her to be at the green stables, despite the fact that her future husband rode for the blue team.

He tapped the brush against the wall to free some of the hair, and Dulcia waved a hand in front of her face as dust rose. 'Sorry.'

She waved off the apology also. 'How are you feeling?'

He leaned on the door. From that angle, he could see the full length of her, right down to her sun-kissed toes.

'Do I look all right?' she asked, plucking a horse hair off her garment.

How was he supposed to answer that? He was torn between falling at her feet and walking off to spare himself any embarrassment. 'That colour suits you.' It was all he could manage.

She looked up, searching his eyes for a moment before turning and grabbing a wrapped package from a shelf behind her. When she turned back, he saw light in her eyes, even though she was not smiling.

He nodded towards the linen bundle wrapped with ribbon. 'What have you got there?'

She held it out to him. 'Fruit tarts.'

For a moment, he was distracted by the enormous silver

ring on her finger. The one he had given her was gone. 'My favourite.'

Her lips turned up in a smile. 'I know. That is why I made them for you.'

His eyes travelled up to meet hers, then returned to her perfectly painted mouth. 'You made them for me?'

'As a thank you.'

'For what?'

'For walking me home.'

He shifted his feet, putting more weight on his elbows. 'Which time?'

She thought for a moment. 'All of the times, but especially the other day. I could not ask for a better friend.'

*Friend*. He straightened. 'You don't have to thank me for that.'

She did not move. 'I know.'

He stared at the gift, wondering if her arms were tiring. He was about to take it when he heard footsteps approaching. Dulcia lowered her hands and stepped back from the door just as Nerva came into sight.

'What are you doing here?' he asked, bending to kiss his sister. He wore a green tunic beneath his toga in support of his team.

'Wishing Nero luck.'

Nerva peered into the stall, taking in Amator. 'Gods, look at him. What a handsome boy.'

'I'm going to assume you're talking about Amator,' Nero said.

Nerva chuckled. 'You are looking quite fit also.' He turned back to Dulcia, eyes narrowing on the package in her hands. 'What is that?'

She looked suddenly guilty. 'Fruit tarts.'

'Ah, trying to impress Manius with your culinary skills?' Nerva patted her arm like one did a child. 'Look at you, playing the game so well. Who knew you had it in you?' He glanced over at Nero. 'Some comfort food when he loses.' He returned his attention to his sister. 'I thought you would be seated by now, enjoying your prime viewing spot.'

'Prime viewing spot?' Nero asked.

'Did she not tell you? Our little Dulcia will be sitting on a balcony with the Liberia family today.'

'Really, Nerva, I have not been little for some years.'

'I'm surprised you're even attending,' Nero said, his mood completely ruined. 'You hate the circus.'

'Many women attend for the social outing, a chance to show off their garments and jewels,' Nerva said. He took Dulcia's hand, studying the ring. 'You will be weighed down by this stuff by the time you are wed.'

Nero turned back to Amator. 'You had better go give Manius his tarts.' He tried to keep the bitterness from his tone—and failed.

'We better leave him,' Nerva said. 'He gets race day jitters far worse than me.'

Nero stole a glance at Dulcia and found her scowling back at him. He resumed working.

'Come,' Nerva said, draping an arm over her shoulders. 'I will walk you.'

She did not say goodbye, simply left. He could hardly blame her. The problem was every mention of Manius, or even his family for that matter, fanned the jealousy inside him. Sure, she would have everything she deserved, but none of it provided by him.

He drew a breath and shook the thoughts from his head. Taking hold of Amator's halter, he looked the stallion in the eye. 'You better beat that arse of a man today.'

～

DULCIA FELT like a duck amid swans. Every direction she turned, she was blinded by jewellery or suffocated by expensive perfume.

The balcony was located in a wing reserved for senators, equites, high-ranking military personnel, and anyone rich enough to buy their way in. People lounged on plump cushions, with every comfort on hand. Slaves waited nearby, ready to fill their cups and bring them food. Others fanned their masters with lotus leaves and enormous feathers from exotic birds Dulcia did not recognise.

'It is too hot,' Livia whined, gesturing for the girl fanning her to speed up.

Dulcia kept her eyes on the procession, afraid her face would expose her thoughts.

First came the boys of the nobility on horseback. They were followed by future infantrymen on foot. Behind them were the athletes who would race, box or wrestle.

'Here comes Manius,' Junia said.

The charioteers wore team colours. Impractical cloaks draped their shoulders, spilling all the way down to the floor of the chariot. Their arrival brought the crowd to their feet, though not the people around Dulcia, who were apparently far too comfortable to bother standing.

Four matching grey horses pulled Manius's chariot. They were as impressive as Nerva's so far as breeding, size and condition. Junia cheered when Manius slowed in front of the balcony, bringing disapproving stares from her mother, who clapped modestly.

'I would prefer to see him in a senator's toga than a blue cloak,' Livia remarked.

Claudius raised a cup to his son, though he seemed more interested in watching the slave girl tending his wife.

'You had better clap,' Junia said over the noise.

Dulcia found a smile, and her hands came together in what she hoped was convincing applause. Manius nodded once in her direction before moving on, and she was left with a hollow feeling in the pit of her stomach, a reminder that it was all an act. Every smile felt like a betrayal of herself.

Nerva's horses followed with their new driver. Her brother had been rather unlucky in that regard. The last man had been thrown from his chariot and trampled by horses. By some miracle he had survived, though his right leg had not.

She knew Nero would have jumped at the chance to race, but everyone was rather keen on keeping him alive. When Nerva had tried to bring it up during a meal together, Remus had remarked that he already participated in enough life-threatening activities. It was a well-known fact that Nero was fearless to the point of reckless. Some intervention was necessary.

Music from aulos and lyre players pulled her attention back to the procession. Dancers trailed behind the musicians, wearing purple tunics and carrying spears. They performed war dances, some wearing wings, others helmets with crests. Then came the Sileni in woolly tunics, goatskin loincloths and ridiculous hairstyles. They mocked the dancers, making the audience laugh out loud at their antics.

Junia leaned in close and whispered, 'Now the part we have all been waiting for.'

Dulcia turned to her, confused, then followed her line of sight to the gladiators. They raised their shields and beat their chests, playing up to the crowd. The cheers were deafening.

Junia raised her cup as they passed. 'They call that one Romulus. A fitting name for that body. Goodness, did the temperature just rise?' She flashed a devious smile at Dulcia, who turned to look at the man.

'He might die today.' And she would be forced to watch.

Junia took a drink from her cup. 'But if he lives, he will be invited to the dinner party afterwards, a win for everyone.'

'You know, we can all hear you,' Livia said, not looking at her daughter.

'So?' Junia turned to Dulcia. 'She marries me off at age twelve, then complains when I do not play the virgin in my twentieth year.'

Dulcia frowned. 'I did not know you were married.'

Junia shrugged. 'Not anymore. Otto died in battle two years ago.'

Dulcia looked down at her drink. 'I am so sorry.'

'Do not be,' Junia replied, sounding upbeat. 'The man was a pig.'

Livia tutted. '*He* was due to be promoted.'

'The man once dragged me by the hair from my bed after I miscarried.' She was speaking to Dulcia but spoke loud enough for her mother to hear. 'Apparently it was my fault.'

Pity swelled inside Dulcia. 'Why would he suggest such a thing?'

Junia blinked, her eyes shiny. 'The slave he was bedding told him my bathwater had been too warm, that I asked for more hot water to be brought in.'

Livia straightened, her mouth pursed. 'It is a well-known fact—'

'Mother, please. I cannot hear it again.'

Everyone fell silent for a moment.

'Your sister used to be a gladiator, did she not?' Livia asked, changing the subject.

'A long time ago,' Dulcia replied. 'Before women were banned.'

Livia tutted once more. 'Poor Lady Prisca. What a horrendous way to die. I still feel the grief as though it happened yesterday.'

Junia rolled her eyes. 'She could not stand the woman,' she whispered to Dulcia.

'I heard that,' Livia snapped.

Junia waved her cup, and a servant rose to fill it. 'I must

say, it is difficult to imagine you as the sister of a gladiator. You are so...'

'Weak?' Livia offered.

Junia turned to glare at her mother. 'I was going to say *timid*.'

'Are they not the same?'

Dulcia's cheeks heated. Perhaps they were the same.

Junia patted her hand. 'Ignore her.'

Incense burners walked in front of litters carrying statues of gods. They were taken to a wooden platform and displayed. As soon as the procession finished, the *spatium* was cleared, ready for the first event.

'I do hope they open with a gladiatorial battle,' Junia said, looking around. 'I find the boxing rather comical.'

'I find it tedious,' Livia sighed. 'Hand the men some weapons and be done with it.'

Dulcia closed her eyes against the words, wondering how on earth she was going to survive the day.

A horn sounded, and the crowd cheered.

# CHAPTER 11

The new charioteer's name was Chares, and Nero liked the way he handled the horses with respect and care.

'They seem skittish,' Chares said, stepping up into the chariot and gathering the reins. He slipped them over his head and wrapped them around his middle for better control. His fingers brushed the knife at his side as though checking it was still there. The weapon might save his life if he fell.

'They're keen to get going,' Nero said, holding Amator's bridle with one hand and rubbing his forelock with the other in an attempt to calm him. A groom stood on the other side doing the same. Every now and then, an impatient hoof clipped the gate.

The sound of more horses arriving made Nero look up. It was Manius, his chest pushed out to twice its normal size. He nodded at Nero, who returned the gesture.

'Easy,' Chares called to Vita, one of the middle mares, who was throwing her head up.

Manius looked over at the flighty horse, then at Chares. 'First time racing with new horses is always hard.'

Chares did not even glance in his direction. He was experienced enough to know the man was simply trying to get in his head, and did not look the least bit nervous. Nerva had chosen well.

'Grow wings and fly,' Nero whispered to Amator before stepping back. No one wanted to be in the way of the horses when those gates opened. He went to stand behind the chariots, twelve in total, three from each faction. Drivers made final adjustments to their grip and repositioned their feet, evenly distributing their weight. A horn sounded, and the gates flung open to the roar of one hundred and fifty thousand spectators.

The chariots lurched forwards, forming a clean line as they headed for the spina. The handlers followed them out onto the track. They would wait in the centre, better positioned to capture runaway horses or assist the injured if the need arose. Nero slipped between the stone barrier and wiped his hands on his tunic as the drivers settled into their first positions. The thunder of hooves, combined with the resounding noise from the crowd, made his ears ring.

As the horses approached the *metae*, Nero changed position to get a clearer view. He watched as Manius pulled on the inside rein and squeezed between two chariots, a move that put him in third position. Chares remained in sixth place coming out of the turn, but with plenty of time to catch up.

The horses spread out on the straight as they galloped back towards the starting gates. Chares reached for his whip and pushed the horses hard down the outside, overtaking the two white faction chariots and putting him in fourth place.

'That's it,' Nero said aloud.

The horses rumbled past him, lost in dust and excitement. A bronze dolphin lowered at one end, a marble egg at the other, each counting down the laps so spectators could keep track of progress.

Six to go.

The drivers managed two entire laps without incident, but during the third, the lead chariot clipped the spina on the turn and lost a wheel. The driver managed to free himself of the reins before his chariot flipped coming out of the turn. He rolled free of the approaching horses, and the moment the track was clear, two men ran out and helped him to safety. The loose horses continued at full speed, the broken chariot bouncing wildly behind them. Eventually they would tire enough that their handlers could capture and remove them from the track.

The incident put Manius into first position. Nero slapped the pillar with the palm of his hand and cursed under his breath. Another dolphin and egg fell.

Four laps to go.

During the next lap, Chares moved wide on the straight once more, sneaking into second place. Nero paced between the pillars, his heart thudding hard in his chest. He knew Manius would do whatever was necessary to ensure he remained in the lead. The man was as dirty a driver as the next during a race.

Chares took the turn much too fast, trying to compensate for the fact that he was on the outside. By some miracle, the horses remained upright, and both wheels of the chariot stuck thanks to some clever weight management. Nero reminded himself to breathe as they entered the straight. He was certain Chares would take the lead before the next turn, but Manius was no fool. Predicting his opponent's move, Manius swung his horses wide, blocking Chares, who was forced to pull up in order to avoid a collision.

Nero cursed again, head shaking.

Chares used the opportunity to try and take the inside position, but Manius glanced over his shoulder and pulled his horses left, blocking him once again.

At the far end, another chariot upturned. The driver

disappeared beneath horses before being spat out the other end, a pulp of broken flesh and bones. Two men ran out onto the track with a wooden stretcher, but they were immediately forced back by approaching horses that had no choice but to leap over the wreckage. But a chariot cannot jump, and it flew up in the air on impact. The driver held onto the sides, his legs flailing for a moment before landing inside the chariot as it hit the ground. It took him a moment to collect the reins and regain control of the horses. The crowd leapt to their feet, their cheers deafening.

Chares and Manius were still fighting it out on the straight, Manius lashing the backs of his horses, edging them forwards until his chariot was level with his opponent's. Nero saw him glance at Amator, and a bad feeling rose inside him.

'Don't you dare,' he said, taking a few steps forwards. He froze as Manius swerved right, clipping Amator's leg.

The crowd howled in protest, the noise suddenly tenfold in Nero's ears. Then nothing. He could not hear a thing, not even the roar that tore from his throat. Amator ploughed chest first into the dirt, pulling the other horses down with him. Leather snapped, and Chares was thrown from the chariot as it rolled. There was a collective gasp as the horses twisted and crashed against one another before finally tumbling to a stop amid a cloud of red dust.

Nero leaped over the barrier and took off at a run straight for them, his eyes fixed on the horses. High-pitched whinnies rang out across the sand, bringing the few spectators who were still sitting to their feet for a better view. With his stomach in knots, Nero ran faster.

~

DULCIA'S NERVES had gotten the better of her. She looked everywhere but at the race, her damp palms pressing against her thighs the entire time. She drank the wine, picked at the grapes—anything not to watch the two leading chariots gallop at full speed, their wheels occasionally bumping.

There were still four laps to go. She could not bear to see any more horses fall.

Plucking another grape, she ignored Junia's distracted glances in her direction, but the collective gasp of the people around her made her look up. She immediately wished she had not. Her fingernails dug into the flesh beneath her garments as she watched her brother's horses slam into the ground, the driver expelled from his chariot, rolling a few times and then going still.

Amator had been the first to fall, the others dragged down with him. She heard the snap of leather or bone—she could not tell which. Dust rose in front of the balcony, staining her vision. Standing, she stepped between the seats and rushed to the edge of the balcony. As she gripped the banister, she spotted Nero sprinting down the track towards the crash site.

The insane thing was that the race just carried on as though nothing had happened. The remaining nine chariots were simply expected to navigate the crash sites, and the men responsible for clearing the wreckage were forced to dodge the chariots. Two such chariots passed either side of the accident, taking up nearly the entire width of the track as they came back together. Nero did not stop, or even slow down for that matter. His gaze was fixed on the horses that he cared for like children.

'Ah, Dulcia,' Junia called. 'What are you doing?'

Dulcia could not reply. She continued to grip the barricade, afraid she would fall down if she let go. Nero disappeared between galloping horses, and Dulcia's hand went over her mouth to hold in a scream. He reappeared a few moments later, now moving at a jog, waving away the dust. When he reached the horses, he fell to his knees beside

Amator, then pulled out a knife and began cutting through the leather straps. By that stage, some other men had arrived and were trying to detach the chariot. Horses approached, and they dragged it out of the way just in time, calling to Nero to move. He remained where he was, cutting through the straps, trying to free the horses.

*Move.*

He looked up as the horses neared, then continued cutting as though he had not seen them.

'Nero!' Dulcia shouted. 'Get out of the way!'

There was no way he could hear her in a venue that size.

'What in heaven's name is she shouting about?' Livia said behind her. 'Sit down.'

Dulcia did not even glance back at her. Nero was directly in the path of an oncoming chariot. The driver managed to veer around the wreckage at the last minute, but the chariot behind was not so lucky. The horses had no choice but to leap over the fallen animals. Dulcia's heart stopped as Nero dropped flush against the ground and they flew overhead. The chariot was propelled up in the air, breaking apart on landing, its driver ejected into the stone wall barrier.

Nero leapt to his feet as more men poured out onto the track to help him. Together they freed one horse. Two horses. Vita was bleeding from the head and nose, struggling against the confines of the harness, while Amator was completely still.

'Sit down this instant,' Livia said, her tone growing more abrupt.

There was no way Dulcia could turn her back on the scene playing out in front of her. She watched as Nerva jogged out onto the track to join the effort. Nero was on his knees next to Amator's head, the knife in his hand moving at an extraordinary speed. Nerva stopped at Vita, and he and another man began rocking the horse, encouraging her to get up. They did not have much time, as more chariots were approaching.

'They need to stop the race,' Dulcia whispered, one hand pressing against her stomach.

Nerva glanced in the direction of the advancing horses, then took hold of Vita's bridle and pulled while the other man pushed. Finally, the mare got up on shaky legs and was led away. Nerva ran over to Nero, who had finally managed to cut Amator free. But still, the stallion did not move.

Another dolphin went down. There was only one lap to go with seven chariots remaining in the race. They would not slow for anything now.

Nerva grabbed Nero's arm and tried to pull him away, but Nero shrugged out of his grip, took hold of one of Amator's legs, and tried to drag him. Unsurprisingly, the twelve-hundred-pound stallion did not move. Nerva caught his arm once more, and again Nero pulled himself free. Nerva shouted something at him, then had no choice but to move or be trampled.

Dulcia could barely believe what she was seeing. 'Move!' she screamed, pounding on the banister with her fist.

'Dulcia,' Junia said. 'Come sit down.'

*Shut up*, she wanted to shout. Instead, she watched the remaining chariots move into a line on the final straight. Whips went back and forth as they each tried to get in front. There was no space between them, no room for error. Without thinking it through, she leapt over the barrier and dropped down onto the track. She landed in a crouch, the air leaving her lungs in an *oomph*.

'Dulcia!' It was Junia above her.

She was already running towards Nero. If anyone could make him move, it was her. But she was barely a quarter of the way there when someone caught her around the waist.

'What in heaven's name are you doing?'

It was Nerva.

101

She pushed at the arm around her, trying to free herself. 'Nero!' she screamed, needing him to look at her. He must have heard her that time, because his head snapped up, eyes locking on her. 'Move!'

He glanced at the approaching horses, then down at Amator before getting to his feet and taking off at a run towards her. Nerva dragged Dulcia farther back, struggling to keep a hold of her. She looked at the chariots storming towards Nero, then back at him, her hands jumping to her mouth as she realised he was not going to make it in time.

He must have realised it too, because he stopped running and turned to face the horses.

'Nero!'

Nerva backed them up against the wall as Nero disappeared from sight. He was swallowed up by thundering horses and flashes of colour. As quick as they had arrived, they were gone again, leaving only dust in their wake.

'Let me go,' she pleaded, pushing at Nerva's arm once more.

He released her that time, because it was the last lap and they would not be passing again. She took off at a run into the settling cloud of dust, looking for a body on the ground and panicking when she could not find it. 'Nero!'

A hand caught her wrist and she spun around to see him standing there, his panicked eyes moving over her. He let out a shaky breath.

'Have you lost your mind?'

'Have I...' Her free hand went over her mouth, stifling a sob. 'I thought you were dead.'

He pulled her to him, his arms going around her. One hand spanned the middle of her back while the other cradled her head. A veil of murky air protected them from prying eyes. 'I'm fine,' he whispered into her hair. 'We need to get you off the track.'

The moment he released her, she wanted his arms around

her again. He took her hand instead and led her back to Nerva, who was searching for them. Her brother looked past them to Amator, who lay on the track, his broken body covered in dust. The great stallion was unrecognisable.

Nerva's arm went around his sister, shielding her vision. 'Let us go.'

Her legs obeyed, but she could not look away from Nero's broken expression. She wanted him to follow, but instead he turned and headed for the dead horse.

Thunderous applause shook the air around them, and Dulcia looked up, confused.

Nerva tightened his grip on her. 'It is Manius,' he said. 'Your betrothed has just been crowned the winner.'

# CHAPTER 12

'*L*eave it,' Nerva had told him. '*He is not the first charioteer to use dirty tactics.*'

No, Manius was not the first to win a race with dirty tactics, but he was definitely the first to kill Nero's favourite horse in the process.

By some miracle, Chares was alive, but he would never race again. Neither would two of the mares. They would likely be sold to wealthy fans, a living keepsake. Only Vita would make a full recovery. It would take a lot of time and money to replace the horses they had lost.

No, Nero could not let it go. In fact, he only grew angrier over the days that followed.

With three horses gone, he continued to train Vita at the Trigarium, always on the lookout for Manius. He had no idea what he would do when he ran into him, but at the very least he would let him know that he saw him for what he was—a coward who relied on cheap tactics instead of skill. One thing he knew for sure was that Manius would never be good enough for Dulcia. She deserved someone with some integrity.

His opportunity to confront the man came three days

after the race. Manius made an appearance around noon, just as Nero had finished putting Vita through her paces. He was easily recognisable across the field, with his ridiculous silk cloak pushed back over one shoulder. Every muscle in Nero's body tightened at the sight of him.

'Take Vita back to the stables, would you?' he said to the groom.

The groom looked over to where Manius stood, arms crossed at the edge of the field, waiting for his chariot like the rich fool he was.

'What are you going to do?'

'I don't know,' he replied honestly, striding off in that direction. He knew the moment Manius spotted him, because that cocky smile on his face faded.

'Nero,' the charioteer called when he was close. 'How is the general's driver fairing?'

Nero did not slow down. With his hands curled into fists and his jaw set, he marched straight up to Manius, unsure at what point he would stop. Before smashing his face in or after?

'Nero?'

The sound of Dulcia's voice stopped him in his tracks. He turned and found her standing with a horse some twenty feet away. Her look of surprise melted into confusion as she took in his body language.

'Dulcia.' He relaxed his hands. 'What are you doing here?'

She glanced at Manius, giving him his answer.

'I collected Dulcia on my way here,' Manius said. 'She likes the horses.'

As if Nero needed educating on Dulcia's likes and dislikes.

He watched as she went to stand next to Manius, looking painfully uncomfortable at his side. Nero felt a surge of protectiveness in that moment. He had not seen her since the day she jumped the banister at the Circus Maximus, because he had no idea what to say to her. He had overheard Nerva lecturing her after the event, and she had probably received the same lecture again from both her parents, perhaps even Manius's family. He feared anything he said or did would only make things worse.

'I was just asking after the welfare of your brother's driver,' Manius said, taking Dulcia's hand and placing it on his arm.

Nero's eyes followed the motion, the sight of her arm through Manius's fanning that flame inside of him. She did not pull away, just stood there—like a dutiful wife.

'He's lucky to be alive,' Nero said, his tone like ice.

Manius tutted. 'The things we charioteers do for the love of the sport. Be thankful Nerva has never let you compete. Much safer to be tending the horses than racing them.'

It was said without malice, but that did not stop Nero from wanting to knock that smug expression off his face. His gaze flicked to Dulcia, who was staring at her feet. Surely she saw him for what he was.

He narrowed his eyes on Manius. 'You did that, not the sport. You realised you were about to lose, so you took out the lead stallion.'

Dulcia looked up at that, eyes wide. 'Nero, stop.'

She seemed genuinely surprised by the accusation. 'You were there. You saw it.' It was unfair to put her on the spot, but he was beyond propriety.

'We are all upset about the loss of Amator,' she said. 'It was a terrible accident.'

Nero threw his hands up. 'He deliberately ran his chariot into the horse.'

Manius took a step forwards. 'You will kindly address your grievances to me, not my betrothed.'

The nerve of the man to act like she needed protecting from *him*. Nero shook his head, losing patience. 'What? You speak for her now?'

Dulcia closed her eyes and looked away while Manius lifted his chin. 'If you think I am going to stand by while you attack my future wife, you are mistaken.'

Dulcia's hand went to her stomach, the way it always did when there was conflict. Nero's chest grew heavy.

'We are done here,' Manius said, placing his hand on Dulcia's back. 'Let us go.'

She stiffened at his touch. It was so subtle, but enough for Nero's mind to snap. With his hand already clenched into a fist, he stepped forwards and punched Manius in the face, sending the charioteer hurtling sideways to the ground. He did not stop there. In the next breath, Nero had his knee in Manius's side and a small blade pressed to his neck.

Dulcia ran forwards and grabbed his arm. 'Stop,' she pleaded. 'Get off him.'

Nero reached up with his free hand to move her out of the way, afraid she would get hurt, but it was more of a shove than he intended. Out of the corner of his eye, he saw her fall back into the dirt. His anger evaporated, and his hand went limp around the dagger. He turned his head, saw the shock frozen on her face. All he wanted to do then was go to her, help her up, apologise, erase his actions completely. But before he could get to his feet, Manius's fist smashed into his cheek, sending a spray of blood across the dirt and the dagger flying. It sailed through the air and landed like a dart in the sand, a hair's breadth from Dulcia's leg.

Manius seemed oblivious to the fact as he pushed himself up and went to swing again, but that time Nero was ready and blocked the blow with his arm. They continued that way for a few moments, rolling about in the dirt, fists swinging.

Dulcia scrambled to her feet. 'Stop it. Nero, please.'

But he could not stop. He was going to strangle the man with his bare hands. The dagger had almost hit her, and now he was going to choke the charioteer with his own pompous cape.

Large hands grabbed hold of him, pulling him off. Nero fought to get free but failed. He turned his head to see who had hold of him and found a scowling Albaus. Felix was beside him, a hand outstretched to Manius. The charioteer propped himself up on his elbows, two streams of blood pouring from his nose. He ignored the offer of a hand and rose slowly to his feet. He spat blood onto the ground.

'You will pay for this, *Rat*.'

Felix looked between them. 'I am sensing some hostility between the two of you.'

Dulcia walked over to Manius and tugged on his arm. 'Let us go.'

Nero could not believe what he was seeing and hearing. 'You're going with *him*?'

She glanced over, her cheeks red and her expression wary. 'Stay back,' she warned.

'Dulcia—'

Manius stepped in front of her. 'Your days of telling her what to do are over.'

That time Albaus took a step in his direction, but Felix raised a hand to stop him. 'They were just leaving.'

Dulcia took Manius's arm, but he pulled free, his pride too wounded. 'I am fine.'

She nodded, her trembling hand returning to her side as she stepped away from him. Nero hated that he had done that to her.

'Dulcia,' Nero called once more, wanting her to go with *him*, to care for *him*, to choose *him*. He wanted to tell her he was sorry for pushing her, check every inch of her body for injury. If he could just hold her for a moment, kiss her hair, make everything better between them.

He moved to go after her, but Albaus caught his arm again, and Felix's stern expression held him in place.

'Leave it.'

Nero's shoulders fell as he realised he had no choice but to let her walk away.

~

DULCIA SAT with her mother on the laundry floor, their backs against the wall. It was the least attractive room in the entire household, and yet it had served as a refuge of sorts her whole life. She was reminded in that moment that she valued comfort over luxury, the familiar over the new.

'I should never have permitted you to spend time with that boy,' Tertia said, reaching out and taking Dulcia's hand. 'I should have known he was trouble by the way your sister was drawn to him.'

'He is not trouble.' Dulcia studied the cracks on the wall opposite. 'He is just misunderstood.'

'He is damaged, and some things cannot be fixed.'

Dulcia closed her eyes. 'Do not say that.'

Tertia turned to look at her. 'You cannot see him anymore. It is not safe for either of you. Manius has every right to be jealous.'

Dulcia frowned. 'Jealous of what? Nothing has happened between us.' A lie. More than ever she realised it now. She recalled the panic she had felt when he had been on the track, the way her mind had broken apart at the prospect of losing him. She was not the type of girl who jumped over banisters and ran into danger. That was something her sister would do.

'Whatever it is or is not, you must let it go.'

Dulcia shook her head, rejecting the sentiment. She had known things would change, but imagining a life without Nero made her stomach solidify and her chest tighten. Who would she talk to? Play games with? Laugh and climb trees with?

'You are children no longer,' Tertia continued. 'It is inappropriate. You endangered yourself at the circus, and you embarrassed a lot of people.'

'He almost died.'

'It is the circus. Men die all the time there.'

'Charioteers die.'

Tertia blinked. 'He is not even a charioteer yet, and he has worked for Nerva for how long?'

'He cares for the horses, trains them. It is a very important job.'

Her mother looked sceptical. 'And does he still fight? Gamble?'

'How is that relevant?'

Tertia shook her head. 'They are more reasons for you to stay away from him.' She thought for a moment. 'What did Manius say at the party afterwards?'

'He was just happy about his win.' He had said nothing of the accident or of her actions. No one had. Livia's relentless icy glare had communicated her thoughts on the subject. Junia had said nothing of Nero, but had casually mentioned that crashes happened all the time and were part of the thrill of going.

Nero had blamed Manius for Amator's death, but that was surely just the grief speaking. It was an accident, a horrible accident, and her heart broke for him. Mila had told her he had slept in the stallion's empty stall since it had happened. She had tried to go see him there, twice, then thought better of it each time.

'Do not be reckless with all that has been handed to you,' her mother said. 'The gods smile down on you.' She brushed a lock of hair back from her daughter's eyes. 'You are the sensible one, remember? You must keep the balance.'

'Mila's sensible.'

Tertia exhaled. 'She has calmed down a lot since becoming a mother, I will give her that.'

'She is also happy.' How could she not be? Look at all she had.

Tertia reached out and squeezed her hand. 'As you will be, my sweet girl.' She drew a breath. 'You deserve this. You know that, right?'

Deserving it was one thing, wanting it was another. She recalled the look on her father's face when he had broken the news of their engagement. It had bordered on pride. *Pride.* 'I might not take up swords and fight like Mila did, but I believe in all she fought for.'

A knowing smile spread across Tertia's face. 'You want the dream she fed you. The reality is not so glamorous.'

Dulcia's brow creased. 'What do you mean?'

'She lives in an apartment with three children, four men and no help.'

Dulcia could not believe those words had come from her mother. 'In case you have not noticed this about your eldest daughter, she does not need help. Anyway, the four men *are* her help.'

'Bodyguards, perhaps.' Tertia reached up and tucked Dulcia's hair behind her ear. 'I am not suggesting she is not happy. I know she is. Remus is a wonderful husband and father.'

'I feel a *but* coming.'

'*But* that is *her* dream. It is all right for you to want more.'

Dulcia tilted her head. 'More than an adoring husband, healthy children and loyal friends who would lay down their lives for me?'

'You make me out to be shallow because I want an easier life for you. Wealth does make for an easier existence. You will never struggle to make ends meet with Manius. You will want for nothing, and your children will carry the Liberia name.'

'Excellent. Instead of love, I get a name.'

Tertia laughed and pulled her daughter into an embrace. 'You get both. From all reports, Manius adores you.'

'From all reports? You have not even met him.'

'A man of his status dining with a slave pushes the boundaries of propriety, even for Manius, who is very progressive in his thinking.' Seeing her daughter's expression, she added, 'Give him time. The incident today has everyone on edge.'

Dulcia did not want to think about earlier. She knew Nero never meant to push her, knew by his expression, by the way his entire body went limp at the realisation. She had conveniently left that part out when relaying the story to her mother. No need to fuel the fire.

'I know Nero can be kind, that he cares about you, perhaps even loves you in his own way.'

Dulcia wanted to object to that last part, but of course it was love. Why else did she feel so light in his presence, look forward to seeing him every day, and miss him when she did not? He was friend and family bundled into one. He was her safe haven.

She held her breath, bracing for the second *but*.

'But your father has chosen Manius as your husband.'

'Because he asked.'

'And Nero did not.'

The words were like cold water thrown over her. No, he had not. Perhaps friendship and family were enough for him.

Seeing Dulcia's expression, Tertia added, 'Has he ever told you he loves you? That he wishes to marry and take care of you?'

He always took care of her. There had never been a need to announce the fact. 'Perhaps... perhaps Manius simply got in first.'

There was pity on her mother's face. 'Does Nero seem like the sort of man who would show restraint with his feelings? I believe today was evidence of the contrary.'

She honestly did not know the answer. At times she sensed restraint, but the question was why.

'*Dulcia*' he had said as she left with Manius that afternoon. One word that had almost tripped her. What he had not said was "*Stay with me. Love me. Marry me.*"

Dulcia rested her head on her mother's shoulder, and Tertia stroked her hair.

'I think there is a reason Nero has never asked for your hand.'

Dulcia swallowed against the large lump in her throat. 'What reason is that?'

The soothing strokes stopped. 'He too knows you deserve more.'

# CHAPTER 13

*N*ero did not want to go to the tavern. He did not want to go home. He did not want to be around people, to feel their disappointed gazes on him, or worse, their pity. So he stayed away, remaining at the stables despite there being no need for it.

He sat with his back against the wall in Amator's spotless stall, listening to Vita eat on the other side of the wall dividing them. He missed the company and antics of the great stallion—missed a lot of things.

The realisation hit him hard once more. He had lost Dulcia also.

Manius had a firm hold of her now, and once they wed, he would likely never see her. Maybe from a distance, maybe if she were permitted to visit with her sister, maybe if he could be in the same room as her without losing his mind. By then, would he find a way through his blinding jealousy and learn to be happy for her? He did not think so.

The stall door creaked, and Nero turned his head, expecting to see a groom. Instead, Dulcia stepped inside, eyes meeting his amid the shadows. He pushed himself to his feet, too surprised to speak for a moment. She narrowed her eyes on him, and he saw the anger and disappointment in them.

*Gods, not more disappointment.*

Marching over to him, her breaths coming in laboured bursts, she shoved his chest with both hands. His feet did not move, despite her best effort. Visibly frustrated by the fact, she went to shove him again, but that time he caught both wrists. He had never seen her like that before. She was not a fighter.

'For heaven's sake, Dulcia. Use your words.'

She tore her arms free with surprising force. 'That is rich coming from you. Only you can push and shove, is that it?'

Shame tore through him, the memory of her falling and the dagger next to her so vivid. 'Today, I... I'm sorry.' Nothing he could say would be enough.

She drew a shaky breath, stepped right, left, then stopped. 'Why did you not object?'

He shook his head, confused. 'Object to what?' He tried to read her, figure out what she needed from him.

'To Manius.' She resumed pacing, holding her hips for balance. 'To the wedding, to everything.'

He crossed his arms. 'It wasn't my place to object.'

'Was it not?' She turned to him, a plea in her eyes.

*Honesty.* That was what she needed from him in that moment.

'Do we not watch out for one another?' she continued. 'You think him some sort of monster, yet you say nothing.'

Her voice cracked and he took a step towards her, careful not to scare her away.

'I don't get to pick your husband. Your father does, remember?' How he kept his voice so calm and even, he had no idea.

'So you admit you hate him, and yet you said nothing.' She pressed a palm to her forehead. 'Actually, not true. You said *congratulations*.'

115

He lifted his shoulders in an exasperated shrug. 'If I'd pissed on your parade, I would have been the worst person in the world.' He never swore in front of her, and he could tell she was taken aback by it.

'Tell me honestly.' Her voice was quieter now. 'Why do you hate him?'

He thought for a moment. 'He's a wealthy fool who's had everything handed to him, and still he wants more. Losing that race would've been inconsequential for someone like him.'

She stared at him. 'I might be new to the circus, but I thought the point was to win.'

There was that famous sarcasm. 'The best man on the day wins. It can't always be him.'

She threw her hands up. 'So you hate him because he wins all the time. You are jealous, is that it?'

Yes, he was jealous, but admitting that aloud would only make him look ridiculous. 'He ran his chariot into Amator. He's the reason this stall is empty, and the two next to it,' he added, pointing behind her. 'All because of his ego.' He paused. 'And I don't think he's capable of loving you the way you deserve.'

Her shoulders fell. 'And yet you say nothing when I tell you he will be my husband.'

They were going round in circles.

'No one asked me what I wanted,' she said, her voice barely above a whisper. 'Not Manius, not Rufus. Not even my own mother. They all just assumed, because what smart woman does not want a wealthy husband?'

He did not reply, just waited for her to finish.

'Marriage is what women my age do. When an offer is made, you consider it. When a very good offer is made, you accept it.'

'That what your mother told you?'

She blinked, her lip trembling as she turned away. 'I thought…'

She was visibly struggling to get the words out, so he took another step towards her, so close he could feel the heat from her body.

'You thought what?' The volume of his voice matched hers.

'I thought you might offer.'

For a moment he was not sure what she meant. *Offer what?* Whatever he had was hers if she wanted it. Then his arms fell to his sides. 'To marry you?'

She said nothing, but eventually nodded, her eyes on the wall.

Gods, he wanted to touch her in that moment. She looked so vulnerable, and his need to reassure her was overwhelming. He would ask for her hand if he thought he stood a chance, if he thought he was even halfway good enough. 'Who would have said yes if I had? Not your father. Not your mother.'

She turned to look at him, swallowing before she spoke. '*I* would have. I would have said yes in a heartbeat.'

The confession winded him. It was not the revelation of feelings, but rather that he had not realised the depth of them. There was a throaty edge to her voice that made heat pool in his stomach.

An embarrassed laugh escaped her. 'Was it just me? All this time? This feeling of lightness, the hum in my bones?' She waited for him to speak, and when he did not, her hands went over her face. 'This is so humiliating.' She turned to leave, but he caught her arm. Stilling, she kept her eyes on the door.

He knew whatever came out of his mouth next would ruin them both. No good would come of his confession, but it was too late for lies. He could not have her believe she was alone in this. 'I felt it too.' His voice was low and deep. 'All of it. I felt it then and now.'

She found the courage to look up at him.

'I keep waiting for it to ease,' he continued, 'to let go of me. Just enough to build a life without you.' His hand went to her face, fingers brushing her cheek and jaw. Her skin was like silk beneath them. 'But it doesn't go away.' His hand moved down her neck, following the shape of her hair that fell down one shoulder. She was exquisite, and she did not belong to him.

Tilting her head up, she said, 'For a moment, I thought I was crazy.'

His hand slid up her arm, stopping on the back of her shoulder. 'You're not crazy.'

'And now it is too late,' she breathed.

He shook his head. 'I never had a chance with you.'

Before he realised what was happening, she pushed herself up onto her toes and pressed her mouth to his. There was nothing timid about the action. It was not the soft kiss he had imagined so many times. There was no reluctance, no awkwardness, just sheer heat that fuelled the fire inside him. Her hands slid up his neck, and she pulled herself up, lips parting. Hips brushed his, igniting all of him.

Gone was that shy girl he knew, replaced with this woman who was a lot for him in that moment. He could not think through the sensation, the scent of her, the intoxicating taste of her open mouth. His hands slid to the middle of her back, fingers splayed and palms pressing her closer until everything else faded.

He had kissed women before, but not like this. Never had his body reacted so entirely to anything in his life. He was certain the slightest shift of her hips would finish him.

A cough sounded from somewhere, and Dulcia pulled away with a small gasp. Two uniformed men stood in the doorway. A stern-faced Nerva glared at him. Beside him stood Marcus, a member of his cavalry unit. He smiled wryly, shaking his head.

Yes, it was extraordinarily unlucky timing.

Nero let go of Dulcia, who had paled at the sight of her brother. He had really done it this time.

Nerva looked between them, not saying anything for a moment.

'This...' Dulcia began. 'I know how this looks.'

'Well, I guess this explains today's fallout with Manius.' He looked at Nero. 'Not about the horses, then?'

Nero drew a breath, but before he could respond, Nerva turned to Marcus and said, 'Take my sister outside. I need to speak with Nero—alone.'

# CHAPTER 14

They sat in their usual spot on the steps of the temple, watching the street. A honey cake lay wrapped on Dulcia's lap, an offering for Vesta. She had needed an excuse to get out of the house. It had never felt so claustrophobic. There were only so many disapproving glances from Nerva she could stomach.

'What did your sister say on the subject?' Licinia asked, squinting against the sun.

Every day was warmer than the last. Soon it would be too hot to sit on the steps.

'About which part? The kiss? Or Nero losing his job?'

Nerva had taken her straight to Mila's apartment, seemingly so he could lecture her in front of an audience. Everything was a mess—and it was all her fault.

Licinia glanced sideways at her. 'Both.'

Dulcia shooed some flies away from the cake. 'Mila spent the entire time pleading with Nerva to keep Nero on. He loves that job, and he will be lost without it.'

'Perhaps he could find employment at another stable.'

News travelled fast in the city, and if people had not

already heard about the fight with Manius, one look at the wealthy man's colourful face would set tongues wagging.

He had been furious when they had left the Trigarium, his ego in tatters. Manius had barely uttered a word as he put her in the litter and sent her home. She had not been invited to dine with him that evening.

Licinia glanced at her when she did not reply. 'Do you suppose he would have lost his job if Nerva had shown up and found the two of you talking instead of…' The conversation was not entirely appropriate for someone of her status.

'He attacked a charioteer *off* the track, a charioteer who also happens to be my betrothed. Nerva cannot have men in his employment who go around punching charioteers in the face.'

The smallest of smiles from Licinia, her eyes going to the honey cake. 'That is quite an offering for Vesta.'

'Well,' Dulcia sighed, 'in case you have not noticed, I am making some rather large mistakes of late. I need all the favour from the gods I can get.'

'A bribe cake, then?'

Dulcia suppressed a smile, her cheeks flushing. 'I would have brought a much larger cake if it were.'

Licinia bowed her head at a group of passing men. 'We all learn lessons in our own time. The important thing is you learn.'

Dulcia played with the corner of the wax paper for a moment. 'I love him. Nero, that is.'

'I know.' Licinia did not look at her.

'And he loves me too. But I suspect you knew that also.'

A smile came to and immediately left Licinia's face. 'What are you going to do?'

She was silent a moment. 'I am engaged to Manius.'

'Yes.'

'If I stray from that arrangement, I will both embarrass and shame my family, and Manius's for that matter.'

'Yes.' Licinia glanced across at her. 'Some people would be very upset with you.'

'Exactly.'

'But there is also a chance you might get to marry the man you love.' The words sat between them for a moment. 'Engagements are broken all the time, but once married, no amount of honey cakes will appease Vesta if you stray.'

Dulcia had to look away. 'If I refuse to marry Manius, there is every chance Rufus will banish me from the house.'

Licinia regarded her suspiciously for a moment.

'What?' Dulcia asked, growing self-conscious.

'You still cannot call him Father. Even now.'

Dulcia stretched her neck to one side, hoping to ease some of the tension she had held for weeks. 'I called the man *erus* for the first twelve years of my life. *Father* is a big leap from *master.*' She straightened the cake on her lap. 'I feel like he sees me now. For the first time in my life, I am visible.' She paused. 'When I was young, it was all I wanted.'

'A father?'

Dulcia shook her head. 'Not just any father. Nerva's father, Rufus Papias, the man with the same eye colour as me, the same mouth. He is quiet, you know—like me. That is something I have noticed over the years.' She waved a hand over the cake once more, and flies took off. 'Then the moment it happens, I jeopardise everything.'

'It does seem that way,' Licinia agreed.

A small laugh escaped Dulcia. 'You did not need to agree quite so quickly.'

'Would you prefer me to lie?'

Dulcia's cheeks heated. 'Of course not.'

An old man hobbled past. He held a stick for balance, and a dog with a half-chewed ear followed at his heel.

'I should go,' Dulcia said, standing. Licinia stood also. 'I promised my sister I would take care of the twins while she runs errands.' She handed the priestess the cake. 'My bribe.'

Licinia gave a tight smile and touched a hand to Dulcia's arm. 'May Vesta watch over you.'

~

'I WILL BE BACK AS SOON as I can,' Mila said, grabbing her basket and gesturing for her daughter to follow. Asha's golden hair was brushed out, reaching all the way to the middle of her back. She looked excited at the prospect of time alone with her mother.

Dulcia could not resist pulling her in for a hug as she passed. 'Enjoy the peace,' she whispered, planting a kiss on her niece's rosy cheek.

Asha smiled up at her. 'Don't tell the boys, but we are going to watch the gladiators train at Ludus Magnus.'

Dulcia straightened and looked over at Mila, who had heard the exchange. 'I thought you were running errands.'

'We are.' Mila gestured for her daughter to come to her. 'One of those errands is ensuring Asha can defend herself if the need ever arises.'

Dulcia crossed her arms in front of her. 'Here I was thinking you were going to get your daughter some new clothes or something.'

'She has clothes. Now she just needs a pretty dagger to go with them.'

Dulcia was not amused. 'And does Remus know his daughter is hanging around gladiators?'

Mila tilted her head. 'Take a moment to consider how ridiculous that statement is.'

Fair point. Every person living in the apartment had fought in an arena at some stage. 'I give up.' She hesitated. 'Before you go, who shall I expect home this afternoon?'

The possibility of running into Nero was equal parts exciting and terrifying. She had no idea how it would be between them given what had happened the night prior. She had practically thrown herself at him. Her hands grew clammy at the memory, as if his body were still pressed to hers, heating every inch of her. She needed to lock such thoughts from her mind before she got them both into more trouble.

'If you are wanting to know where Nero is,' Mila said, a knowing look on her face, 'he is working with Remus. We thought it best to keep him busy.'

Dulcia nodded and looked around the room. 'How did he seem this morning?' What answer was she hoping for?

Mila shook her head as she thought, a worried expression on her face. 'Quiet.' She sighed. 'If you intend to marry Manius, then I think it best you give him space for a while. We underestimated his feelings for you.'

Dulcia knew something about that. 'If I *intend* to marry Manius? You make it sound like I have a choice.'

Mila ushered Asha through the door, then turned to look at her properly. 'There is always a choice. Each with its own consequences.'

Dulcia felt her throat closing. 'I think I have really messed up.'

Mila leaned on the door for a moment, her expression softening. 'I wish I could tell you what to do, but I cannot. Walking away from Manius, defying Rufus—' She broke off for a moment. 'I cannot predict how that will end for you.'

There Dulcia was in her nineteenth year, still hoping her sister would have all the answers.

'I will say this,' Mila continued, 'Manius's pride has already taken a knock. If you try to end things with him, he *will* lash out.'

'So I am to consider pride in all this?'

Mila nodded. 'Manius believes he is handing you the world. If you tell him "no thanks", then take up with Nero, a man with no status or wealth—even employment, for that matter—you had better be prepared for retaliation.'

She understood then. 'You are afraid for Nero.'

Mila glanced at the twins playing on the floor. 'If you embarrass that man, he is not going to go after Senator Rufus Papias's daughter. He has his future to consider. He will go after the people you love, the people who don't matter in his world.'

A shudder passed through Dulcia. Manius did not seem the vindictive type, but what did she know?

The smell of simmering lentils wafted through the open door. Mila sniffed the air, then shook her head. 'Now the entire building smells of soup. Why does that woman not cook outside like the rest of us?'

Dulcia smiled. 'At least it smells enticing.'

'Today it does. Yesterday the apartment stank of boiled offal.' Mila gave the boys a stern look as they leapt off the floor and began running circles around Dulcia. 'Behave, or I swear to the gods, your father will hear all about it.'

The boys immediately stopped running, holding in their giggles as they looked at one another, seeing who would crack first.

'Mila,' Dulcia called as she turned to leave. Her sister looked back, waiting. 'I cannot win either way, can I? I marry Manius and break my own heart, and Nero's, or refuse and place a target on his back.'

Her sister rested her head against the edge of the door for a moment. 'Nero has already done that himself. Manius Liberia knows his outburst yesterday did not stem from the death of one horse.'

Dulcia let her sister's words sink in. 'But everyone knows he loved that stallion.'

Mila pushed off the door. 'Perhaps that is why Manius did it.'

'It was not intentional. It was an accident.'

Mila tilted her head, like she should know better. 'I have to go. Hopefully the boys sleep for you.'

They had already resumed running circles around Dulcia. 'They do not seem overly tired.'

'Stop running,' Mila pleaded, then looked back at Dulcia. 'They have already broken everything of value in this room. Good luck.' She disappeared through the door, pulling it closed behind her.

Dulcia bent and tried to catch the boys. 'You want to run? Let us go outside, then. Where is your ball?'

Both boys took off in an excited flurry to look for it. Time with her nephews was always the perfect excuse for Dulcia to release the child within.

They kicked the ball in the courtyard, and when it got too hot, they played *Rota* to cool off. It did not take long for the twins to grow bored, so they went downstairs once more for some skipping games.

'Let's hunt insects!' Atilius cried. They had stopped to rest for a moment, falling to the ground, panting.

It was mid-afternoon when they returned to the apartment with their collection of cicadas and scarab beetles. Dulcia set the pot of insects on the balcony.

'We will release them after we eat.' She knew they had a habit of holding on to them until they eventually died and wanted to spare the insects the torment of a slow death at the hands of eager, inquisitive boys.

They sat on the floor, legs crossed, eating coarse bread with goat's cheese and slices of pear. Then, with their stomachs full, they had a final game of Rota before she finally convinced the boys to lie on the bed with the lure of a story.

'A scary one,' Atilius insisted, nestling into the crook of her arm.

'If it is too scary you will not sleep.'

'We will,' Caius insisted. 'Promise.'

She told them the story of the hero Aenieid, who visited the underworld. It was one Nerva had told her when she was eight, but she had been much easier to scare than the twins.

They lay either side of her, restless but listening. She knew if she could just get them to lie still for long enough, sleep would eventually take them. They resisted for as long as they could, but eventually their little bodies began to twitch, and they drifted off to sleep. Trapped beneath them, and exhausted from the drama of the past few days, Dulcia drifted off also.

It was late in the afternoon when Dulcia's eyes snapped open. Her vision was blurry, and her heart pounded against her ribs. Something was wrong.

She felt for the boys on either side of her, finding them still there. She coughed, her throat dry, then blinked again, her vision not improving. Then she realised why—the room was filled with smoke. She sat up with a gasp and looked around.

'Wake up,' she said, shaking the boys. Atilius merely stirred, and Caius coughed. 'Now,' she said, louder that time, but trying to keep the panic from her voice. 'We have to go.'

Caius coughed again, then began to cry. Atilius sat up, rubbed two fists into his eyes, then looked around the room, confused.

Scooping them up awkwardly in her arms, Dulcia stood with one on each hip. 'I need you to hold on, all right?' She coughed into her shoulder and headed for the door. Fear danced up her spine when she realised the smoke was much thicker in the communal room.

'Fire,' Atilius said.

Dulcia kissed his bewildered face. 'You are safe with me.'

Making her way over to the front door, she awkwardly pulled it open. Heat hit her like stone, and black smoke poured into the room. Orange flames licked the stairwell. Kicking the door closed with her foot, she leaned against it for a moment, but the temperature of the wood forced her upright. Her mind raced, and panic tore through her. She knew how quickly fire could spread through structures like

127

this. The wall-to-wall wood was the perfect fuel for blazes, which could last for weeks. She also knew people disappeared in fires—entire families, never to be seen again.

Caius began to cry, then Atilius.

'It is all right,' Dulcia soothed, rushing towards the balcony and nudging the shutters with her foot. She slipped through the narrow gap.

The air was more breathable outside, but she knew it would not remain that way for long. The fire was beneath them and would eventually consume the balcony they stood on.

Peering over the banister, she called, 'Help! Help us! Please!' She paused to listen for voices, but all she could hear was the crackle of fire climbing the walls below.

Placing the twins on the ground, she crouched to their height. 'I need you to stay here. I will be right back. Do not move.' Before they could object, she held her breath and ran back inside. She went to one of the bedrooms and snatched up a blanket—Nero's blanket. Returning to the balcony, she found the boys wailing, their tears forging black paths down their puffy cheeks. She wrapped the woollen blanket around them and leaned over the balcony once more. 'Help! I have children up here! Please!'

Coughing, she crouched down to the boys, gathering them in her arms and pulling the blanket over the three of them. She peered through the gap in the banister, trying to judge the distance to the ground. Even if they managed the drop, there was no guarantee they could escape the court-yard. The only thing she knew for certain was that they had a higher chance of survival on the ground. 'I am going to need you both to be very brave.'

Caius continued to cry, but Atilius stopped to listen. 'Like a gladiator?'

'Yes.' She nodded enthusiastically. 'Exactly like a gladiator.' Seeing he was the most together of the two, she focused on him first. 'I am going to lower you over the balcony, and then you are going to do a big jump to the ground. We are only one floor up. Can you land like a cat?'

He peered out from the blanket, his three-year-old brain ticking over. 'On my feet?'

'Yes. Then I want you to go straight to the water pump and get yourself nice and wet while you wait for me. Do you think you can do that?'

She could barely hear her own voice over Caius's crying. Atilius did not respond, just continued to stare through the gap in the blanket. They had no time to waste, so she stood and fixed the blanket around Caius, her bare feet growing hotter. Snatching Atilius up, she peered over the edge and wondered how far she could lower him before she would be forced to let go. With no time to think on the matter, she swung him over the rail, her chest squeezing when he began to whimper. He stared up at her, eyes wide, and she attempted a smile. 'It will be all right.' Then she prayed to any god listening that it would be.

Atilius clung to her arm as she lowered him. When she could stretch no farther, she peeled off his hands and, holding him by one arm, reached her other hand through the gap in the banister to catch him. She would be able to get him closer to the ground that way. Lying flat on the hot floor, with Caius wailing next to her, she lowered Atilius as far as she could, her entire body sweating and trembling with the effort. She peered through the narrow gap in the banister, the one Remus had intentionally narrowed to ensure little bodies could not slip through. His feet were around five feet from the ground thanks to the added length of her arm. While she had seen him jump from that height before, she knew this was different.

'Look down,' she called to him. 'Look how close you are. I am going to let go, and you will land on your feet, like you always do.'

The whimpering ceased. Holding her breath and praying, she let go. He landed on his hands and knees. Tears ensued.

'Well done,' she called. 'You are so brave. I am so proud of you.' She could barely see him through the smoke.

'My knee,' Atilius cried.

'It is just a graze. Go to the water pump. Nice and wet, remember? Go! I will be there in a moment.'

He scrambled to his feet and ran off.

Dulcia faced Caius, who looked terrified.

'Right, your turn.' Despite her best smile, he began to cry harder. 'Quickly now.' Getting to her feet, she picked him up. Arms and legs went around her, clinging for dear life. She tried to peel him off, one limb at a time, coughing violently as she did so, but it was no good.

'I stay with you,' he screamed in her ear, then gasped for air.

She tried again, managing that time to get both his arms off her. But he became so hysterical she found her arms going around him instead, his body trembling against her chest. Covering her face with one hand, the soles of her feet nearly melting where she stood, she broke down.

They were going to die.

# CHAPTER 15

*J*udging by the smug look on Gallus Minidius's face, he knew exactly why Nero was there. Gallus sponsored the games in Caelimontium, a small arena that Nero had been fighting at for a number of years, despite Dulcia's blatant disapproval. He also had a lot of contacts and ties with other venues.

Not knowing his true family name, Nero had long ago adopted Latinius, and all that was associated with it. It was a fighting name, two generations of gladiators who would not be forgotten any time soon, and a name Gallus liked to exploit.

Nero did not mind the exploitation when it was convenient, or put another way, when he needed the coin—and there he was, a new height of desperate. He was not content relying on Remus for a wage, even though he knew the business and could offer hard work in return. He helped because he was family, not for coin.

'You made quite a mess of Manius Liberia's face.' Despite the disapproval in Gallus's tone, there was glee in his eyes.

It amazed Nero how quickly the news had travelled. 'I

might've lost my temper. That's not to say the man didn't deserve it.'

'They usually do.' Gallus rocked on his feet and winced, his arches suffering under the weight of him. 'Though I am surprised you acted on the fact. Most men are not that brave —or foolish,' he added, studying Nero. 'I gather Nerva Papias was less than pleased by the report.'

That was putting it mildly. It was made worse by the fact that he had shown up to discuss the matter, only to find his sister in Nero's arms. He cleared his throat. 'He has suggested some time away from the sport.'

'He sent you marching.' Not a question, a statement. 'That is why you are here, is it not?'

No point wasting time on discretion. 'You once told me you could organise a biga chariot, make me a charioteer.'

Gallus waved a plump finger at him. 'I said I could make you an *essedarius*. There is a big difference.'

'Both put me in a chariot.'

'True, but the latter requires you to hold a weapon instead of a whip, and your opponent will likely be on foot.'

'Sounds like an act that pays well.'

Gallus laughed and clapped him on the shoulder. 'So much like Remus.'

'It's just until I find something else.'

Gallus tapped his nose. 'That is what they all say, until they realise they can earn more from one spectacular fight than most men make in a week.'

'It's just a performance, right? No one is going to die?'

Gallus grinned. 'The valuable ones do not die. Certainly no man trained by Remus Latinius himself.'

'Actually, I was trained mostly by his wife, Mila.'

Gallus stared blankly back at him.

'Libertas,' Nero said, offering her gladiator name.

'Ah.' A smile stretched across Gallus's face, his cheeks rising like mountains. 'The slave girl rescued by our hero. I was there that day.' He sat with the memory for a moment. 'She fought her first fight in this very arena, you know.'

Nero had heard the story before. 'If my memory serves me correctly, she fought Felix.'

'Won too. Started her career, I did. Albeit short.' His expression turned serious, and he sniffed the air. 'You smell smoke?'

Nero's brows came together as he looked around, spotting black smoke rising in the distance.

'Oh dear,' Gallus said. 'Let us hope they contain it before it spreads.'

Nero narrowed his gaze. 'What region would you say that is?'

Gallus looked around, getting his bearings. 'Ten? Eleven?'

His home was in region eleven. 'I have to go.' He wanted to make sure Mila and the children were safe.

'Come by later,' Gallus said, but Nero was already jogging for the exit. 'Where are you running to?'

Nero dashed around the corner without replying and ran towards the smoke. A part of him knew Mila could handle herself and the children in a crisis, but he was also painfully aware of how quickly fire could move through the city.

When he reached his region, he was forced to slow down as people fled in the opposite direction. He clipped the shoulders of men hustling their families away from the danger and merchants loaded with whatever they could carry. The closer he got, the more anxious he became. Not only was the fire near his home, but the smoke was sitting directly above their residence. When he turned that final corner and stepped onto his street, he saw his insulae alive with flames. Black smoke spilled like liquid from doorways and windows. The *Vigile Urbani* were out front armed with men, buckets, hooks and levers to tear down buildings either side in an attempt to contain it. The men shouted, pushing back spectators who were forced to watch their belongings burn.

Surely Mila would have gotten out in time. She was probably far away by now. Still, he pushed forwards, searching the street for familiar faces as he did so.

'Nero!'

He turned to see Remus jogging towards him. 'Where's Mila?' Remus asked as he came to a stop in front of him.

Nero forced himself to remain calm. 'She would've fled at the first sniff of smoke.'

Remus leaned on his knees and tried to catch his breath. Wherever he had come from, he had come at a run. His eyes searched the crowd.

'Remus!'

Both men turned at the sound of Mila's voice. Whatever relief Nero felt vanished when he caught sight of her. Something was wrong.

'Father!' Asha shouted, appearing from behind her mother. She ran to Remus, and he caught her.

'Where are your brothers?' he shouted over the noise.

Mila finally pushed through the people blocking her. 'They were in the apartment.' She struggled to catch her breath. Wherever she had come from, she had come at a *sprint*.

'The twins?' Remus asked.

Her gaze went to the burning building. 'Dulcia has them.'

Nero's heart stopped beating for a moment.

Remus put Asha on the ground. 'They were inside?'

Nero turned to stare at the flames climbing the insulae walls, his heart drumming wildly as the pieces came together.

Mila spun in a full circle, searching. 'They must be here.' She pressed a hand to her forehead. 'She would have smelled the smoke.'

Remus took off, tearing through the crowd, head jerking

side to side as he went looking for them. Mila went in the other direction, screaming her sister's name. 'Dulcia!' Asha ran after her mother, grabbing a handful of skirt before they were swallowed up by bodies.

Nero's hands went into his hair as he tried to think logically. Where would she go? If anyone could get into her mind, surely he could.

'Move back!' a uniformed man shouted. 'Unless you want to be crushed.'

The Vigile had the ballistae ready to smash through the building. It was the most effective way to prevent it spreading.

'Wait!' Nero had taken care of the twins enough times to know they usually had a sleep in the afternoons. Perhaps she had fallen asleep also. Maybe she had not learned of the fire until it was too late. He groaned, the realisation that she might be in there almost knocking him down. His eyes met Remus's across the crowd.

'I can't find them,' Remus shouted over the noise.

Mila had returned, horror frozen on her face. 'What if they didn't get out?' It came out like a whisper. She turned to the building, then moved to run off, but Nero caught her arm.

'Hold off the Vigile, and stay with Asha.' Before Mila could object, he took off at a run, shoving aside anyone who was in his path. The heat repelled him, but he pushed against it, knowing nothing could stop him at that point.

'You can't go in!' a soldier shouted, grabbing his arm.

He shrugged out of the soldier's grip and kept running. There was no time to waste. What would she do if she woke mid-blaze with no way out?

*The balcony.*

She would get to the ground and try to exit via the archway. But the archway was a cave of black smoke. He prayed there was reprieve on the other side, some air—just enough to keep them alive.

He did not pause to think it through, just drew a lungful of filthy air and charged through.

Running blindly, he stretched one arm in front of him so he would not collide head first into something. The hair on his body wilted beneath the heat, the air sucking all the moisture from his skin.

One, two, three, four, five. Six. Six strides before the air cleared enough to see his own hand. He stopped and looked around, trying to get his bearings. 'Dulcia!'

Nothing.

He took a few steps in the direction of the apartment. 'Dulcia!' He thought he heard crying. A child, perhaps. 'Atilius! Caius!'

It was definitely crying that time. It sounded like Caius. He had come to recognise their unique cries over the years. 'Caius!' Coughing, he stumbled through the smoke, spotting the two boys by the water pump. He ran to them, snatching them up one in each arm. Their clothes were soaked, and they shook violently as he crushed them against him. 'Where is Dulcia?'

Caius just cried, but Atilius pointed to a pile of debris ten feet away—ablaze. Nero recognised shapes from their balcony. It had collapsed.

*Dulcia.*

He ran for it, the thought of her buried beneath burning planks of wood propelling him forwards. He tripped over something, stumbled, but managed to stay upright. Looking down, he found a barely recognisable Dulcia unconscious on the ground. He went to her, dropping to his knee as the boys coughed violently in his arms.

'Dulcia!' He shouted her name, but she did not move. There was a gash on her hairline, blood running the length of her brow.

He turned to Atilius first, as Caius was still clinging to his neck, like he had done so many times. 'I need you to climb onto my back. Do not let go, no matter what.'

The boy looked ready to fall down, but did as he was told. Nero knew he had little chance of removing Caius. He reached an arm either side of the boy to scoop Dulcia in his arms. She was limp and unresponsive, her head flopping like one of Asha's dolls.

'Wrap your legs around me,' he said to Caius.

Nero blinked, his vision blurring and eyes stinging. Where was the arch? He rose to his feet and looked up to get his bearings.

'Don't let go,' he said again. 'No matter what.'

Wood snapped behind him, and he heard something crash to the ground, sending dust and smoke twisting around him. Debris hit his leg, the sting instant. He cursed but did not slow to see what it was.

The outline of the archway rose in front of him. He drew a breath, but his throat closed in protest. One, two, three, four, five, six strides. The archway went on forever that time. Seven, eight. The three people he was carrying slowed him, as did the smoke, the lack of air. He tried to draw breath, desperate. Blurry shapes and shadows appeared—people, perhaps. He blinked, spotting Mila struggling against two men holding her. Four men had Remus pinned to the ground, a knee pressed to his neck. Asha was crying nearby while strangers attempted to comfort her.

People turned to look at him as he emerged from the blaze, Mila's face contorting into relief as she was released. Remus threw off the men and leapt to his feet. A moment later, they were in front of him, the children lifted from him, Mila cupping her sister's face and saying things he could not understand.

'Help her,' he thought he said.

Remus was crouched down, checking the boys.

Uniformed men stepped forwards to take Dulcia from him. When the weight of her was lifted, the men began to tilt, Dulcia with them.

*Help her.*

Nero's face smacked the dirt, and everything went dark.

## CHAPTER 16

*N*ero woke with a start, eyes snapping open and searching the space for something familiar to anchor him. Panic squeezed his chest, and it took him a moment to remember why.

*Dulcia.*

A horse whinnied on the other side of the wall. The noise made him sit up, wincing as he did so. His head pounded so hard he was momentarily blinded by it. Smoke and soot lined his nose, mouth and throat, prompting memories of earlier events. He was in a stall, but it was not the green team's stables.

'Easy,' Felix said, stepping inside. Albaus was behind him. 'I am under strict instructions to keep you alive until the physician gets here.'

Nero pushed back the blanket, and the small cot groaned beneath him. He frowned at the straw-covered ground. 'Where are we?'

Felix took a seat on the end of his cot. 'Papias stables.'

*Papias.* Nero slid across to sit on the edge. 'Are they alive?' His voice was hoarse, his throat sore. 'The twins? Dulcia?'

'The twins will be fine. Sick from the smoke, but they will be terrorising us again in no time.'

He waited, not sure if he could speak her name again without breaking down. Felix picked up on his struggle, glancing at Albaus before saying, 'Dulcia is yet to wake.'

What did that mean? He looked between the two of them. 'But she is alive?'

Albaus just stared out the door, while Felix cleared his throat. 'Alive, yes. I think everyone would feel better if she would *wake*.'

Nero would certainly feel a lot better. 'Can I see her?'

Felix snorted. 'There is a reason you are surrounded by horses. Rufus Papias's goodwill does not stretch *that* far.' His gaze swept over Nero. 'Normally I would slap you about the head for such a reckless act, but it seems your heroism paid off.'

Nero stared at the door, wanting to go to Dulcia. 'I did what any man would do.'

'Run into a burning building?' Felix turned to Albaus. 'What do you think? Would you run into a blaze on a hunch?'

Albaus grunted and crossed his arms. His body language suggested he was still on edge after the drama.

'Albaus may have,' Felix continued. 'But if the Vigile told *me* not to walk into a fire, I would listen. You are fortunate they did not smash it to the ground with you inside. Luckily, they were too busy holding Mila and Remus back. There were barely any men left to fight the fire.'

Before Nero could reply, Remus appeared in the doorway. It took him a moment to adjust to the light; then, spotting Nero, he walked over and fell to his knees beside the cot. His eyes were bloodshot and weary. He said nothing at first, just pulled Nero into an embrace and held him there. Nero stiffened at first, because Remus was not a hugger, but then he relaxed into it.

After a long moment, Remus pulled back to look at him.

'Thank you.' He patted the back of Nero's head before letting go. The gratitude and relief came from him in waves. The man had almost lost his sons. Mila had almost lost her sister.

'You don't need to thank me,' Nero said as Remus collected himself. 'We're family.'

Remus nodded and pressed his palms briefly to his eyes, sealing in the tears. He rose to his feet and gave Nero's shoulder a squeeze. 'Have a wash. You stink.'

Nero's laugh turned into a chesty cough.

'Lots of water,' Remus called over his shoulder as he turned and headed for the door. He clapped Albaus's arm as he passed, and the tall man gave him a single nod.

Felix exhaled loudly. 'If you think I am going to hang about playing nursemaid, you are mistaken. There is water right there, and your hands appear to be working.'

'What? No broth spoon-fed to me?'

A wry smile crossed Felix's face. 'Albaus has a much steadier hand.'

A grunt from the man who remained leaning in the doorway. The frame creaked beneath the weight of him. Nero's expression turned serious.

'I just need one thing.'

Felix rolled his eyes. 'I swear to the heavens, if you say Dulcia—'

'I need to see her.'

Felix swung himself off the bed. 'If you think you can get past her physician, brother, mother, father, and *betrothed*, then by all means go visit with her. But be warned, they will smell you coming a mile away. Literally. You are like a smoked ham, minus the honey glaze.'

'*Manius* is with her?' He could not hide his disappointment.

Felix threw his hands up. '*That* is what you took from my speech?' He waited for a reply. When one did not come, he said, 'They are to be married soon. What did you expect?'

141

Nero reached for the jug of water and cup. He poured, drank, and spat it on the floor. All he could taste was soot.

'You are going to be coughing that stuff up for weeks,' Felix said, strolling to the door. Albaus straightened, ready to follow. 'Come, my enormous friend. Let us find some food for our young hero and a drink for us old men.'

'Where shall I wash?' Nero called.

Felix paused in the doorway. 'It is a stable. Find a trough.'

~

WHEN DULCIA OPENED HER EYES, she thought she might be blind. It took her a moment to realise it was dark. Her chest pounded as she tried to get her bearings.

*The twins.* Where were the boys?

She recognised her mother's familiar breaths and turned to see her asleep in a chair, one arm draped over the bed and her head resting on it. Dulcia went to speak, but her tongue stuck in her mouth. All she could taste and smell was stale smoke. The memory of the fire rushed in, making her breath catch and fingers press into the bed. She could still feel the heat of it.

Kicking off the blanket, she sat up and took a lungful of air, relieved when she could. She took another breath, and another.

Tertia stirred, opened her eyes, and relief flooded her face. Pushing herself up, she reached out and grabbed hold of Dulcia's face with both hands. 'Thank the gods. They must have finally tired of my prayers.'

Dulcia rested her pulsing head against her mother's. It threatened to burst open at any moment.

'Careful,' Tertia said, pulling away. 'You hit your head.'

More memories pushed in, and she grabbed hold of her mother's arm to steady herself. 'The twins—'

'Will be fine,' Tertia soothed. 'You need to drink.' She

reached for the cup of water on the table and held it to Dulcia's mouth.

'I can hold a cup,' Dulcia said, taking it from her and sipping tentatively. Her throat felt raw, and the simple act of swallowing was too much. She went to touch the wound on her head, but her mother caught her hand.

'You needed stitches.' Tertia's brow creased with worry, and then her hand went over her mouth, holding in whatever emotion threatened to spill over. 'If Nero had not found you…'

*Nero?* She rested the cup on her leg. 'Nero was there?'

Her mother sniffed, nodded. 'Ran straight into the flames. Carried all three of you out just moments before the entire structure came down.'

Of course he did. He would walk through fire for her without a moment's hesitation. That was how it was between them. Dulcia felt her heart expand. 'He carried us out?'

A nod.

The cup in Dulcia's hand tilted and spilled. She did not even react. 'Where is he? I need to see him.'

Tertia took the cup from her. 'You are not leaving that bed until the physician says you can. He will be back in the morning.' She squeezed Dulcia's hand. 'Listen to yourself. You can barely talk.'

Dulcia coughed and soot filled her mouth. 'You are sure the twins are all right? There was so much smoke. Caius was in my arms when it collapsed. I… I tried to jump.'

'They are both going to be fine.'

Dulcia shook her head. 'I just could not get them out.'

'You kept them alive. You did everything you could.' She touched a finger to her daughter's chin.

Dulcia glanced at the curtain. 'Where are they?'

'Rufus had a room made up for them, just for tonight.'

Dulcia's eyebrows rose. 'He let *Remus* stay in the house?'

'He has a heart.'

'What about Nero?' Dulcia searched her mother's face. 'Is he here?'

'In the stables with Felix and Albaus. They are not to come anywhere near the house. If Aquila finds out, it will not end well.'

Dulcia tried to stand. 'I must see him.'

Tertia grabbed her arm, holding her in place. 'You will do no such thing. What if Manius returns to see you?'

'He came to see me?'

'Of course. He is terribly worried and hoping to check in on you on his way back from dinner, assuming the evening does not run late.'

Dulcia breathed out through her nose. 'You realise how contradictory your words are. He cannot be that worried if he is fitting bedside visits in around his social plans.'

'The man cannot be expected to shirk his responsibilities to wait at your bedside.'

Nero would. He did not even know she was awake. He was probably going out of his mind with worry. 'No. Of course not.' She lay back down on the bed. 'Goodness, I am more tired than I realised.' It was not a lie. She had been dizzy and nauseous from the moment she opened her eyes. 'If I sleep, will you take me to see the twins when I wake?'

Tertia patted her hand reassuringly. 'Of course.'

'You should sleep also.'

Tertia shook her head. 'I want to keep an eye on you.'

Exactly what Dulcia had predicted she would say. 'There is nothing you can do until the physician comes. Please, go to your bed. I am fine.'

Tertia glanced across the room at the neatly made bed. 'The sun will rise before we know it. I suppose a few hours' rest will be beneficial.'

'Yes, rest while you can,' Dulcia agreed, closing her eyes.

She did her best impersonation of sleep, knowing her mother would not leave her side if she remained awake.

Eventually, she heard the creak of the bed, and within a few minutes, soft, even breaths reached her.

Dulcia opened her eyes.

~

NERO UNDERESTIMATED the effects of the smoke. He tried to stay awake, desperate for news of Dulcia, but eventually surrendered to his exhaustion.

He woke just before sunrise with the weight of a body against him. His mind raced with possibilities. It was not uncommon for one of the children to climb into his bed during the night, but they were in the house. The person was too big to be to a child and too small to be a man. He turned his head to look, and the body stirred, then settled. He recognised the scent of her, despite the smoke. His body recognised the feel of her.

*Dulcia.*

He turned, slowly so as not to disturb her. She was facing him, her hands tucked under her cheek, making her face pouty like a child. Her breathing bordered on snoring. He smiled to himself. Gods, she was beautiful in that moment.

And in his bed. Why was she in his bed?

She coughed, and the strangled sound of it scared him. His hand went to her arm, ready if she woke, if she needed him. He would give the air from his own lungs if he thought it would help her breathe easier. But she did not wake fully, settling under the weight of his hand, her shoulder rolling forwards until it brushed his bare chest.

He watched her in the dark, his hand sliding down her back, forming a protective layer around her. She shivered against the warmth of it, so he carefully drew her closer until he felt her breaths on his neck. She sighed contentedly, and then her breathing grew noisy once more. He relaxed his head so his lips rested against her hair. She still smelled of smoke, but the harshness was diluted by soap and a scent he had come to recognise over the years: dough, pears, and cinnamon. It was the smell of fresh bread and lavender, the smell of fresh water and sunshine.

There was no way Tertia would have let her out of bed, let alone out of the house. He should have woken her, told her to return inside to her comfortable bed and the care of her mother. But he was selfish in that moment. He wanted to be with her, to watch over, touch, breathe in and pour his warmth into her.

He wondered about her injuries, her head, if her lungs and throat hurt as his did. Probably much worse given how long she had breathed in that toxic air.

His worry was eased by a sense of peace, a content feeling that spread through his body like he was stepping into a hot bath. There she lay, moulded against him, needing him the same way he needed her. He had thought it impossible for her feelings to match his own, knew the force of them could pull her under. She deserved a safer form of love, one that could be flaunted in daylight.

With that thought, he drifted off to sleep.

～

'DULCIA, WAKE UP.'

The angry whisper made Nero jump, which in turn woke Dulcia. His arms tightened around her as he focused in the grey light. Tertia came into view, a worried expression on her face.

He had fallen asleep, wasted the few precious hours they had together. When he looked down at Dulcia, her heavy eyes blinked back at him.

Tertia tugged on her daughter's arm. 'You need to get up,' she said. 'Now.'

He should have released her, sat up, apologised, made

excuses, but he did none of those things. If those moments were all they had, he would hold Dulcia for as long as she needed.

'The physician will be here soon. *Manius* will be here soon.'

Dulcia's expression was solemn. 'Give me a moment.' Her voice was hoarse, barely audible. She turned in his arms and stared up at her mother. 'Please. Just give me that.'

Tertia exhaled. Looking at Nero, she said, 'She better be outside in two minutes,' then quietly slipped from the stables.

Albaus and Felix were asleep in cots pressed against the other walls, Felix fitting nicely, while Albaus's trunk-like limbs hung over the edges. They did not even stir. That was what came of living with children; you had to learn to block out the noise of early risers.

'Are you all right?' Nero croaked, inspecting the cut on her head.

She smiled weakly, eyes on his mouth. 'You sound as bad as me.'

'I was so worried about you.'

'I know.'

He searched her face, noticing a graze on her cheek. 'You're really all right?'

A small nod. 'You saved us.' She reached up and brushed her fingertips over his lips. 'I owe you my life.'

He could not help himself, kissing the tip of one finger. 'You should go. You need to see the physician.'

She looked so disappointed with his response, but he needed her well. 'And Manius?'

She was testing him. 'Only if he has healing powers I'm unaware of.'

Another small smile from her. 'I suspect you have healing powers.'

If he did, he would use them to take away the dark circles

from her eyes, the cuts and bruises, to restore her lungs to perfect breathing order. 'I wish I did.'

She regarded him for a moment, one finger stroking the stubble on his jaw. 'I do not want to marry him.'

She said it so quietly he had to concentrate in order to hear her. She was looking at him as though he had the power to grant her wish, but he did not. He was nothing, nobody. All he could offer was a fleeting moment of comfort. 'I know' was all he said.

They watched one another. He wanted so badly to kiss her, to tell her she did not have to do anything she did not want to do. But that was not the world they lived in. He was unemployed, homeless, weak, with only the clothes on his back and the few coins left in his pouch. To snatch away her only security and offer nothing in return was reckless. 'You should go to your mother.'

Her eyes seemed to hollow out for a moment. 'That is all you have to say? "Go to your mother"?'

*Stay. I love you. Let me take care of you.*

He was sleeping in a stable thanks to the generosity of her father, a gesture Rufus would regret if he learned the whereabouts of his daughter at that moment. 'You need to see the physician.'

She blinked, a plea in her expression, one he was forced to ignore. He felt her body pull away from him, and it took all his strength not to drag her back again. He had to let her go.

As she sat up, he took hold of her elbow, because she was moving like everything hurt.

'I don't need your help.' She pulled her arm free of his hand.

He slid to the edge of the bed, ready if she needed him. She stood on trembling legs, pulling the palla tighter around her despite the warm air. He gripped the edge of the bed to stop himself from reaching for her, from drawing her into his lap and burying his face in her neck.

'Now is not the time,' he said.

She looked down at him, her expression wounded. 'Time for what?'

He glanced around the stall. She was going to make him say it. 'To be reckless.'

She nodded, hugging herself tighter.

'You think I want you to marry him?' His voice was laced with all the pent-up frustration and jealousy he had carried for so long. 'What sort of man would I be if I asked you to walk away now?' He forced himself to look at her, finding her eyes glassy with tears. Gesturing to the wall, he added, 'I'm sleeping with horses.'

Another nod. 'I understand. Good day.'

He stood, coughed, and watched her leave. His feet threatened to go after her, and the moment she was out of sight, a heaviness grew in his chest, spreading to his arms and legs. He collapsed back down, head bowed and hands in his hair.

'I suspect Dulcia would happily sleep on the streets, as long as it was with you.'

Nero turned to look at Felix, finding him propped up on one elbow, watching him. He had been awake after all. 'I can't do that to her.'

'Oh, I know that. But would it have killed you to admit you were at least *tempted?*'

'Feed her false hope?' He hung his head again. 'I won't destroy her.'

Felix rolled his eyes. 'Must you be so dramatic?'

Nero raised his head. 'Right now she needs a roof over her head.'

The dwarf sat up and pushed the blanket aside. 'All I am saying is, if you do not wish to see that girl married to your nemesis, you had better make a plan—and quickly. Once she exchanges nuptials with Manius Liberia, there will be no second chances.'

Nero stared at him. He was right, of course. Soon she would be untouchable. If he was crazy enough to think himself worthy of her, mad enough to try, the time was now. He just needed a few weeks to get back on his feet, to make some money and figure it all out.

'Dulcia's not going to marry Manius.' He nodded as he thought. *She's going to marry me.*

# CHAPTER 17

The sun had grown teeth. The women stood in the shade at the back of the temple. Licinia had her arms folded, watching the blue rock thrush flitting around them in search of insects.

'You are not saying much,' Dulcia said, eyeing the priestess. 'Your silence is not much of a comfort.'

'Is it really comfort you seek?' Licinia looked sceptical.

Dulcia shook her head. 'Fine, counsel, then.'

Licinia smiled. 'You want me to talk you into marrying Manius, is that it?'

Dulcia glanced around, worried someone would overhear them. 'He visited me daily for the entire week I was bedridden. Everyone is singing his praises.'

'Everyone?'

She hesitated, twisting the ring that hung from her neck, the one she should not be wearing. 'Well, my mother, at least.'

'Ah.' The birds flew off, and Licinia turned to face her. 'You have a choice, but the choice is not between Nero and Manius. That would be too easy. The choice is between Nero and your *family*.'

That was true. Her mother had made it perfectly clear the

day she had dragged her from the stables, unable to look at her. *'If Rufus finds out about this, you will be exiled so quickly, you will be left spinning on the street. What were you thinking, going to him?'* Tertia had seethed.

She had been thinking only of Nero: his warm arms, lips, breath. The way his voice hummed on her skin when he spoke. How was she to make sensible choices when she could not think past him?

*'Lust,'* Tertia had called it. *'It can reduce the most sensible person to a juvenile state. You are smarter than that.'*

Her mother had reduced everything she felt down to a physical impulse. Dulcia might have been young, but she recognised the enormity of her feelings.

'Did they find an apartment?'

A nod. 'It's tiny. Only two rooms, but they make it work.' Remus and Mila had refused the offer of coin from Nerva.

'But you have not seen Nero since the night you…'

The fact that Licinia could not even finish the sentence spoke volumes.

'Nothing happened, you know.' Not entirely true. She had bared her soul, and he had sent her away. Now three weeks had passed without a word.

The birds returned, snatching Licinia's attention once more. 'You answer only to Vesta.'

Dulcia felt her eyes prickle. She had been on the verge of tears for days. 'Families will be returning to the city soon, tiring of the quiet and salty air. Mother has bought fabric for the gown. Manius's sister even gifted me a necklace for the event.'

Licinia studied her for a moment. 'And yet you have never looked more miserable.'

Dulcia brushed aside a tear that escaped. 'Nero said that now is not the time, but time is running out. They are talking about a date four weeks from now.'

A bird hopped closer, its tail flicking and head tilting to get a better look at them.

'He is being practical,' Licinia said. 'The more time that passes, the higher the stakes.'

Dulcia drew a long breath. 'I can be practical too. I have already thought about the fact that I would need to find work.'

'If you are truly being practical, then consider the possibility that people might not be prepared to employ you, or use your services, when they learn of your situation.'

The words slammed into Dulcia's middle.

Seeing the effect of her statement, Licinia added, 'But you have skills, youth and good health on your side.'

'But not my own mother.'

Silence.

Approaching footsteps made them both turn. Dulcia felt cold at the sight of Manius coming towards them. *What on earth is he doing here?*

'They said I might find you here,' he said, coming to a stop in front of them. He bowed his head at Licinia, who returned the gesture. 'I am afraid I must steal Dulcia away.'

Licinia regarded him for a moment before replying. 'We were just finishing up.'

He was the last person Dulcia felt like seeing. 'I thought I was joining you for dinner this evening.' She struggled to keep the annoyance from her tone.

He bent, kissing her cheek. It left a damp spot on her skin, and she had a strong urge to wipe at it.

'Can I not surprise my soon-to-be wife during daylight?'

Licinia looked away. 'Please excuse me.' She bowed her head once more.

Dulcia wished her friend would stay, but knew she could not avoid being alone with him forever. 'Good day.' She lowered her head.

The priestess gave her a fleeting sympathetic glance before leaving.

Dulcia felt only dread as she looked at Manius. It was a blazing contrast to the butterflies in her chest whenever Nero made impromptu visits. She knew she would never play games, climb a tree, or even laugh with the man standing before her.

'Come,' he said, offering her his arm. 'I have something to show you.'

She stared warily at the extended limb before finally stepping forwards to take it.

~

THE DOMUS WAS in region thirteen, close to the Liberia household, though around half the size. Dulcia stood in the middle of the newly refurbished atrium, feeling detached from the scene. Her gaze settled on the fountain in the middle of the room. 'Who lives here?'

'We will,' Manius said, a wide grin spreading across his face as he came towards her. 'In a few short weeks.'

She really ought to have smiled, or at least reacted. Instead, she watched the pride play out on his face, his teeth seeming five shades whiter in that moment. So happy with himself. What an awful person she was, unable to even muster a few words of appreciation.

'You did not think we would live with my family, did you?'

What did she know? She still shared a room with her mother. 'I had not given it much thought.'

'A senator must have his own domus if he is to entertain.'

She pressed her lips into a thin line to stop herself from speaking. He was not a senator yet, but it was probably smart not to point out the fact.

Manius strolled around the room, radiating importance.

'After the wedding, your father will discuss the matter with Severus himself. What a successful match we are.'

She watched him circle her, feeling like prey. 'Yes.'

He returned to her, taking her face in his hands so she was forced to look at him. 'This is not just business, you know. I also get you, and you get me.'

The angle was uncomfortable, so she shifted her feet, waiting for him to let go. Instead, he bent his head and kissed her, more feverishly than previous times. His prime reason for marrying her might have been for the senate, but there was no denying his attraction to her. That only made her feel worse. At least if it were pure business, she could remain detached without guilt. She felt like an awkward statue standing there in the middle of that large room while he ravaged her mouth. Finally, he pulled back, but kept hold of her.

'Would you like to see the bedrooms?' There was no mistaking the innuendo. 'The beds are *most* comfortable.'

She swallowed against his fingers. 'Careful. Senators must be of high moral character.' She had meant to keep her tone light. 'Perhaps you can show me the kitchen.'

'Of all the rooms in the house, you ask to see the kitchen?' He pulled her back to him, his hand gliding over her breast. 'Why do you deny me still?'

She leaned away from him. 'Because we are not married yet.'

He laughed. 'In a matter of weeks it will not matter.'

She pulled free of his grip. 'I should go.'

He caught her wrist, holding so tightly she had to bite the inside of her cheek to stop from crying out.

'I bring you here, to our *home*, and you offer up nothing but bland conversation and indifferent glances before walking out on me?' He seemed genuinely confused. 'It is as though you have forgotten what you are.'

She watched as her hand changed colour. 'And what is that?'

'A freed woman. A *slaveborn* woman.' He let go of her arm, and she pressed it to her chest, covering it protectively with her other hand. 'When a man like *me* invites you to bed, you should be gleefully lifting your skirts.'

She took a step back. 'Can you hear yourself?'

He looked away, suitably ashamed.

'Perhaps there are some women who show their gratitude in that way, but I am not one of them. Is that really the type of woman you want to marry?'

He was quiet a moment, then cleared his throat. 'I only pray your hesitation has nothing to do with some childish fling.'

She did not have to ask what or who he was referring to.

'We cannot erase our past feelings or actions,' he continued, 'but we can put them behind us for the benefit of our futures.' He paused. 'I trust you will be able to do that. I might seem like a progressive man, but I will not accept you in parts. You will belong to me entirely or not at all. In return for your blatant devotion, you will have a life many only dream of.' Another pause. 'Do you understand what I am saying?'

She nodded, then backed away from him. 'I have to go home and prepare for this evening.' She was barely aware of what she was saying.

Manius waved her away. 'The litter will take you home.' She was almost at the door when he called out, 'And wear something nice.'

There was no shortage of criminals in Rome. Those sentenced to death via combat were often sent to Gallus Minidius, who wanted to pay Nero handsomely to be his star executioner. The sponsor organised a horse and chariot and made Nero a spectacle, one that drew people from all corners and classes to watch Remus Latinius's apprentice deliver justice.

'I'm not interested in playing executioner,' he had said at first.

Gallus had waved his statement away as though it held no weight. 'Common criminals take no toll on your conscience. Your soul will rest easy knowing there are a few less rodents on our streets.'

Nero had been one of those rodents once. 'I'm not a killer.'

'You might change your mind when you meet some of these vile men.'

It had been three weeks since the fire, since he had carried Dulcia's lifeless body from that blaze. Since he had thought her dead. Three weeks since she had come to his bed in the middle of the night, her body fitting so perfectly against his.

'*I do not want to marry him,*' she had said. As if it needed saying.

The only way out was to provide her with a viable alternative, offer her something more than a section of mattress in a cramped apartment. That was why he took the extra coin Gallus threw his way—and the job that went with it.

It was his third visit to the Amphitheatrum Neronis, an arena that was five times bigger than the amateur pits he had fought in previously. He waited in the tunnel with two chestnut mares. They were nervous, not helped by the fact that they could probably smell the blood. One let out a high-pitched whinny.

'Easy.' He stroked the mare's neck.

Gallus wandered up and handed him a helmet, a shield and an assortment of weapons. 'You might need these.' He watched as two guards led a criminal out onto the blood-soaked sand. 'Oh dear. He won't last long.'

Nero had just finished putting his helmet on. He turned to look at the condemned man. 'What was his crime?' He always asked the same question before he rode out.

The sponsor glanced sideways at him. 'Rape.'

'Really?'

Gallus's cheeks ballooned with exasperation. 'I am not given detailed accounts of their sins, you know. Just pick a crime that suits your conscience. Murder, perhaps?'

Nero drew his brows together. 'Maybe he stole food to feed his starving family.'

Gallus scoffed. 'Stop. You know as well as I that death via combat is saved for a particular variety of men. Start thinking otherwise and you will get yourself killed.' He gestured for Nero to climb up. 'You are much more valuable to me alive.'

Nero stepped up into the chariot and gathered the reins. 'Nice to know you care... about your profits.'

The gate began to open. The horses stirred. Applause started before the crowd had even set eyes on the horses.

'I will have you know that I care a great deal for your welfare,' Gallus shouted over the noisy crowd, now on their feet. 'Because if you die, your gladiator friends will come for me.'

Nero shook his head and picked up the spear. A sword turned in his opponent's hand. He held a shield in the other. Guilt pooled in Nero's belly. He had to remind himself that the man would die eventually. That was how it worked. If Nero died first, they would send someone else out to finish the job.

'Ha!' Leather reins slapped rump, and the chariot lurched forwards.

~

'Nero.'

He really did not want to open his eyes.

*Smack.* 'I know you can hear me.'

He forced his eyes open, blinking a few times until Mila came into focus, her arms crossed, mouth set in that particular way. Oh, he was in trouble.

Pushing himself up onto his elbows, he sighed. 'No "good morning", then?'

She held a coin pouch in front of his face and shook it so it jingled. 'What is this?'

He looked around at the empty beds. Felix and Albaus had abandoned him.

'They are not here,' she said, reading his mind.

He cleared his throat. 'Who?'

She whacked him across the head with the coin pouch. 'Where did you get all this money?'

He sat all the way up, hand going over the side of his head. 'That actually hurt.'

She took a menacing step towards him, preparing to hit him again. He raised his hands in surrender.

'I didn't steal it, if that's where you're headed.'

She tossed the pouch down on the bed next to him, somewhat subdued by his statement. 'Then where did you get it?'

'I earned it.'

'How?'

He swung his legs over the edge of the bed, every muscle sore, every bone aching from the fight which had ended on his feet next to a dead horse. 'You know how. Gallus Minidius.'

She crossed her arms again, which meant she did not believe him. 'Oh, I know Gallus, and he does not pay gladiators this well.'

'Some came from the crowd.'

She shook her head, disappointment replacing the anger. 'What does he have you doing that would pay such a sum?'

He leaned forwards, his hamstrings protesting at the slightest stretch of his legs. Two fights in one evening was the answer to that question. He straightened his arms and winced. Gods, he was sore. He sighed and leaned on his knees. 'I fight well.'

'And what does that entail, exactly?'

The look on his face must have answered her question.

'Gods,' she said, stepping back. 'What have you gotten yourself into?'

'Delivering justice for the people.'

She laughed, a harsh noise. 'You even sound like him now. That man is a snake.'

'*You* fought for him once.'

She threw up her hands. 'Yes, when I was young and desperate.'

He tilted his head, eyebrows raised. 'Well, now *I'm* young and desperate.'

'You are not that desperate. I was trying to earn my freedom.'

Nero stood. 'And I'm trying to save your sister from a man she doesn't want to marry.'

Mila's face fell at his words. 'Oh, Nero.'

'Don't.' He snatched up his tunic and slipped it over his head.

'Does Remus know what you have been up to?'

'I imagine he will by the end of the day.' He stepped past her into the other room, where the children were eating *cena* on the floor.

She followed him out. 'What about Felix and Albaus?'

Silence.

Mila exhaled. 'Wait until I see them.'

He did not want to be around for that conversation. 'Where are they?'

Asha got up off the floor and went to hug him while the twins continued eating. He bent to kiss the top of her head, wincing as a rib twinged.

'They are working,' Mila said, leaning in the doorway. 'Honest work.'

He picked up the knife and cut a thick slice of cheese. 'It's just for a little while. Until I get some more coin saved.'

She stared at him. 'She does not need wealth to be happy.'

'No, but she needs a place to live when her father casts her aside.' He put the knife down. 'And before you say it, you know as well as I that she can't live here. There's barely room to move as it is.' He reached for the bread. 'I've found an apartment.'

She walked into the room. 'What apartment?'

'Two rooms with a shared courtyard.'

Mila's hand went to her brow. 'Oh, Nero.'

He cut through the bread, then put the knife down.

Breaking the cheese in two, he placed one piece on the bread and shoved the other into his mouth. 'She doesn't want to marry him. Told me plain as day.'

'She might not have a choice.' Mila glanced at the children to check if they were listening. Asha was, of course. The boys were happily playing. 'You are risking your life in the arena in hope that she will walk away from her obligations.'

He continued as if she had not spoken. 'It's close by. Ground floor. I don't ever want her trapped upstairs if there's a fire.'

Mila's expression was filled with pity. He had to look away.

'Don't look at me like that. If I offer her an out, she'll take it.' He watched Mila's reaction to his words.

'For whatever reason, Rufus has decided to behave like a father. That means it is not up to her.'

Asha began tugging on his hand. He tore his gaze away from Mila and looked down at her. 'What is it?'

She gestured with a finger for him to come closer, so he bent, bringing his ear to her mouth.

'Just marry her,' she whispered. 'Tonight. Consummate it so it will be too late for Rufus to do anything but give his blessing.'

'Asha!' Mila said from the other side. 'Who on earth taught you about consummation?'

She looked innocently at her mother. 'Felix.'

Nero smirked, and Mila shook her head.

'Well, I will be having words with Felix later.' Mila looked between them. 'And you should not encourage him.'

Asha held on to Nero's hand. 'But he loves her. He's always staring at her when he thinks nobody is watching.'

'No I don't,' Nero said, covering Asha's mouth with his free hand.

'Yes you do,' Mila replied, walking over to the table.

Asha pushed his hand away. 'But it's all right, because she does it too. So you *have* to marry her.'

Mila wrapped the cheese. 'Before you follow the advice of a six-year-old, are you prepared for what will happen if Dulcia *does* walk away from Manius?'

Nero straightened. 'I'll marry her today if she agrees to it.'

'I am talking about Manius's reaction.'

Just the mention of his name put him on edge. 'I can handle Manius.'

Mila did not look convinced. 'In a fight, sure.' She dragged a bowl to her, lifted the tea towel and poked at the dough. Satisfied, she upturned it onto the floured part of the bench. 'But he will not attack with his fists.'

'I told you,' he said, taking hold of her shoulders and squeezing. 'I can handle him.'

Mila pounded the dough with her fist.

'She's angry kneading,' Asha whispered up at him.

'I am not angry kneading.' Mila looked between them. 'I am just worried.'

Nero leaned on the bench, watching her for a moment. 'Perhaps you think she *should* marry Manius. I wouldn't blame you.'

She stopped and looked at him, her expression softening. 'There is no better man for my sister than you. I would love nothing more than to see you both happy.'

Nero gave her a lopsided smile. 'In that case, I forgive you for pounding me across the head earlier.' He winked and strode off.

'Where are you going?' Mila called.

'She will be at the nundinae. If I hurry, I might catch her.'

Mila sighed, then waved him away. 'Go, but be careful.'

# CHAPTER 19

*N*ero watched her from afar. The merchant was leaning forwards over his produce in order to hear her. Nero's hands fisted when the man's eyes dropped below her face for the third time. Dulcia leaned closer, repeating herself yet again. The merchant must have heard her that time, because he straightened and smiled at her. Nero had no choice but to swallow down his jealousy. He could not blame the man. Her beauty was visible to everyone: men, women, children. Hell, dogs stopped in the streets to watch her pass.

The merchant loaded the items into her basket, as if she were incapable of lifting a pear without his help. Then he kept hold of the handle for a moment, smiling as he chatted away. What on earth was he saying? There were buyers lined up, waiting.

Unable to stand it any longer, Nero strode towards them, eyes on Dulcia, who was shrinking farther away while the loaf of a man kept hold of her basket. A few more strides and he was at her side.

'I'll take it from here,' he said, yanking the basket from the merchant's hands.

The man's eyes widened with surprise. Then, reading Nero's face, he nodded and turned to the next customer. Nero watched him a moment longer, just in case he dared to look at her again. When he turned to Dulcia, he was met with crossed arms and a scowl.

'Let's go,' he said, gesturing for her to go ahead of him.

She shook her head before walking off.

The last time he had seen her, she had looked so pale, so fragile. She seemed better, though the dark circles remained around her eyes. Perhaps she was not sleeping, or woke smelling smoke, like he did sometimes.

'What are you doing here?' she asked over her shoulder.

'Looking for you.' A nervous excitement churned his insides. 'I want to show you something.'

She stopped walking and looked around. For what, he had no idea. She reached out and took the basket back from him, then sighed. 'I should really get home.'

'It won't take long.'

She was trying very hard not to look at him, but finally her eyes met his and her expression softened. 'All right.' The words came out in a resigned breath.

He took the basket back from her. 'This way.'

They strolled side by side, Dulcia keeping more distance between them than usual; less eye contact, less conversation —less everything. She was closed up so tight he worried he would not get through to her.

'Where are we going?' she asked as they entered the rowdy streets of Subura. 'I gather not the river.'

He shook his head. 'Not the river.' Touching a hand to the small of her back, he guided her through a narrow alleyway. She walked closer to him then, nervous eyes searching the shadows. The neighbourhood did not exactly have the safest reputation, but the apartment was on an open street. 'Almost there.'

'Almost *where*?' She glanced over her shoulder again.

He leaned closer. 'Patience.'

They emerged from the darkness onto a busy street. Children played, and women stood in clusters gossiping, pausing occasionally to yell at their offspring. Yes, it was still Subura, but he liked to think of it as the classy part.

'Now where?' she asked, looking up at him.

He gestured to the building on his left. 'We're here.'

She turned to look at the building. 'We are?'

He took her hand and pulled her through an archway at the base of the insulae. Instead of going up the stairs, he led her behind them to a small door.

Her hand tightened on his. 'What is this place?'

He fiddled with the handle of the door for a few moments before giving up and throwing his shoulder into it. It whined as it swung open. 'Just needs oiling.' He gestured for her to go ahead of him.

She stared into the room, not moving. 'Who lives here?'

'No one yet,' he laughed. 'But me, soon.' He did not say *us*, did not want to risk her fleeing before she had a chance to see its potential.

'You?' Her brows formed a suspicious frown.

He drew a breath. 'Please go inside.'

She walked into the apartment, stopping in the middle of the room and looking around. She said nothing.

Nero went to the small window on the opposite wall and pulled back the curtain. The fabric came apart in his hand, and a cloud of dust whirled around him. He coughed, and she flinched at the noise.

'Sorry,' he said, waving a hand in front of his face. 'It's not much yet, but it will be. Two rooms. The second opens to the courtyard.' He stepped in that direction. 'Come.'

'Yours?' Her feet were seemingly anchored to that one spot.

Nerves pelted his gut. 'I've paid the first six months' rent.'

Her eyes went to him then, cutting through him. 'Six months?' A pause. 'Where did you get the coin?'

He shrugged. 'I've been working.'

Dulcia looked around the room, unreadable.

He could not handle the silence, the waiting, the not knowing. 'I got it for us.'

At first he thought she did not hear because she did not react. He reached for her hand, lacing his fingers through hers. Her gaze fell to them, and he waited for her to say something.

Nothing.

The nervous feeling in the pit of his stomach grew. 'You could sew us new curtains.' He had no idea why he said that, and it was clearly the wrong thing to say, because she burst into tears. Retracting her hand, she faced her back to him. He immediately turned her around again, lifting her face so he could read her.

'I'll find another apartment,' he said, 'a better one.'

She took a step back from him, head shaking. 'It's not the apartment.'

His heart was drumming in his ears. 'Then why are you upset?'

Her hands fell to her sides and she stared at the roof instead of him, lips pressed in a thin line as she tried to stop herself from crying. 'Because it is too late.'

His hands closed, opened again. 'No it's not.'

'Yes it is.' She looked at him. 'It really is.'

'Why? Did you secretly wed Manius?'

'No.'

'Then it's not too late.'

She pulled away from him and walked off into the other room. He followed but paused in the doorway, watching as she opened the door to the courtyard. Sunshine spilled into the room, bathing her in golden light. His heart seemed to stop beating for a moment as he imagined seeing her that way every morning, when the sun was at that exact angle.

She looked around, hugging herself. 'Yesterday, Manius surprised me also.'

He stepped into the room and walked over to stand beside her. He leaned his back on the doorframe so he could see her face and waited for her to continue.

'He took me to an enormous house upon a hill in region thirteen. Soon to be our home.'

Nero looked around the apartment, which suddenly seemed smaller. 'Well, I can't compete with that.'

She turned to face him. 'I felt physically ill as I tried to imagine my life there, sharing that home with him. I was supposed to be happy, grateful, excited, feel all the things a woman like me should feel.'

He frowned. 'What do you mean, *a woman like you?*'

'Slaveborn. Worthless. A nobody.'

He blinked, not believing what he was hearing. Her hair was out and swept to one side. She had never looked more worthy of a grand house. He reached out and touched her hair. 'Is that what he told you?'

She did not reply.

He would pummel that man next time he ran into him. 'You're not worthless. You're a goddess. And if he hasn't told you that, then he doesn't deserve you.'

She pushed hair back from her face, tucking it behind her ear. It immediately sprang free again. That was when he noticed the purple bruise enclosing her wrist. Catching her elbow, he narrowed his eyes.

'What happened to your arm?' He was tiring of Aquila's outbursts. Dulcia was an easy target for a scorned woman like her.

Her silence made him suspicious, because she always just told him the truth without a moment's hesitation.

'A mishap in the kitchen.'

She really was a terrible liar, and there was only one reason she would lie—she was protecting someone. 'Who did that to your arm?'

She put her arm behind her back and turned away from the courtyard. 'I have to go.'

'Dulcia—'

'Let it go. It does not matter.'

'Of course it matters.' He reached for her face, but she pushed his hands away.

'I really have to go.'

He stepped in front of her, linking his hands on top of his head. 'Are you telling me no? You don't want to marry me?'

When she looked up at him, there was anger in her eyes. 'Oh, was that a proposal?'

He tried to recall what he had said to her in the moments prior. *Fool.* It had been a far cry from the speech he had planned in his head. He took both of her hands in his and dropped to his knees. He would beg if that was what it took. Once she walked out that door, his chance would be gone.

'I'm sorry. You deserve flowers and sonnets, but I forgot about the flowers, and I'm a terrible poet.' He paused, his mouth dry. 'Don't marry Manius. Don't. Marry me instead, and I swear to the gods, I will spend the rest of my life trying to make you happy.' He swallowed. 'Please. Trust me.'

She looked down at him, eyes glassy, bottom lip trembling. 'I can't. I told you before, it is too late. Just being here with you is risky.' She glanced at the door behind him. 'Manius is understandably threatened by my... past feelings for you. He has made it very clear that—'

He snatched her bruised arm and held it between them. 'Is that what this is?' He struggled to keep his voice calm. 'Did he do this to you? Felt the need to pull you into line?'

She yanked her arm free. 'Why does everyone feel the

need to hold on to me while lecturing me?' There was hurt in her eyes. 'I can hear just fine without being handled.'

His shame almost knocked him backwards. Slowly, he raised his hands, showing that he would not touch her again. He was no better than Manius in that moment. 'Don't go.' His voice was a deep plea.

She shook her head, eyes welling again and spilling over. 'I have to.' She brushed the tears away. 'Do you not understand what I am trying to tell you? It is too late. Now I must return home to my mother, and she is going to ask me where I have been. And you know what a fantastic liar I am.'

'So tell her the truth.'

'The wedding date is set. The dress is being made.' She looked around, exasperated. 'Manius bought us a house.' She sniffed. 'What do you think will happen if I walk away at this point?'

Nero moved closer, wanting to grab her, but knowing that was not a good idea. 'You think I can't take care of you? Is that it?'

'I never needed to be taken care of. I only ever needed you.' She took a step back. 'And you wait until a few weeks out from my wedding day to figure out your feelings.'

'That is absolute shit and you know it.'

A pained noise escaped her. 'I am going.' She walked through to the other room and snatched up the basket.

'Stay.' A final plea.

'It is too late. If you do not realise that, then I cannot help you.'

He grabbed her arm again, unable to stop himself. His chest felt like it was being torn open.

She spun on him. 'Stop touching me!'

He immediately released her, eyes going to the bruise. 'He'll pay for leaving that mark on you.'

She waved away his words. 'You already beat him up once, remember?'

His palms went over his eyes, his frustration palpable. 'How could I forget? You practically laid yourself over him like a human shield.'

'Someone had to stop you. Heaven forbid you show some restraint for once in your life.'

He could not believe what he was hearing. 'I've been showing nothing but restraint since I arrived back here.' He took an unsteady breath, stepped back. 'I see what you're doing. You're trying to make walking away easier. Is that it?' He nodded, as if he had just figured it all out. 'If you can just find a way to hate me, then you can go to your rich house on the hill and not feel guilty for walking out.'

Her face reddened. 'You think this is *easy*?' More tears escaped. 'I feel like I am dying inside.' She pressed a hand to her chest. 'Every day betrothed to that man has been a small death. I never wanted a wealthy husband, a big house. I am embarrassed to travel in a litter, uncomfortable at parties, waited on by slaves I am supposed to ignore, just like I was ignored my entire life.' She sucked in a breath, a sob tearing through her. 'I only ever wanted *you*.'

He held his hands in front of him, as though offering up the broken pieces of himself. 'Stay. We'll figure this out.'

She shook her head, then said slowly, 'It is too late.'

He groaned, dragging his fingers through his hair. 'Fine. Go. Go marry Manius. He can have you. Whatever problems you encounter along the way can easily be solved with money.'

Her hands went over her ears. 'Stop.'

'Make Rufus really proud of the daughter he ignored all those years. That's what this is about, after all.'

'Stop it!'

'*Congratulations*, your wedding guests will say. Your father finally loves you for one reason only—you married well.'

She staggered back from his words, then turned and ran

for the door. He forced his feet to keep still, to not chase her, to not fall at her feet and beg her forgiveness.

'Dulcia,' he called. He was surprised when she froze in the doorway. One word with so much power. She turned, panting and broken. 'You can leave the door open.'

*A*nother dinner. Another evening pretending she belonged. This time it was a different circle of friends, but Dulcia could barely tell the difference between them. Same excess of food, fabric, jewels and wigs made from the hair of conquered civilisations. She sat beside Manius on the lounge, stifling a yawn. The fight with Nero, the tears, the heartbreak—it had left her exhausted.

'Oh, are we keeping you awake?' Livia said from across the table, her tone dripping with sarcasm.

Junia waved her cup, gesturing for more wine. 'Oh, Mother, leave Dulcia alone. She is allowed to feel tired.'

Livia held her cup up also, then turned to the woman beside her. 'Tiredness can be a sign of infertility, you know.'

'Mother,' Manius said. 'Dulcia was at the nundinae this morning, then took a long walk through Subura. Junia is right. She is allowed to be tired after such an eventful day.'

Dulcia's gaze snapped to him, her heartbeat increasing. She had not told him where she had been that day.

He glanced sideways at her.

Aquila had an army of spies running about the city, so it made sense that a man like Manius had eyes all over Rome.

'*Subura*?' Livia's nose crinkled. 'You are lucky you were not robbed.'

Dulcia fought the urge to roll her eyes. 'My sister lives there now.'

Manius turned to her. 'But you were not with your sister, were you?'

So he meant to embarrass her. 'No, I was with a friend.'

Claudius leaned forwards, plucking an olive off the tray in front of him. 'I am sensing a scandal.' He met Dulcia's gaze and winked.

She immediately looked down at her lap.

Manius took a long drink from his cup before speaking. 'With her friend Nero. The one they call *Rat*.'

Everyone's eyebrows seemed to rise in unison, and the other guests stopped talking.

'The rodent working for Gallus Minidius? Well, that is neither safe nor appropriate,' Livia tutted. 'Must we endure the rumours?'

Dulcia's chest tightened as she gripped her drink with both hands.

'For goodness' sake, they were clearly in a public place,' Junia said.

'*Were* you in a public place?' Manius asked. There was a coldness in his tone that suggested he already knew the answer to that question.

Dulcia looked at him. Instead of guilt, which would have been a far more appropriate reaction, she felt annoyed at the invasion of privacy. As if the day had not been difficult enough, she was now on public trial by the very man who should have had her back.

She set her cup down and stood. 'As pleasant as the evening has been, I think I am going to leave.'

Livia's eyes gleamed. 'Oh, dear,' she murmured into her cup. 'Trouble so soon.'

'Sit down,' Manius said tiredly.

She remained standing. 'I am leaving.'

'I will walk you out,' Junia said, preparing to stand.

Manius raised a hand to stop her. 'No. *I* will walk her out.'

Dulcia thanked her hosts, saying her farewells amid whispers and smirks, then returned inside and walked briskly towards the entranceway.

'You are not to see him anymore,' Manius said, closing the gap between them.

She stopped walking, his words like cold water on her back, then turned to face him. 'That is not reasonable. He is family.'

Manius leaned in. 'You are lucky you left that apartment in tears today or we would be having a very different conversation.'

She lifted her chin. 'Is that what your spies told you?'

His hand shot up and came down across her face. It was not hard, not compared to Aquila, but it stung. Her trembling hand went over her cheek, and she fought hard to stop the tears.

Manius calmed himself. 'What is the matter with you lately? You are becoming as openly rebellious as your sister. Am I to ban you from seeing her also?'

She lowered her hands and held her ground. 'Is this what I am to expect from our marriage? Spies and distrust? A good slap when I step out of line?'

He brought his face inches from hers, his voice hoarse with anger. 'You dare lecture me on trust?'

She blinked, then looked at the floor. He was right not to trust her. She was not in control of herself around Nero, and the problem was only getting worse. 'You are right.' It came out as a whisper.

He leaned away, eyes widening for a moment. 'And there it is.' He shook his head. 'You admit it. I chose you for your virtue, and you turned out to be just another whore.'

She flinched at the word he flung at her, then drew a

courageous breath. 'I am sorry, but I cannot marry you.' She felt instant relief the moment she said the words aloud.

Confusion passed over his face, but then his eyes narrowed into slits. 'No, you do not get to walk away from me.'

'I do not love you.' The confessions were spilling out of her now. 'And I cannot imagine a time when I will.'

He laughed, and the sound echoed around the atrium. 'Do you honestly believe a woman like *you* gets to marry for love?'

She refused to cry, refused to let him tear her down any more than he already had. 'Yes, I think it is possible.'

He reached up, palm on her red cheek. 'Really? A woman with nothing to offer a man like me except her beauty and virtue?' When she went to speak, he brought his thumb to her lips, silencing her. 'We can forget the virtue now.' His hand fell away. 'Tell me, what does your priestess friend say of your fornication?'

Dulcia lifted her chin, not bothering to indulge him with an answer.

He stepped back, rubbing at his temples. Drawing a long breath, he said, 'I think I drank too much wine. Go home, and I will call on you in the morning.'

She did not move. 'I meant what I said. I cannot marry you.'

'Do not embarrass yourself further. The litter will take you home. We will talk tomorrow.'

'I do not want to talk tomorrow.'

There was that confused expression again. 'Let us see what your father has to say on the subject, shall we?'

Dulcia fought hard to keep down the food and wine she had consumed. 'I already know what he will say.'

'I doubt that.'

'I understand the consequences.' She looked around the atrium for a moment. 'This is going to devastate my mother

176

and probably lose me the roof over my head. But that is a price I am prepared to pay to live honestly.' She turned from him, walking towards the door on shaky legs with her heart thudding and hope soaring. 'I do not need the litter,' she said over her shoulder. 'I will walk.'

'Take the litter,' he called to her back. 'I will be by in the morning.'

Her pace quickened when the door opened in front of her. She gripped her palla as if the fabric were holding all the broken pieces together.

Down the steps, she went straight past the waiting litter. She would risk being murdered before setting foot in it again. It was not that far to her home anyway. There she would wake her mother and tell her the news. Perhaps Tertia would surprise her. Maybe she would offer comfort, and help Rufus to see that Manius was not a good match for her.

She realised at that moment she was running, charging down the street like a wounded animal. When she reached the Papias house, she stopped at the bottom of the steps, panting. She stared up at the door, so familiar, despite many layers of paint over the past nineteen years. On the other side of that door was her father, her mother, her domina, occasionally her half-brother. There was also the kitchen she loved, and the cook she had grown to love, as well as many other servants she was raised with.

'*I will come by in the morning,*' Manius had said.

Perhaps he thought sunlight could erase the evening—the harsh words, the accusations and bold statements. She considered the possibility of starting over the next day, trying again with the man and making everyone happy. How many times had she tried to convince herself that she could do it? She could have a comfortable life in a grand house filled with servants. All she had to do was give Manius what he wanted, and it was not much. A virtuous wife who hung from his arm and smiled in a way that made every other husband envious, who entertained, and marvelled at his accomplishments. She could spend his denarii on garments and jewels, host dinner parties for his friends, smile, laugh at their crude jokes, look away when they struck a slave for the smallest thing. She could lie with him, turn a blind eye at his indiscretions and never have any of her own. She could bear his children and raise them to be miniature versions of the very people she despised.

Six steps. Then she would be at the door.

Tomorrow Manius would call, and she was confident she could fix whatever was broken between them. He was jealous, needed reassurance that he was the better man, the more desirable man for *a woman like her*. She could reassure him that she was still virtuous, then go on to have the life her mother could not and the approval of her father. Rufus might even call her *daughter* at the wedding.

Six steps. One, two, three, four, five, six, then through the door. It should have been easy.

But her feet did not move.

## CHAPTER 21

$S$tanding in the middle of the room, Nero looked around at the pristine apartment. He had spent the afternoon cleaning it and fixing everything that was broken. He had torn down the remains of the curtains and resisted the urge to set them alight, cursing himself for not cleaning it up prior to bringing Dulcia to see it. Not that it would have made much of a difference to the outcome.

In the evening, Felix and Albaus had come by to drop off some of his belongings. Hearing that all did not go to plan, they tried to convince him to join them at the tavern, but he could not face people, could not face anyone in his current state. They must have been concerned, because soon after they departed, Mila and Remus appeared on his doorstep. Mila reminded him that he always had a home with them. It took some convincing that he was fine and would not fall apart over a woman, and yet when they finally left, he collapsed against the door with his body threatening to do just that.

He replayed the argument with Dulcia, angry at himself for not being more patient. He should have given her time to sit with the idea, reassured her. She was afraid, and she had every right to be. He should have blocked the door and told her he loved her, repeated it over and over until it was all she knew. Had he actually said the words? He could not remember. But he remembered telling her to go, and every cruel word that followed. He had assumed she knew it, felt it. So many foolish assumptions before pushing her away.

Nero closed his eyes, his head resting against the smooth wood. He had blown it, even though every fibre of his body told him they belonged together. No one could love her like he did—especially Manius. His mind scrambled with a way to fix it.

*It is too late.*

A knock at the door vibrated against his back. He opened his eyes. Who else was left to take pity on him?

It was late. The streets had grown quiet. He turned to face the door and considered not opening it. The strength required for conversation was beyond him at that point. Leaning his forehead against the door, he closed his eyes again. Hopefully they would think him asleep and leave.

Another knock sounded, louder that time.

*Go away*, he wanted to say. Instead, he straightened, took a deep breath, and opened the door. It was smooth and quiet that time.

Dulcia stood on the other side, eyes on the freshly oiled hinges.

'You fixed it.'

He followed her line of sight, trying to hide his shock. 'Yes.'

She looked at him, eyes glassy and lips a little swollen. She had been crying. His chest grew heavy at the thought.

'And the curtains?'

He glanced over his shoulder at the bare window. 'I can make do without curtains for a while.'

She looked past him into the candlelit room. He crossed

his arms and leaned his shoulder on the doorframe. 'What are you doing here?'

She drew a breath, hands clasped in front of her. 'I told Manius I cannot marry him.' She looked down at her feet. 'I left.' Slowly, she raised her eyes to him. 'And came straight here.' She exhaled slowly. 'I am going to be in a lot of trouble when that sun rises.'

Lucky he was leaning on the doorframe or he might have fallen over. She had come to *him*. He tried very hard not to jump to any conclusions.

Clearing her throat, she asked, 'May I come in?'

He straightened but did not get out of her way. 'You want to come inside?' He had to check he had heard right.

She nodded. 'Yes.' Her eyes searched his for a moment. 'I need to measure the windows for those curtains.'

He swallowed and looked away, trying hard to keep his emotions in check, then moved aside.

She hesitated before entering. Instead of walking past, she stopped in front of him.

'I should not have left today,' she whispered, eyes on the floor.

He uncrossed his arms and lifted her face so he could see it. He turned her head both ways, noticing one cheek was redder than the other. He blinked and reined in his anger. The last thing he wanted to do was scare her. As he ran two fingers over her cheek, he knew he would never let anyone hurt her ever again—including him.

She struggled to meet his gaze, but instead of pulling away, she moved closer, falling against him. His arms went around her, drawing her in, his lips pressing her hair.

'I am going to marry you,' she murmured into his chest. 'I am going to love you openly and proudly for the rest of my life.' Her voice broke, and she took a moment to gather herself. 'You are the best man I know.'

His throat closed, and he felt like he was choking. He was silent for the longest time. 'I don't deserve you.'

She looked up, crying now. 'You don't get to do that anymore. I choose you, and I will choose you every time.'

He tipped her head back and brought his lips to hers, the sensation spreading like hot liquid. Her hands travelled up his neck, pulling him closer and deepening the kiss. She was so soft, so trusting despite the day she had endured. He reached out and pushed the door closed, her grip tightening on him at the momentary absence of his hand. As if he could leave her at that moment. He could barely think through his need as his hands caressed down her back and buttocks before locking on her thighs and lifting her off the ground. Her legs wrapped him and her stomach pressed against his. The instant warmth of her took the remaining air from him. He had to stop, had to do the right thing, but then she shifted her hips and the softest of moans came from her lips. In a moment it would be too late.

'Should we stop?' He spoke the words into her open mouth.

She pulled back, eyes bright and expression serious. 'No one is stopping. No one is slowing down. I love you. Just let me love you.'

Gods, what had he done to deserve her?

Walking over to the bed, he sat on it, needing her closer. His mouth found her throat and he consumed it, driven mad by the fingers woven through his hair and the scent of her skin.

'I need more of you,' she whispered.

His hands travelled beneath the fabric, finding the soft flesh of her thighs. Nails dug into his shoulders.

'You can have all of me,' he said. 'I'm yours.' He pulled back to look at her. 'Marry me.'

She smiled the sweetest of smiles. 'I thought you would never ask.'

Nero's hands pushed beneath the fabric gathered at the top of her legs. 'Tomorrow.' His mouth was drawn to the bare skin of her shoulder where her tunic had slipped down.

'The order of things is not so important.' It came out as a laugh.

He looked up at her, waiting for her body to still again. 'I love you. I have loved you for so long.'

Another smile, but that time accompanied by a mischievous glint in her eye. 'Show me.'

A grin spread across his face, his entire body responding to those two words. He leaned back on the mattress and pulled her down with him.

DULCIA WAITED for the guilt to arrive and strip her of her good mood. She waited for the remorse, the shame, that feeling in her gut that told her when she had done something very wrong. But all she felt was safe, warm, untouchable. She felt truly free for the first time in her life, with her back against Nero's bare chest and one leg stuck between his. Not so free then, but utterly and blissfully trapped.

She opened one sleepy eye, noting the changing light. Soon the sun would rise, and she would be forced to face the consequences of her actions. She had a plan of sorts. First she would go to her mother, who would know the best way to handle Rufus. Perhaps he would break the news to Manius. Perhaps he would break a stick on her back first.

'It is too late,' she would tell them. She was a ruined woman. The only sensible thing for her father to do was to let her marry him, even if he banished her afterwards.

Nero propped himself up on one elbow so he could see her face. 'What are you thinking about?'

She twisted to look at him. 'I cannot predict Rufus's reaction.'

He lay back down and drew her closer until she could feel his breath in her hair. 'He's not going to rush out and buy us a wedding gift.'

She turned in his arms. He looked half dead, but so content. 'I should go alone.'

'No.'

'If I show up at the house with you looking so pleased with yourself, it will only aggravate the situation.'

His lips curled into a lazy smile. 'I *am* pleased with myself. Look at you. I have a goddess in my arms.'

She watched him for a moment before speaking. 'It will be all right.'

'You telling me or asking me?'

She thought. 'Asking, I think.'

He pulled her so close she struggled to draw breath. 'If it's not all right, we'll leave the city.'

'And go where?'

Light came to his eyes. 'Anywhere you want. I don't care, as long as I'm with you.'

She felt so much affection for him in that moment. Arching her back, she stretched to kiss him. 'We'll need coin.'

'I have some coin.'

She pressed her lips together, thinking. 'How much is passage on a ship?'

An amused expression settled on his face. 'Depends. Where will the ship be going?'

'Alexandria.'

His grin matched her own. 'You really want to see those pyramids.'

'Yes.'

He smoothed down her hair with his hand. 'Then Egypt it is.' Planting a kiss on her nose, he added, 'Let me worry about the coin. All you have to do is tell your mother the good news.'

Fear settled in her belly once more. He must have seen it, because his expression turned serious.

'You're not alone in this anymore. I'll be right there with you.'

'I am not sure that is a good idea.'

He propped himself up on one elbow. 'I can't hide away while you suffer alone. I won't do it.'

'You want to suffer alongside me, is that it?'

He pressed a hand to her belly. 'Haven't you figured out by now that your suffering *is* my suffering?'

She reached up, holding his stubbly cheeks. 'I love you.'

His grin widened. 'Show me.'

*a* fist pounded on the door. Dulcia's eyes snapped open at the same time Nero leapt from the bed and threw on his tunic.

*Bang, bang, bang.*

'What if it is Manius?' Dulcia asked, reaching for her clothes. 'He knows about this place.' Seeing his confused expression, she added, 'He had me followed yesterday.'

Nero's face hardened. 'Of course he did. Stay here.'

Light poured through the window. They had carelessly fallen asleep.

*Bang, bang, bang.*

'It's Mila. Open up.'

Dulcia exhaled with relief, and Nero threw her a smile.

'Only slightly less threatening,' he whispered. The moment he opened the door, Mila burst through it.

'Is my sister here?'

The urgency in her voice made Dulcia freeze momentarily before hurrying into the room. 'I am here.'

Mila took in her dishevelled appearance but said nothing of it. 'I have news of Licinia.'

Dulcia frowned. 'Licinia?' She knew it was not good news

by the look on her sister's face. Nero must have known it too, because he took her hand. 'What news?'

Mila swallowed. 'She has been found guilty of fornication and sentenced.'

Dulcia shook her head. That made no sense. 'What?' Perhaps she had not heard right. Nero's hand tightened around hers.

'They are marching her through the city as we speak,' Mila continued.

Dulcia pulled her hand free and pressed it to her breast-bone. 'Fornication? Licinia is the most chaste woman I know. She would never…'

Mila stepped forwards and grabbed her by the wrist, pulling her through the door. 'They are going to bury her alive.'

A cold sensation filled Dulcia's belly as she was led out onto the street. Buried alive? It had to be a misunderstanding, one Dulcia would set straight.

She glanced over her shoulder to ensure Nero was following. He caught up and gave her a reassuring smile. 'It's just a mistake.'

Dulcia nodded. Yes, a mistake. They would not bury a priestess alive without adequate proof. 'I will speak on her behalf, clear her name.'

Mila let go of her arm and broke into a run. 'If that is your plan, you better hurry.'

The three of them ran through the streets and alleyways, making their way towards the forum. She was not there, but it did not take them long to spot the party as they marched towards Colline Gate. People were lining the streets, some sombre and silent, others spitting on the road where Licinia walked, her hands bound in front of her.

'Whore!' shouted one man.

Dulcia took in the sight before her: the raised fists, the tears, the shaking heads. All that anger, heartbreak and disappointment aimed at her friend, who kept her eyes ahead and chin raised. But her tear-streaked face gave her away.

'Mila!'

The sound of Remus's voice pulled her from her trance. He pushed through the growing crowd to get to them. 'They are saying there is a witness.'

'That is not possible,' Dulcia said. 'She is innocent. I know she is.'

Remus and Mila exchanged a look.

'Someone claims they caught her with a man,' Remus said.

Dulcia shook her head, rejecting the words, then tried to move closer to the road. 'Licinia!' Her voice only added to the noise.

'Dulcia, wait,' Nero said, catching her hand.

She pulled free of his grip and slipped between two men. 'There is no time.' Stepping around a crying woman, she heard Nero curse behind her. He was too big to fit through the gaps.

The guards either side of Licinia looked at each other in surprise when Dulcia stepped out in front of them.

Licinia's eyes widened, then teared up. 'I didn't do it.'

Dulcia reached out and took hold of her bound hands. They were freezing despite the heat. 'I know.'

'Out of the way!' one of the men said.

Dulcia turned to him. 'She is innocent.'

The guard rolled his eyes and waved her on. 'Save your breath. She was caught spread-legged with a man.'

'What man?'

'He wasn't caught, and the girl refuses to give his name.'

Tears welled in Licinia's eyes. 'Because I have no name to give. There is no man. I was caught with no one.'

Dulcia stepped between them, her body like a shield. 'I am telling you there has been a mistake, and I am not moving until I have spoken with the emperor.'

Both men laughed.

'Oh, she wants to speak with the emperor,' one said.

The other shook his head. 'You go do that. In the mean-time, move before we have you thrown into Mamertine.'

Nero had finally broken through the crowd and came to stand beside her, his eyes fixed on the men. Remus walked up beside him. Dulcia tried to think. Her best chance of success was to find Nerva. He would get her in front of the right people, but by the time someone agreed to an audience, it would be too late. 'If you carry on, you will be burying an innocent woman. All I ask is that you delay a while. Please.'

'I said move.'

Nero and Remus both took a step in his direction, and the man's feet shuffled back a little.

'My father is Senator Rufus Papias, my brother General Nerva Papias.' It was not something she usually did, but she was desperate enough to throw their names out and see what happened. 'If you refuse to listen, I will make sure they hear about it.'

The guards paused and looked her up and down. She could not have appeared less like a Papias in that moment if she had tried.

'Rufus Papias doesn't have a daughter,' one said, his expression hardening. 'Now get.'

One of the guards went to grab her, but Nero intercepted and knocked his hand away. 'Touch her and see what happens.'

Visibly fed up, the other guard stepped forwards and grabbed her by the arm. She instinctively kicked out, striking his shin, hurting her toe more than she probably hurt him. He cursed and flung her aside. She landed on the road on her hands and knees. Ignoring the sting of grazed flesh, she pushed herself up onto her feet. As she turned, she heard the sickening sound of a fist hitting a face. She watched as the guard was knocked backwards onto the road, his hands going over his nose and blood seeping through his fingers.

*Nero.*

The other guard drew his sword, but before he had a chance to use it, Remus jumped between them, swiftly disarming the man.

'Let's everyone calm down,' he said, holding the weapon upside down between two fingers to show he meant no threat.

The guard with the bloody nose stood and drew his sword. He swung it angrily at Nero, who ducked, then knocked the blade from the guard's hand. It landed with a clang next to Dulcia. Without hesitating, she snatched it up and went to stand in front of Licinia.

'Show me who accused this woman, and I will show you a liar.' Her hands shook as adrenaline coursed through her.

'Dulcia,' Licinia said, fear in her voice. 'Move aside.'

'I will not step aside while you are wrongfully put to death.'

Nero took a step towards her. 'Give me the sword.'

She ignored him, her gaze moving between the guards, daring them to come for her friend.

'Dulcia,' Nero said, firmer that time.

She finally looked at him.

'Listen.' His eyes pleaded with her. 'There are more guards on their way. You need to leave.'

*Leave?* She shook her head. Even the sound of footsteps approaching did not soften her resolve, not when her friend was about to be buried alive. But then Mila appeared out of nowhere, knocking the sword from her hand before grabbing hold of her arm and pulling her off the road.

'We need to go.'

Dulcia's feet grew roots. 'No. Mila, please. They are going to kill her.'

Her sister spun around to face her. 'And you with her if you do not get out of here.' She pulled her, harder that time, but it was too late. A ring of guards appeared around them.

Remus and Mila exchanged a glance as the soldiers took the men into custody.

'And the women too,' the guard with the bloody nose called. 'Troublemakers, the lot of them.'

'No.' Nero tried to pull free of the two men either side of him.

Remus was only slightly calmer. 'Let the women leave.'

The guards ignored him.

'Please,' Dulcia pleaded with the guard closest her, 'do not let them bury her. She is innocent, and you will anger Vesta if you contribute to her death.'

At that moment, a tall body pushed through the gathered crowd and took one of the guards by the throat, lifting him off the ground. *Albaus.* Three guards went for him just as Felix arrived, struggling to break free of the crowd. He turned to glare at them.

'Would it kill you to look down once in a while?' He straightened his tunic, then took in the scene in front of him. 'Oh for the love of…' He shook his head at Albaus, who was using the soldier like a shield against the guards closing in on him, waiting for their opportunity. 'If I had known you were going to throw yourself into this mess, I would have waited at the back.'

Nero managed to get an arm free, punching the guard to his left and shoving the other sideways in an attempt to get to Dulcia. But two fresh soldiers tackled him to the ground before he reached her.

She flinched at the sound of his body slamming against stone.

Felix put his hands up in an attempt to calm everyone. 'Might I suggest a civil conversation before this takes a serious turn?'

Nero had a knee on his neck and the full weight of a man on his back.

'You are hurting him,' Dulcia said, trying to pull free. The guard yanked her arm, and she winced.

'For goodness' sake,' Felix said to Albaus, 'put the man down before someone opens you up on the street.'

Albaus grunted before releasing the man. He landed on his knees, coughing and clutching his throat. The guards surrounding Albaus kept their weapons pointed at him, but none were brave enough to attempt an arrest.

'What in heaven's name is going on here?'

The sound of Manius's voice made Dulcia turn. He stepped through the circle of guards and came to stand in the middle, looking around before his gaze settled on her.

One of the original guards spoke up. 'All under control.'

Manius's brow creased with scepticism. 'Really?' He walked over to the man. 'Then why is my betrothed being restrained by your men?'

The man paled at the revelation. 'Your betrothed?' He shared a surprised look with one of his comrades before continuing. 'She was the cause of the disruption.'

Manius glanced across at Nero, whose wild eyes were fixed on him. 'Release her.'

The guard hesitated before letting go of her. She ran straight to Manius and fell at his feet. 'Please, tell them Licinia is innocent.'

She was met with a cold stare and clenched jaw, but she was not beyond begging in order to save Licinia's life.

Instead of pulling Dulcia to her feet, Manius crouched down, an arm resting on one knee to balance himself.

'What is it you want me to do?'

'Defend her.'

He glanced at the priestess, who was as pale as her robes. 'They have an eyewitness.'

Dulcia shook her head. 'What witness? Who?'

'A woman.'

'That is a lie,' Licinia said, struggling to bring volume to her voice. 'I lay with no one. Vesta's home is as pure as the day I arrived.'

Manius glanced in her direction. 'Am I to trust the word of one convicted?'

'Trust my judgement,' Dulcia said, her desperation growing. 'I know she is innocent. I ask only that you delay her sentence until I can gather proof.' Out of the corner of her eye, she could see Nero growing restless beneath his captors.

Manius narrowed his eyes. 'Trust *your* judgment?' He leaned closer, as though inspecting her face.

'Dulcia,' Nero called, struggling once more.

She did not dare look in his direction.

Leaning close to her ear, Manius whispered, 'I trust *your* judgement *least* of all. You are as big a whore as she.'

A shiver ran down Dulcia's spine.

Nero arched his back, struggling. 'Get away from her—' He was silenced with a fist to his face.

Dulcia stared boldly back at Manius. 'My sins are mine alone. Please help her.'

His eyes seemed to darken a few shades. 'If only there was something I could do.' He paused. 'A mutually beneficial outcome.'

Nero worked an elbow free and threw it into the guard's leg. The man cried out before digging his knee harder into Nero's neck.

'Not helping,' Felix hissed in his direction.

Manius waited for Nero to still before continuing. 'What say you, *wife*? Shall we go figure a way out of this mess together?'

'Dulcia, don't.'

She looked over at Nero. His face was pressed against the scorching road, every muscle in his body straining against the weight of the men. They were not going to just let him walk away.

Her gaze went to her sister, who needed to go home to

her children, her safe life, the one she and Remus had worked so hard to build. Dulcia was jeopardising everything. This was not their fight.

'Please—' Her throat closed, and she swallowed against the sensation. She turned to Manius. 'Please ask them to let everyone go. This has nothing to do with any of them.'

Manius nodded as though agreeing with her assessment, then cleared his throat. 'If you come with me now, I will make sure everyone here walks free.' He paused. 'I will even speak up on Licinia's behalf.'

'Dulcia.' There was a plea, a warning in Nero's voice, but then his words were strangled once more.

She closed her eyes for a moment, unable to stomach it. 'You know I love him. You know where I was last night. Why would you help me?' She kept her voice low so only Manius could hear her.

He brought his lips to her ear. 'I will not be made a fool of. Look around you. How do you think this will end?'

'Don't listen...' Nero was struggling again.

Her eyes snapped open as she fought the urge to crawl to him.

Manius's hand landed on her shoulder, his grip firm. 'You go to him, and I will make sure that when he is locked up, the key disappears.'

She felt like her heart was lodged in her throat.

'Licinia will be buried in a chamber, never to be seen again by the Roman people,' Manius continued. 'Given the circumstances, we both know your father is going to take my word over yours. And it will not stop there.' He paused. 'I will come after your sister if I have to. A mother separated from her children is a terrible thing.'

She looked at Nero's red face, listened to his laboured breath. It was clear she did not have a choice, that she never had. Like Manius said, he would not be made a fool of.

'And you will ensure they all walk away? Every one of them?'

Manius took hold of her arms and pulled her to her feet. 'I have enough money to make any problem disappear.'

So much power—none of it hers. She could not tear her eyes away from Nero. 'But we had a plan,' she breathed.

Manius took a step back from her, his patience gone. 'Take the priestess to the Campus Sceleratus. Imprison the others.'

The moment the words left Manius's mouth, Remus tore free from his captors and ran towards Mila. But she did not need his help—she already had the soldier on his knees and the sword she had stolen from him pressed to his throat. Albaus produced a knife from gods knew where and was crouched down, ready to fight his way out. Felix was turning in circles, no doubt realising he could not talk his way out of the mess. They dragged Nero to his feet and turned Licinia away, preparing to march her off in the other direction.

*This is not happening.* Dulcia's entire world was coming undone in front of her. She struggled to draw breath, a feeling that brought back memories of the fire.

'I will go with you,' she said, reaching for Manius's arm. 'Whatever you want or need from me, you have it. Please, just let them go.'

'Dulcia no!' Nero threw off one of the guards, but two more were immediately upon him.

Manius watched her for a moment. 'I need to know you come of your own free will.'

Was he insane? Of course she had to agree. He had left with her no choice.

'Dulcia, no,' Nero called again.

Felix stepped in front of him, blocking his view. 'I will hang you myself if you do not shut up.'

'Yes.' Dulcia gripped Manius's arm like it was the only

thing holding her up. 'Of course. We are betrothed, after all.' She swallowed down the rising bile. 'My place is at your side.'

Nero threw his body sideways, sending two men flying. 'Dulcia, stop.'

Manius threaded her hand through his arm. 'So we have an understanding?'

She would have agreed to anything in that moment. 'Yes. I… I was confused, but everything is clear to me now.'

She felt the muscles in his arm relax slightly, and then he brought his mouth to her ear once more.

'If there is ever a repeat of last night, I will rain fire down on everyone you love until there is nothing left but ashes.' He pulled away slightly so he could look at her. 'Understand?'

She could not stop her body from trembling. 'Yes.'

He patted her hand and turned back to the guards. 'Detain the vestal until we get to the bottom of this. The others can be released when they are calm. First sniff of trouble, lock them up.'

Dulcia's eyes met Licinia's. Tears of relief poured down her cheeks.

Everything seemed to move in slow motion from that point. Weapons were handed over, words exchanged. She could not comprehend any of it. They finally let Nero go, and he ran straight for her. Of course he did. There had never been a doubt in her mind that he would fight for her. He was captured by the guards once more. Then Felix and Albaus were in front of him, saying things she could not hear over the screaming in her ears. Mila stood in the same spot, silent, watching, heartbroken on her behalf. She knew the cost of walking away. Remus was at her side in the next breath, holding his unresponsive wife.

Manius looked at Nero in a way Dulcia had never seen him look at anyone. It was pure hatred, a warning. Then she was walking off in the opposite direction, her eyes pausing on Nero a fraction longer than she had intended. Manius pulled on her arm and she faced forwards again. The crowd began to disperse, revealing a litter.

A final look over her shoulder, a forbidden glance at everything she was leaving behind. Albaus kept hold of Nero while Felix shouted up at him, trying to talk him off the ledge.

People refilled the space between them, and then he was gone from sight.

# CHAPTER 23

*D*ulcia stood opposite her mother, body stiff and mind struggling to focus on the raised voices on the other side of the door. Rufus was telling Manius to calm down, and Manius was telling Rufus that they should wed that afternoon, that he wanted it done, that waiting would only invite more trouble. Then he said other things that made Tertia look away.

'You are very lucky he is still prepared to marry you after your disappearing act last night.' She shook her head. 'You have jeopardised everything.'

Dulcia's closed fists were pressed into her stomach, helping to fill the emptiness. She did not reply.

'You were supposed to be the one who broke the cycle.'

That got Dulcia talking. 'For goodness' sake, Mother. You are disappointed. I get it. So am I.'

Tertia leaned against the wall, hugging herself. The men's voices were no longer raised but a consistent hum. They were safe to loiter with Aquila out of the house. She had left to avoid the drama, but not before throwing a filthy look in Dulcia's direction.

'I think it will be all right,' Tertia said.

Dulcia felt a surge of annoyance. 'Will it? All right for whom?'

Her mother looked up. 'For everyone. You made a mistake, but you are not the first, and it is not the end of the world.' It sounded as though she were trying to convince herself.

Dulcia sucked in a breath. 'I love Nero. I think you knew it before I did. And you must know I cannot just turn it off because everyone has decided I should.'

Tertia looked taken aback. 'You are confusing your friendship for something more.'

'No I am not.' Dulcia stepped away, releasing some of the pressure on her stomach. 'I had planned to come here this morning, to tell you everything. I cannot marry Manius, because I belong to Nero, mind and body.'

'Shush.' Tertia rubbed her forehead. 'If they hear you—'

'Manius already knows, and Rufus *must* know.'

Tertia pushed off the wall, her mouth pressed into a thin line. 'How could you be so careless? So short-sighted?' She was whisper-yelling. 'That man is prepared to treat you like an empress. He wants you to be happy.' Her hands went over her face, then fell away. 'Last night...' She could not finish. 'That was not like you. Nero seems determined to destroy your future, and like a fool, you let him.'

'Do not put this on him.' She stared at her mother, feeling nothing but disconnect. The numbness made her brave. 'I went to him when I realised I could not go through with the wedding, and we made a plan.'

Tertia walked over, bringing her face inches from Dulcia's. 'That was your big plan? Fall into bed with him, throw away your future, and hope it works out in the end?' She pointed a finger at the wall. 'The only reason the wedding is still going ahead is because those men are trying to contain the damage. The alternative is public humiliation on both sides.'

'To be clear, the only reason *I* am standing here is because *that* man, the one whose praises you sing, threatened the lives of everyone I love.' She paused, panting. 'I would not be surprised if he framed Licinia himself to ensure this exact outcome.'

'He did no such thing.'

'Of course *you* would defend him. You worship the man like a god, despite the fact that he would have thrown your other daughter into prison without a second thought if I had not agreed to his demands.'

'His demands?' Tertia threw her hands up. 'Do you understand the shame you will bring on his family if people learn of your indiscretions? Manius did what any responsible man would do. He looked past your shortcomings and his own pride for the greater good. He controlled the situation and protected both families.'

Dulcia closed her eyes, her thoughts fragmented by crushing heartbreak. 'He will likely stop me from seeing Mila.'

Tertia turned away. 'Perhaps that is a good thing. The gods know I love that girl, but she has been a bad influence on you your entire life. And now we have Nero, a product of her terrible choices.'

Dulcia could barely believe the words coming from her mother's mouth. 'That is an awful thing to say. Nero is a good man—'

Tertia reeled back around. 'Good men do not go around stealing other men's wives.'

'I was never Manius's to begin with.' Dulcia was no longer whispering.

Both women jumped at the sound of the tablinum door opening. Manius emerged, his dark eyes fixed on Dulcia. His expression suggested he had caught the last part of their conversation.

He turned to her mother. 'Your dominus wishes to speak to you.'

Tertia bowed her head and stepped past him into the room, her eyes meeting Dulcia's as she closed the door.

'The wedding will take place during the *Ludi Apollinares*,' Manius said. 'Many families will return to Rome for the festival.'

Dulcia nodded. It was only two weeks away. 'Will you not be racing at the event?'

'Yes. We shall celebrate my victory by holding the ceremony afterwards.'

The man loved to be celebrated.

'All right.' It was the only response she had.

Manius cleared his throat before continuing. 'Outside of dinner with my family, you are to remain at the house.'

'Like a prisoner?'

Manius's jaw tightened. 'Like an obedient wife. You have only yourself to blame for your change in circumstances.'

Actually, she blamed him, and everyone standing with him.

'And one more thing. I never want that man's name spoken in our house. He ceases to exist from this moment. Do you understand?'

She took a moment before replying, imagining a life where Nero ceased to exist. How would it feel to never have his name pass her lips again? It was just another form of imprisonment. She would surely wilt to nothing without him. But there was only one answer to give, one answer that would appease her future husband. 'I understand.' The words soured on her tongue, and she had to look away for fear he would see how much she struggled to speak them.

'I will leave one of my men to watch over you in my absence.'

A bodyguard. A spy. A thug. He framed it as a favour.

'All right.' She no longer cared. If he felt better having her watched, then he could go right ahead. 'I am quite tired. Would it be all right if I stay at home this evening?'

His expression was more accusing than sympathetic. 'Of course. I shall leave you to rest.'

'Before you go.' A question sat on her tongue. She had to ask, and she was certain she would see it on his face if he were lying. 'Was it you?'

He frowned, confused. 'Was what me?'

Her breath was so shallow she worried she might not be able to speak. 'Did you falsely accuse Licinia to regain control of me?'

'No.' He glanced behind him before continuing. 'The information was brought to me.'

'And you used it to your advantage.'

He shrugged. 'I saw an opportunity.'

She could barely look at him, even though he appeared to be telling the truth. 'She is innocent, you know. That is why I took a stand.'

He nodded. 'It seems you made the right choice, then.'

He did not kiss her goodbye, just turned and left.

# CHAPTER 24

*D*ulcia and Mila were across the street from the
Papias house being watched by one of Manius's
men. Mila had wanted to take a walk, but Dulcia did not
want to test Manius's limits too much for fear of how he
might react.

Mila frowned at the man watching them. 'And he just
stares at you all day?'

'When I step outside. Inside the house, the role falls to
Mother.'

'He waits outside *all day*?'

Dulcia did not want to think about it. 'They come and go.
This afternoon someone else will arrive to take his place.'

Mila turned back to her sister, her frown softening. 'I
wanted to tell you in person that we are returning to India.'

She had seen this coming, but her heart sank nonetheless.
It was just like the last time her sister had uttered those
words, except this time she could not muster a smile. 'Oh.'
Nor words, apparently.

Mila took Dulcia's hands and squeezed them encouragingly. 'We came back for you, because Nerva left and I
promised you I would return.' She paused. 'Now you are all

grown up, and you have proven you are more than capable of handling yourself.'

'You are wrong. Now I need you more than ever. Do not be scared off by Manius.'

A sigh slipped from Mila's lips. 'I am not afraid of him, but I do have to be sensible. I have the children to consider now.'

'I would never let harm come to any of you.'

'Not intentionally, but this new arrangement needs time to settle. It seems Manius is prone to tantrums.'

She could not argue with that.

Mila squinted against the blazing eastern sun. 'We always return eventually. Rome has a way of keeping a firm grip on those born within its walls.'

Dulcia pulled her hands free. 'I am sorry I put you all at risk that day.'

*That day.* The day Nero's distraught face had imprinted on her mind. It was still so fresh she could barely believe five days had passed since.

'Stop. You saved your friend's life that day.'

Dulcia stared off down the street. 'Her gratitude has likely waned by now. She was banished from the city upon her release.' How much loss could one person withstand? The announcement of her sister's departure was pushing her towards a tipping point.

Mila must have picked up on the fact, because she pulled Dulcia into her arms. 'I am very proud of the way you stood up to those guards. I always suspected beneath that timid exterior lay the heart of a lion.'

Tears prickled Dulcia's eyes. 'What am I to do without you?'

Mila held her at arm's length, her eyes filled with mutual affection. 'You do what you have always done. Be brave and smart. Manius is a powerful man, and that power will only grow as he moves up in the world.'

Dulcia hesitated before asking, 'Is Nero going with you?'

Mila let go of her. 'If we can convince him, I think it best. He needs family right now, but as you know, he is not very good at walking away.'

'No.' The thought of him being all the way on the other side of the world made Dulcia's chest tighten.

'If he stays here, he is going to get himself killed.'

Dulcia nodded in agreement. 'Yes. He should go with you, move on with his life.' If only she could speak the words with conviction. 'When do you leave?'

Mila glanced over at the man watching them. 'In two days. We have organised passage on a grain ship.' Her lips curled into a smile. 'I am afraid we will miss the social event of the season. Though I doubt Manius would have let me in the door anyway.'

The wedding. How on earth was she supposed to get through it alone? 'Lucky you. You escape Livia's ridicule and Claudius's leering.' She shook her head. 'You will not be missing much. It is just an excuse for Manius and Rufus to make a big display of their partnership.'

'I do not doubt it.' She smiled coyly. 'Why else would Manius marry a *ruined* woman?'

Dulcia blushed. 'Careful. You sound like Mother.'

'I am only teasing.' Mila exhaled loudly. 'You will survive this, you know.'

Dulcia pressed her lips together to keep her emotions in check. 'I hope so. Right now it feels like a life sentence.' She glanced at her bodyguard, then lowered her voice. 'I am afraid to ask how he is.'

Mila did not have to ask who she was referring to. 'Nero is a survivor. You do not worry about him. He must be working a lot, because whenever I go by the apartment, he is rarely there.'

'Working for Gallus?'

A nod.

'Do I want to know what that work entails?'

'No.'

Dulcia was silent a moment. 'I was naive to think this could end any other way. I see that now.'

Mila scraped her sandal along the road. 'I wish the world was different, but wealth and power usually win. The only alternative is to be an outcast like me.' She smiled. 'One positive thing has come out of this. Rufus is finally taking notice of you. Rebellion has its perks.'

'Yes. All I have to do is tear my beating heart from my chest and leave it outside our marital home.' Dulcia smiled sideways at her sister.

'There you go. Just fill the gaping hole with jewels and silverware.'

Dulcia laughed, but then the pain pressed in once more. She waited for it to pass before speaking. 'Make sure Nero leaves with you. It is better for everyone if he does.'

Mila studied her. 'You will not feel abandoned?'

'Oh, I will definitely feel abandoned.' She attempted a smile and failed. 'But he hates the city. He would only be staying for me, and that is a terrible reason to stay.'

Mila reached out and squeezed her sister's arm. 'See? So grown-up. Feels like just last week you were sitting on your bed playing with your dolls, and now you are breaking hearts all over the city.'

Crossing her arms, Dulcia said, 'Mother gave all my dolls away to the poor a few years back. I came home one day and they were gone.'

A smile spread across Mila's face. 'You must have been devastated.'

'A little.' Her cheeks reddened.

'From dolls to men, seemingly overnight.'

The colour on Dulcia's face deepened. 'Must you?'

'Absolutely,' Mila laughed. 'You are too adorable not to tease.'

Dulcia could not stop her own smile, proving to herself that it was possible. 'I am going to miss you more than I can put into words.'

Mila pulled her sister into her arms once more. 'I will miss you too, but at least I leave knowing you can take care of yourself. You found your fight.' She fell silent a moment, holding tighter. 'This might seem like the lowest point in your life.' Her voice was just above a whisper. 'But speaking from experience, that's a good thing, because now things can only get better. And when we leave, there will be no one left to defend but yourself. I have every faith in you.'

Dulcia pulled back to look at her sister. 'The fight is over. Manius won.'

Mila tucked her sister's hair behind her ears, the way their mother always did. 'He only won that battle.'

She shook her head, confused. 'Are you saying I should keep fighting this?'

'I am saying that with no one to use against you, the power shifts. The fight is not over until you lay down your weapons or die.'

'Careful. You are sounding a lot like a gladiator.'

Mila smiled. 'Well, my gladiator blood runs through you.'

'Hmm. I shall remember that next time someone hands me a sword and challenges me to a battle.' Her chest tightened at the realisation that she had to say goodbye. 'Enjoy your paradise. You have earned it. You all have.'

'We have to survive the voyage and Felix's seasickness first.'

Dulcia drew a long breath. 'I will let Mother know of the news so she can visit before you leave.'

Mila nodded. 'You should go inside so that bodyguard of yours can relax.' She leaned in to kiss her sister's cheek, bent to pick up her basket, and then looked at Dulcia one more time. 'Brave and smart. Remember those two things and you will be fine.'

'*H*eavens, Manius,' Livia said, 'Dulcia grows more sombre by the day. A woman should be at her *happiest before* the wedding. That is when she is blissfully unaware of the tedious years ahead.'

They were dining with one other couple, a senator and his wife whose names Dulcia had already forgotten. The wife tutted and smiled into her cup. The senator exchanged a light-hearted glance with Claudius.

'You must forgive my wife,' Claudius said. 'She started early on the wine today.'

There was light laughter, except from Livia, who continued to watch Dulcia with disdain.

'What a dampener on the evening you are. How about entertaining us for once? Perhaps you could sing something.'

Dulcia took a long drink, letting the liquid numb her. 'I do not sing. I am afraid your guests would be most disappointed.'

Another tut from Livia. 'Does not sing, does not dance, does not even talk. I am still trying to figure out what attracted Manius to the girl. We all know it is not her pure bloodlines.' She glanced at her friend. 'She is half slave, you know.'

'Mother,' Junia said, hand going to her brow. 'Every dinner you make it your personal mission to tear the poor girl down.'

Livia looked around the room, aghast. 'Am I wrong? I cannot be the only one who finds her dull of late.'

Dulcia placed her cup on the table, perhaps a little too hard, for the wine sloshed over the side. She stood. She could feel everyone watching her, even Manius, who had remained silent through the entire conversation. 'My cue to leave.'

As she went to step past Claudius, he caught her hand.

'Do not let Livia scare you off, my dear.'

Dulcia looked down at the hand wrapping her wrist. 'I am not afraid of your wife. I am afraid of what I will say if I stay. The slave half of me will tolerate her insults, like every slave in this household. But the Papias half will not sit quietly forever.'

Claudius let go of her. Junia smiled into her drink.

'Always the quiet ones who surprise you,' the senator's wife said.

Everyone laughed except for Livia. Manius stood, but instead of defending her, he said, 'I will have the litter take you home.'

Whenever he touched her, she always had the same instinct—to pull away. It was a reaction she could no longer afford. She let him guide her from the room and out into the atrium where the air was not stifled by the scent of cured meats and snobbery.

'What is the matter with you?' Manius asked once they were alone. 'You do not normally let my mother get to you.'

Dulcia drew a breath. 'To be clear, she always gets to me. There are only so many evenings in a row that I can bow my head and take her insults.' Dulcia stared up at him, her frustration building. 'And you let her speak to me however she pleases.'

'What would you have me say?'

'I should not have to ask you to say anything. Is it wrong to assume you might speak up without being prompted?' When he did not reply, she added, 'Unless you are enjoying the ridicule as much as she is. Is this your way of punishing me?'

He looked around, visibly agitated. 'It is difficult to defend your honour given recent events.'

She could not bring herself to regret the night she had spent with Nero. On the contrary, she found herself playing it over and over in her mind, terrified she might forget some of the details. Shame made her look down.

'Come with me,' Manius said, reaching for her hand and leading her away.

She glanced in the direction of the garden. 'Where are we going?'

He did not reply, instead ushering her through a door at the far end of the room.

Dulcia looked around at the table scattered with parchment and scrolls. 'What are we doing in here?'

He tugged her around the corner and pushed her against the wall. Before she could say anything, he was pressed against her, kissing her, one hand pinning her shoulder, the other gripping her ribcage. It was an entirely new level of kissing for them, one where his tongue probed forcefully. She wanted to pull away, but the wall was behind her, and she could go no farther. His hand went to her thigh, pulling up her skirt. She pushed against his chest with both hands and turned her head to the side.

'What are you doing?' Her attempts to separate their bodies were futile, the weight of him making the task impossible.

'You can skip the act now. We both know you are not the

virtuous maiden you painted at the beginning of all this.' He moved to kiss her again, and she ducked under his arm and slipped out of the tight gap.

'Have you lost your mind?' she asked, wiping at her painted mouth. 'What if your father walks in?'

He exhaled, regaining control of himself. 'My father is not a shy man. He will likely just carry on with whatever it is he came in for.'

She knew that was probably true. He was the sort of man who would take a seat and watch with interest. 'I… I am not comfortable here.'

'Fine.' The patience was gone from his voice. 'Let us go somewhere else.'

She swallowed down the word *no*, which threatened to come out as a scream. 'We… we should wait.'

He turned, leaning on one foot, and regarded her for the longest time. 'With *me* you wish to wait? The man you are to wed?'

She knew it made no sense, but she felt a deep sense of betrayal to Nero with every kiss, every touch. The night she had gone to him, she had bared every inch of herself, and he had claimed every part of her. There was nothing left for Manius. 'I might have made mistakes in the past, but I can make better choices now.'

Running his hands down his face, Manius stepped back. 'But *he* did not have to wait, did he?'

Nero had waited three years—they both had. 'I thought we were never to mention him again?'

'Difficult when he remains between us.'

She hugged herself. 'I have agreed to everything you have asked of me. Must I give you this too?'

He walked over and sat on the edge of the table. 'Fine. Leave.' He waved his hand, unable to even look at her. 'Take the litter and go.'

She turned for the door.

'But Dulcia.' She stilled, waiting. 'Once we are wed, you will have to let me in. I expect to visit your bed, and I expect an enthusiastic partner with children to show for it. These are not unreasonable requests of a wife.'

She nodded. 'I understand.'

He ran a finger along one of the scrolls as he considered his words. 'The incident at the forum, with your friend.'

*Licinia.* He could not even say her name.

'I did what I had to do.' Looking up, he added, 'You will thank me one day.'

She frowned, searching for signs of remorse. 'If I had refused to go with you that morning, if I had said no, would Licinia have been buried alive?'

'Yes.' He answered without hesitation.

She closed her eyes for a moment, unable to continue looking at him. 'I find that difficult to swallow, that you would do that to an innocent person.'

'It was not just my reputation I was protecting, but yours and your father's. You really should be thanking me.' He drew a breath. 'I want a place in the senate. Your father wants my support, my money, and wants you to marry well. Everyone wins.'

Everyone except for her. 'I should go.'

'I have not finished.'

His tone stopped her more than his words. 'All right.'

He cleared his throat. 'If you had refused, I would have named the man she fornicated with.'

She looked at him tiredly. 'There is no man. The entire thing was fabricated.'

'I would have named him nonetheless.' His jaw ticked. 'Do you know what would have happened to that man?'

A nod. 'He would have been buried alive with her.'

'Yes.'

She realised at that moment who he would have named. 'Do you really hate him that much?'

He thought for a moment. 'It would have been so easy. He loiters around that temple like a bad smell, waiting for you.'

She tilted her head. 'Why would you tell me such a thing?'

'So you understand.' Walking over, he cupped her face and kissed her gently. 'Look at the life I am offering you. All you have to do is take it and not look back.' When she stiffened beneath his touch, he added, 'Do not be naive. I did what any man would do in that situation.'

She stepped away, reaching behind her for the doorframe. 'You are wrong. Not every man would do such a thing.'

He rubbed at his jaw. 'Let me tell you something about your orphan rat. He is just like me. We all want what we want, and we all fight dirty to get it—even him.'

'Good evening, Manius.' With that, she left the room.

# CHAPTER 26

*T*he water ran red beneath Nero's hands as he rubbed them together. Blood stained his cuticles and fingernails, a constant reminder of who he had become.

'It seems to be all here,' Gallus called.

Nero shook the water from his hands. 'Of course it's all there.' He turned. 'I'm no thief.'

Gallus walked over and clapped him on the back. 'Of course not.'

He was many other things, but not a thief.

Coins jingled in the sponsor's hand. 'Payment.' He dropped them into Nero's open palm. 'Best take the evening off.'

Nero shook his head. 'I want to fight.'

Gallus's eyebrows rose. 'Fight?' He nodded towards Nero's swollen hand. 'Can you even hold a sword?'

Nero stretched his fingers out and winced. 'Sure.'

'You must really love this girl,' Gallus laughed.

He really did. And now he had a plan—a very expensive plan. He was going to get Dulcia out of the city. It was not going to be easy with Manius's men watching her, plus many of the city guards were paid directly from the man's deep pockets. Yes, he had learned a thing or two about the charioteer over the previous few days, and he knew the only way he stood a chance of getting Dulcia away from that man was to bribe their way out.

Gallus had been more than happy to oblige with additional work. Unfortunately, that additional work involved collecting unpaid gambling debts. While he was not expected to kill outside the arena, he did inflict pain on men who stood no chance against him. Violence off the sand was something else entirely. The sound of bone breaking and the screams of desperate men were not easy to wash away.

'The price is still fifteen hundred denarii?' Nero asked.

Gallus was not only funding the plan, but helping him to execute it. He too had contacts and deep pockets, and he would pay off all the necessary people when the time came. Nero was painfully aware that time was running out. The wedding date had been set. But he wanted to wait until Remus, Mila, and the rest of them were on board that ship in case Manius decided to play dirty.

'Fifteen hundred due in full before you depart.' Gallus tucked his coin pouch away in a hidden pocket.

Nero was still two hundred short.

'I cannot help you once you leave the city walls.'

Nero shook his head. 'I'll manage.'

Gallus crossed his arms. 'Where will you go?'

Nero was hesitant to share all the details, because information could be bought, and men like Gallus always had a price. But he also needed him to take care of some of the arrangements on his behalf. 'Egypt.' He stretched his neck to one side. 'I'll have the money to you by the end of the night.'

Gallus scoffed. 'Optimistic. Do not forget, I am the man who pays you.'

'We both know the fans pay better than you do.'

A laugh from the sponsor. 'If you are expecting it to rain coin this evening, then you better bring the fight of your life.'

A familiar sinking feeling came over Nero. He knew what he had to do, and he did not like it. But he did not have time for a crisis of conscience. It was time to pay the sponsor and take Dulcia somewhere she would be free.

~

THE WALK home was not pleasant. Nero's arm throbbed where it had been sliced open by a supposedly blunt sword. Then it had been hastily patched up by one of Gallus's physicians before he was ushered back onto the sand for the next fight. Now he moved with a limp, annoyed at himself for getting injured.

When he finally arrived at his apartment, he found the door wide open and heard noise coming from inside. He was too tired and sore to fight off intruders, had nothing left for them. Stepping up to the door, he peered inside, finding two men rifling through his belongings.

'There's little of value in there,' he called to them.

The men looked up from their rummaging, seemingly unaffected by his arrival. They did not look like thieves—too well dressed, and too well fed. They were looking for something, or perhaps someone.

Nero narrowed his gaze. 'What is it you're hoping to find?'

The men glanced at each other before speaking, one slipping his hand into his pocket. There was likely a dagger in there.

'Where is she?'

Nero did not have to ask who. They were looking for Dulcia. 'She's not in that cupboard.' He nodded towards the messed-up linen. 'I thought Manius had her under lock and key.'

They did not reply, just walked over to the door where he stood. Nero braced, ready for a fist or knife. He would find the energy if the alternative was to be beaten or stabbed.

'Wouldn't bother locking your door,' one said. He looked around, clicking his tongue.

The corner of Nero's mouth twitched. 'Why's that?'

The man sniffed and stepped past him, the other following closely. 'Because if we don't find her soon, we'll be back.'

Nero turned to watch them leave, knowing they would not go far.

So, Dulcia had given Manius's men the slip. The question was why? She would be alone somewhere, not wanting to put anyone else at risk. He thought for a moment, then realised he knew where she was.

He left the apartment, aware they would probably follow out of sight. A few minutes earlier, he had been ready to fall down; now, at the prospect of seeing Dulcia, his energy had renewed, his limp less obvious. He went straight to the tavern, checking if Albaus and Felix were there.

'Hello, handsome,' Cassia said, walking up with a jug in each hand. 'If you're looking for the others, they already left.'

Nero gave her a tight smile. 'Actually, I need a favour.'

A sly smile spread across her face. 'Oh?'

'Will you take me out back?'

Her grin widened. 'It's been a long time since you asked me to go anywhere with you. I thought you had a woman.'

He resisted the temptation to glance at the window, see if he were being watched. 'Some men followed me here.' He kept his voice low. 'I need them to see me go out back with you.'

Some men shouted for their drinks, and Cassia silenced them with a glare before looking back at Nero. 'What mess have you gotten yourself into now?' She sighed. 'I heard you were mixed up with Gallus Minidius. You owe him coin?'

He shook his head. 'No. Nothing like that.'

Another sigh. 'I go out back with you, and then what?'

'You wait a while, then return inside and get back to work.'

Disappointment settled on her face. 'So there is a woman, then?'

He shifted his weight from one foot to the other. 'Yes, there's a woman.'

'I hope she's worth all this trouble.' Cassia stared at him for a moment. 'Let me put these down, and then I'll be back.'

'Thank you.'

No reply. She walked over to a table of waiting men and placed the jugs down while swatting away drunk hands. When she returned to Nero, she took his hand and looked up at him. 'Follow me.' She led him through a door into the kitchen where the owner, Copa, stood stirring a pot of stew, sweating and red-faced.

'And where do you think you're going?' she called, a fist perched on one hip.

'I'll be back in a moment,' Cassia replied, waving her off.

Copa narrowed her eyes on Nero, who smiled back at her before disappearing through the next door. It opened into a small alleyway that reeked of garbage and urine.

He glanced both ways, then turned to Cassia. 'I owe you.'

Cassia crossed her arms, looking less than impressed. 'Go on, then.'

He kissed her cheek and jogged off.

The streets were quiet aside from a few rowdy drunks, likely expelled from their drinking holes. He kept up a decent pace all the way to the river, stopping only to catch his breath and check his surroundings. When he was certain he had not been followed, he headed to the path that led down to the water. He walked beneath the tall trees until he arrived at the one they had claimed as their own, then glanced in both directions before looking up and searching the branches. He narrowed his gaze on what appeared to be a swinging foot.

Grabbing hold of the branch above, he began to climb. She was humming, a song he had heard a thousand times before. It was the same song Mila always hummed when she was cooking. He knew the moment she heard him because she fell silent and her leg stopped swinging.

'It's just me,' he said, not wanting her to be afraid.

Leaves rustled, and then she peered over her knees, a wary expression on her face. 'Nero?'

He continued to climb, but before he could reach her, she pushed off the branch and landed on top of him. She hugged him, tightly.

'We'll fall,' he laughed, knowing he would never let such a thing happen. He held on to the branch above with one hand while the other went around her. She shook against him, already crying.

'I'm so sorry,' she whispered. 'I'm so very sorry.'

'Stop.' He could not listen to her apologise.

'Please forgive me,' she continued. 'Tell me you understand.'

He would tell her whatever she needed to hear. 'I understand.'

'And you forgive me?'

He drew her closer, cradling her head. 'There's nothing to forgive. I know why you did it.'

That only made her cry more. He gave up on words and just held her while her pain bled out all over him. After a while, the crying stopped and her shoulders stilled. She pulled away to look at him properly, taking in the bruises, bandaged arm and unshaven face. Her brow creased in the middle, the same way Asha's did when she was suspicious.

'How did you know I was here?'

He ran his hand through her hair. Gods, he had missed her. 'Manius's men came looking for you.'

Her eyes closed momentarily. 'They must think me a fool if they believe I would go to you at a time like this.'

'A tree is much safer.'

She almost smiled, then teared up again. 'Sorry.'

'Don't be sorry.' He wiped her wet cheek with his thumb. 'I've been going out of my mind not knowing if you're all right.'

She leaned forwards, kissing his face over and over until he could do nothing but drag her onto his lap and kiss her back.

'Tell me you're all right,' he whispered into her mouth.

She settled herself on his lap, burying her face in his neck for a moment. 'I am fine. I do not want to talk about me. Tell me about you. Why are you covered in bruises and bandages?'

'I've been working.'

She was quiet a moment. 'What sort of work?'

He would not lie to her. 'Whatever Gallus needs to me to do.'

'Why?'

'For us.'

She pulled back to look at him again, her expression serious. 'Us? Nero, please tell me you are leaving on that boat with my sister.'

He guided her head back down to his chest, rubbing his stubble on her hair. 'You should know me better than that.'

She was limp against him. 'Whatever you are planning, it will never work.' Tipping her head back to see him, she added, 'Manius has men all over the city, it seems.'

'I know.' He kissed her again, tasting wine and tears, an insight into her future if he failed to get her out.

'Nero.'

'Yes?'

Her head nestled against him. 'I just wanted to speak your name aloud.'

He kissed the top of her head, resting his lips there. 'Is he hurting you?'

She hesitated before replying. 'No.'

'Why did you pause?'

A sigh. 'Because pain is complicated. He is not beating me, if that is what you are asking.'

He let go of the branch to wrap both arms around her. 'Then tell me what hurts.'

She swallowed. 'He wants me to forget you. He wants to erase you from my mind.' Soft fingers stroked his throat. 'How can I erase you? It is like cutting out a piece of myself.'

A hand went to her thigh, pulling her closer—but not close enough. 'He's a... fool.'

'Did you just stop yourself from swearing in front of me? My, how you have matured.'

He could hear the smile in her voice. 'It had to happen eventually.' He breathed out. 'I have a plan.'

With great effort, she sat up. Her hair was a mess. It reminded him of the morning she had woken in his bed.

'You mean a *new* plan?'

His torso felt cold where her body had lain. 'I can get us out of the city, out of Rome.'

Her brow creased, and he felt certain she would shut the idea down.

'When?'

Not how, but when. All that faith and trust. 'As soon as Mila, Remus, and the rest of them are safely out of the city.'

'Of course. It would be reckless to try anything sooner. I do not trust Manius when it comes to my family.'

'I'll need you to meet me.'

'Someone will follow.'

He tilted his head, a hint of a smile forming. 'You've proven to be rather resourceful in that regard, wouldn't you say?'

'Yes, but Manius will be watching me like a hawk after tonight's escapade.'

He rubbed her hips. 'How did you give them the slip?'

'There was a brawl on the street. I jumped out of the litter while everyone was distracted.' She looked pleased with herself. 'I know a lot of shortcuts and hiding places.'

He leaned in and kissed her. 'Do you trust me?'

A nod. 'Of course. I will follow you anywhere.' She brought her palm to his cheek. 'Just tell me what to do.'

He kissed her again, deeper that time, a familiar hunger igniting inside him. 'You need to find an excuse to leave the house.' He spoke the words into her mouth.

'And when they follow?'

'I'll take care of that.' His expression turned serious. 'Go to the temple of Jupiter, where it's nice and busy.' He felt her withdraw. 'What's the matter?'

She hesitated. 'You will not kill them, will you?'

'Not unless I have to.' He did not want to lie to her.

Dulcia's gaze went to the river.

He sighed. 'Talk to me.'

It took her a moment before she could look at him again. 'I do not want to start our life together with blood on our hands.' She leaned away, watching the impact of her words.

'You want me to tell you no one will die, is that it?'

She nodded, slowly.

'I'm sorry, but I can't promise you no one will get hurt. I'll protect you by whatever means necessary.' He watched the conflict play out on her sweet face. 'When you're safe, when all the threats have passed and this is all over, things will be different.'

Her eyes searched his, and she teared up, despite her best efforts not to. 'I know who you are, and I never want those against us to have the opportunity to say they were right about you.'

He kissed her again, letting his mouth linger over hers for

a few moments longer. She lightly touched his bandaged arm.

'When we leave this place, will you stop?'

'Fighting?'

She swallowed. 'All of it. Everything you are doing for that man against your conscience.'

He swallowed. She really did know him. 'Yes.'

She nodded, her forehead resting against his.

'We can't risk being seen together,' he whispered.

'I can walk myself home.'

He struggled with that notion, but what choice did he have? Before he could object, she brushed her lips over his and began to climb down.

'I will try to get to the temple at noon. You will be there, waiting?'

Nero nodded. 'Of course I'll be there.' He kept hold of her arm until she was out of reach. Dulcia looked up at him one last time, attempting a smile. He smiled back at her.

'I'm sorry I didn't fight for you sooner,' he whispered. Gods, he was sorry.

She stopped climbing. 'And I am sorry for every time you did not feel worthy of saying something.' There was so much affection in her eyes. 'No more guessing and uncertainty. We leave together, and we stay together.'

More blind faith in him.

He nodded, then watched as she climbed to the ground, where she was swallowed up by shadows.

# CHAPTER 27

*H*ow does one say goodbye to her mother without speaking the words? It was in the embrace, the aversion of eyes and the choked tone of her voice. It was in the endless fidgeting, distracted conversations and long stares.

'I know this is hard,' Tertia said. 'But I think your sister's decision to leave Rome is smart. You will be surprised how quickly things will settle down once Nero is out of the picture.'

Another benefit of the timing. She could blame her scattered mind on Mila's departure.

'I really think prayer will help.'

Tertia nodded. 'I am sure Manius will respect your need for prayer at this time. His men will, of course, accompany you to the temple.'

Dulcia pulled her mother to her once more, hugging her.

Tertia laughed. 'I will see you soon.'

'I know.' No she would not. Perhaps never again.

Dulcia stepped back, hands trembling. She needed to keep it together or she was going to ruin everything. Leave the house, walk to the temple, ignore the two men trailing behind her. Not one, but two—her fault. They had doubled after her disappearing act a few nights earlier, despite the fact that she had turned up at the Papias house feigning confusion at the panic.

*'For goodness' sake,'* she had said to her mother. *'I just needed a walk to clear my head. Now everyone is running about like I am suddenly incapable of finding my own way home.'*

It was a shame she was not actually planning on praying at the temple. Prayer might have eased her conscience from all the lies she had told in the past few days.

'See you soon,' she said over her shoulder before leaving the laundry and heading to the front door. She glanced once at the closed door of tablinum and felt a pang of something in her stomach. She could only imagine what Rufus would say when he learned of what she had done.

One foot in front of the other, all the way to Nero. He would be waiting at the temple, ready to get them out of the city. In return, she would spend the rest of her years loving him the way he deserved.

A small flutter of hope stirred.

She closed her eyes as the front door banged shut behind her, then forced them open. Two large bodyguards straightened, ready to follow her. Down the steps, she descended the hill while resisting the temptation to look behind, to fret, to think about all the things that could go wrong.

*Slow down,* she told herself. The urge to run was overwhelming.

The precinct was unusually crowded. Families were visiting the various shrines, altars, statues and victory trophies, fathers passing down stories of their childhood heroes.

As Dulcia ascended the steps, she searched for Nero amid the pillars, careful not to turn her head, look distracted, or do anything else that might raise suspicion. He was not there. She reminded herself that he was hardly going to wait out in the open where he would be recognised.

When she reached the top, she saw a vendor coming towards her. He was pushing a cart with baked cheese, nuts, fish and *garum* on display. The man nodded in her direction before the cart passed behind her, blocking the path of her guards.

'Everything is fresh,' the merchant said to them. 'What can I get for you? Some nuts, perhaps?'

Dulcia's heart rate sped up as she continued forwards. She did not look back, stop, or even break stride.

'Move,' one of the men said, his tone impatient.

'At least taste the cheese,' the vendor urged. 'The honey is still warm.'

As the men continued to argue, a woman fell into step with Dulcia.

'Follow me,' the stranger said without turning her head.

There was no time to ask questions, so when the woman dashed left instead of entering the temple, Dulcia followed. She glanced once at her bodyguards, who looked about ready to throw the cart down the temple steps, and then a pillar passed between them. Dulcia faced forwards, pressing her hands against her stomach, hoping the small amount of food she had consumed that morning would stay where it was.

A hand reached out and grabbed her by her wrist. She inhaled sharply as she was pulled behind another pillar, coming face-to-face with Nero. He threaded his fingers through hers, his grip like a vice.

'Do exactly as I say.'

She nodded. Trusting him was the easy part. Containing her fear was something else entirely.

He turned and led her away in the other direction, his pace brisk but not so fast as to draw attention. They weaved through the crowd gathered in the shade of the portico, moving towards the back of the temple. She was too afraid to turn and look, too afraid she would see the men in pursuit of them. If Nero was scared, he did not show it. His gaze moved in every direction, checking every window they passed, every pillar and person. Outwardly he seemed completely calm.

They descended the steps onto the street, Dulcia concentrating on not falling. She was thankful for the tight grip he had on her, for she was terrified of getting separated. As though reading her thoughts, Nero glanced across at her.

'I won't let go.'

Her free hand went to his arm. 'Good luck prying me off when the time comes.'

A smile flickered as he faced forwards again, all his beautiful features hardening once more. Dulcia found the strength to look back, and she spotted one of her guards. He was jogging between people, eyes darting about, searching. Her head snapped forwards.

'What is it?' Nero asked, reading her.

'Behind us. He has not spotted us yet, but he is close.'

Nero did not say a word, just veered right, ducking into the first alleyway they came across. He picked up pace then, checking behind them to ensure they had not been followed. His grip tightened even more if that was possible.

Dulcia glanced nervously over her shoulder, eyes widening as she recognised the second guard looking back at her. Then she was pulled forwards.

They ran along the uneven stones, turning down the next alleyway. It was so narrow they could hardly fit side by side. She knew she was slowing Nero down, but her legs could move no faster, despite the adrenaline coursing through her. He said nothing, just continued pulling her along.

Stopping suddenly, he tugged her into a doorway. She looked up at him, panting, and he held a finger to his lips. She tried to quieten her breathing, while his was barely affected. He gently pushed her farther back until shadows fell across her face. She waited for the man to run past, for him to flash into sight and then disappear. Instead, the footsteps slowed, and Nero let go of her hand.

Lurching forwards, Nero tackled him against the opposite wall. The man swung at him, but Nero was too quick, dodging the blow and hammering his own fist into the guard's side before grabbing his head and driving it into the stone wall. Eyes rolled back, the guard slumping to the ground.

Nero stepped back, his breaths coming faster now. Turning away, he returned to Dulcia and held out his hand. 'Let's go.'

Her eyes were fixed on the man bleeding from the head. 'Is he… is he dead?'

'He'll be fine.' When she still did not look at him, he added, 'We need to keep moving.'

She nodded absently and took his hand. His fingers closed around hers once more, the firm warmth of his hand calming her. 'There is another one.'

'Yes.' He pulled her out into the alley and broke into a jog. 'And there will likely be others.'

She had no choice but to try and keep up. The toe of her sandal caught the edge of a step, and she tripped. He pulled her upright before her knees touched the ground, all the while checking their surroundings.

'Sorry,' she whispered.

Nero sped up again. 'Not much farther.'

They turned right, and Dulcia was knocked sideways into a wall when the second bodyguard threw himself at Nero. She was stunned for a moment, then looked down at her empty hand. Nero pushed the man off before throwing a knee into his side. The man cursed and shoved him back into the wall, missing Dulcia by a few inches. She felt completely useless as the bodyguard's large hand tightened around Nero's throat.

'Get off him,' she said, shoving at the man with both hands.

He was a solid mass of muscle, the size of the two of them combined. Unsurprisingly, he did not move one inch despite her throwing all of her weight against him. A choking sound came from Nero, one that made her insides scream.

'Back,' Nero managed to get out.

The moment she stepped out of the way, a blade flashed in Nero's hand, slashing the man's arm. The guard released him with a cry of pain, his free hand going over the spurting wound. Nero's foot crashed into his chest, sending him flying backwards into the opposite wall. Before Dulcia had a chance to process what was happening, Nero was dragging her over blood-splattered stones towards the street visible at the end of the alleyway.

She watched as he wiped his face with his hand, then looked down at it. They could not afford to draw unnecessary attention. Dulcia's gaze fell to her own tunic, which was also peppered with blood.

'No one will notice as long as we're calm,' Nero said, wiping again at his face. He squeezed her hand. 'We're almost there.'

Another nod.

They emerged onto the busy street, in an unfamiliar part of the city, with the blazing sun on them. Dulcia blinked against the harsh light. The heat, the noise, the crowd—it was all too much. She brought her free hand to her sweat-covered forehead. Her stomach churned and her hand flew over her mouth.

She was going to be sick.

Nero pulled her into an alleyway just before she vomited. She could feel the fabric of her tunic clinging to her back as she bent, her palm pressing the wall for balance. Nero held back her hair while keeping hold of her. She was fairly certain he was the only reason she was still upright.

'Are you all right?'

Straightening, she pressed her cheek to the cool wall. She needed to get herself together or they were going to get caught.

He gave her a moment, then asked, 'Can you walk?'

She pushed off the wall, feeling a pulse of annoyance when her legs trembled beneath her. Her sister had once fought tigers and giants in an arena, and all she had to do was keep up.

Tears prickled her eyes. 'I am so sorry.'

Nero pulled her to him, holding her close until her legs finally stilled. 'Don't apologise again.'

'You cannot let go of my hand this time.' It was such a childish thing to say, but his hand was the only thing holding her together. 'Promise me you will not let go this time.'

He held her at arm's length, his expression serious. 'I'll only let go if I have to, but I'll always come back for you. Always.'

A few tears ran down her cheeks as she nodded. He kissed the top of her head before pulling her out onto the street.

They continued west until they reached the *Theatrum Balbi*, then crossed the street to a shopfront selling silk. Nero walked straight inside, nodding at the merchant, a tall man with crooked teeth and kind eyes. He gestured to the door at the back. Nero knocked once, and a few moments later a short, large-busted woman stood in the doorway, assessing them. After a painful wait, she finally stepped aside to let them pass.

'He's out back,' she said, waving them through.

They walked into the next room where a balding middle-aged man with ring-covered fingers sat perched on a stool. He stood when they entered, smoothing out his expensive toga, but something about his appearance told Dulcia he was not of noble birth.

'This is Gallus Minidius,' Nero said, gesturing to the man.

That explained everything. She nodded a greeting.

'This must be the lovely Dulcia I have heard so much about,' Gallus said, stepping closer and briefly taking her hand. 'You have your sister's pretty face, though not her muscle.'

'Pleased to meet you,' she said.

Done with the pleasantries, Gallus picked a *loculus* off the floor, dropping it onto the table next to him. 'Food, personal items, a change of clothes.' He glanced at Dulcia. 'It might be a little big on the lady. There's a sword, two daggers and all your travel arrangements down on parchment. The ship will take you to Alexandria.'

Dulcia stared at the satchel that contained the entirety of their new life. 'Alexandria.' They were really going. She felt Nero's thumb rub the back of her hand. True to his word, he had not let go.

Nero reached out and grabbed the loculus. 'How are we getting to Ostia? Boat?'

Gallus shook his head. 'Manius knows you have contacts along the river. He will be expecting you to go via boat. You will go on horseback, but you cannot leave now.'

Nero shifted. 'We can't afford to wait.'

'He already has men running about the city looking for you both. It was not exactly a clean getaway, I hear.'

Dulcia took a step closer to Nero. 'He is not just going to give up when he cannot find us.'

Gallus tapped his nose. 'Of course not. He has likely paid off the guards along the walls.'

Nero's grip on her hand tightened. 'But you'll get us out?'

Gallus raised his hands in a calming gesture. 'Yes, but we will need to wait until evening, when the guards change. You will leave via *Porta Naevia*. Those are the guards *I* have paid off.' He paused for a moment to let them revel in his cleverness. 'If anyone stops you, you tell them your name is

Agrippa Decius. Your horse will be waiting on the other side.'

'What if Manius has also paid them?' Dulcia asked.

Gallus smiled like one does when a child asks a silly question. 'These men are loyal to me.'

Nero looked around the small room. 'Are we safe here in the meantime?'

'Quite,' Gallus replied, tapping the table with his hand as though the sturdiness of the furniture was representative of the fact. 'Rest. Wash. Eat.' He ran his eyes over Nero. 'Definitely wash. You look like you stopped to slaughter a sow on your way here.'

Gallus stepped up to Nero, arm extended. 'You are mad, but I have always liked you, so I wish you both luck.' Glancing at Dulcia, he added, 'Though I question your choice of suitor.' He winked at her as he clapped Nero on the back, then strolled from the room.

# CHAPTER 28

*N*ero wished Dulcia would relax, look him in the eye—at least breathe. But she sat at the table in the middle of the room, watching the door and jumping at every scrape, bang and voice that reached them. He sat on the floor with his back against the wall, watching her.

'Come sit with me.'

Even at *his* voice she jumped.

Standing, she lifted her chair so it would not scrape on the floor, then joined him on the ground. His arm went around her, and he guided her head to his shoulder.

'Talk to me,' he said.

'Soon it will be dark.'

'Yes.' He smoothed her hair down. 'Are you afraid to leave?'

She tipped her face up to look at him. 'If I am caught, I will be returned to my family. The wedding will likely go ahead. There will be consequences, but none of them life-threatening.' She blinked. 'If you are caught, Manius has the power to make you disappear.'

His lips brushed her forehead. 'You're focusing on today and forgetting about tomorrow, next week, a year from now.'

Her eyes searched his face. 'Since I am incapable of seeing past the immediate threat to your life'—there was a hint of smile in her voice—'perhaps you could tell me about tomorrow, next week, and a year from now.' She settled against his shoulder again.

He glanced at the window, keeping an eye on the fading daylight. 'Tomorrow we will board a ship six times the length of the river boats. There will be nothing but water in every direction. The air you breathe on deck will be so raw, so clean, you will wonder how you ever survived breathing anything else.' He ran the tips of his fingers along her arm, watching the bumps appear on her skin. 'Alexandria is like nothing you've ever seen. There are palaces—'

'And pyramids?'

'Not in Alexandria. We need to travel to Giza for those.'

She pressed a hand to his beating heart. 'Then maybe we go to India to be with Mila and the rest of the family.'

His chest grew heavy. 'Not straight away. We'll need to wait.' The decision to run came with consequences. He was making them fugitives of sorts.

'We could get married in Giza.'

His cheek rested on the top of her head and he closed his eyes. 'I vowed years ago to love and protect you, so you're already mine.'

'I don't recall those vows.'

'I never spoke them aloud.'

'Ah. Well, that explains it.' A pause. 'I definitely recall consummating the marriage.'

He kissed the top of her head. The memories of that night were still fresh, because he had replayed them in his mind every day since. He tried to imagine what a life filled with her would look like. 'You're like the sun, giving light to all things.'

She looked up at him. 'Careful. That sounds like the beginning of a poem.'

'Can I make it a dirty one? Like the ones you read?'

Her perfect mouth stretched into a smile. 'If you like.'

He kissed her, tasting the preserved apricots they had eaten earlier. 'You're so beautiful when you smile.' He ran a finger along her jaw.

'As are you.'

He took in her expression. 'You are going to tire of the sight of me smiling.'

'Never.' She tugged his head down into another kiss. His body hummed with the sensation. When she pulled away, her expression was serious. 'When we leave here, you will keep hold of my hand?'

'I won't let go.'

'And on the ship, because I cannot swim.'

His arms went around her, his body a cradle for hers. 'I'll teach you to swim.' He whispered the words into her hair and watched as her eyes sank shut.

∽

'DULCIA, WAKE UP.'

She startled awake in his arms and looked around at the dark room. The woman from earlier stood by the back door, watching the street. Dulcia blinked up at Nero. 'Is it time?'

'Yes.'

He stood, pulling her up with him, then reached for the satchel on the table.

'I will carry it,' she said, holding out her hands.

'Absolutely not. It's too heavy.'

She took it from him and slipped it over her head, struggling to keep her shoulders level beneath the weight of it. 'It is not heavy. See? I will be no help if we run into trouble, but I can carry our things.' Noticing his conflicted expression, she added, 'You will not have time to hand it to me, and we need you ready.'

He reluctantly nodded, then lifted his tunic to adjust the dagger strapped to his thigh. Satisfied with its placement, he took her hand, bringing it to his mouth. 'Tomorrow, next week and a year from now.'

It was their new mantra. 'Tomorrow, next week and a year from now.'

He drew a breath. 'All right. Let's get today out of the way.'

Nero said nothing to the woman as they stepped past her. Dulcia was about to say thank you when she realised they probably needed to remain quiet. She glanced over her shoulder as the door closed behind them. The sound of a lock being turned followed. Nero squeezed her hand, a reassuring gesture she needed desperately. She tried to think about tomorrow, arriving in Ostia and seeing their ship for the first time. She could not tell if it was nerves or excitement that fluttered inside of her. Nero did not say anything, just started walking, his pace brisk but not so fast she would struggle to keep up.

They headed south, where Gallus's contact was expecting them. The walk seemed eternal. She found herself bracing every time someone passed them, so she kept her eyes down and palla hooded over her head, guided only by Nero's body language. He kept her close, as wary as she was. She could tell by the way he stiffened every time someone walked by, his hand brushing over the dagger.

Dulcia held her breath for most of the walk, her damp hands giving away her fear.

At the halfway mark, she began to slow. The weight of her bag was making her shoulders cramp and neck ache. When she stopped to adjust it, Nero took it from her.

'I am fine,' she said.

'It's too heavy for you.'

She reluctantly let go, and he settled the bag on his shoulder as though it weighed nothing at all. Taking her hand again, they resumed walking, and that time she was able to keep up.

When the thirty-foot wall finally came into sight, they slowed down and veered left towards the gate. The city had outgrown the wall. In many ways it was redundant, with the protection of the growing military outside. But the gates were still the only way in or out of the city, and it was easier to guard sixteen points than an open perimeter.

Nero waited for a gap between the incoming carts spilling into the city, then crossed the street. Two guards looked their way, then strolled towards them. Dulcia's heart sped up and her mouth went dry. She really hoped these were Gallus's men or they were going to be in a lot of trouble.

'Where are you off to?' the taller one asked, eyes moving over them.

Nero was calm, his expression friendly. 'Visiting my sister.'

The men exchanged a glance. 'Name?'

'Agrippa Decius,' Nero replied.

The name rolled off his tongue as though he had said it his entire life. The other guard looked at Dulcia. 'This your wife?'

'Yes,' Nero said.

Dulcia was certain they would see her chest pulsing with each beat of her heart. She swallowed, her mouth painfully dry. Finally, the shorter man stepped back from them. 'Watch the carts on your way through.'

Nero nodded and led Dulcia past them. 'Good evening.'

By some miracle, her legs held up as they walked along the thick base of the wall and passed beneath the arch. She glanced once at the guards, then released a long, shaky breath.

'I won't let anything happen to you,' Nero said, keeping his voice low.

Her free hand went to his arm, and fear gave way to a rush of affection. 'I know.' She pressed her forehead to his arm.

*Tomorrow, next week and a year from now.*

❧

NERO STOPPED WALKING. Every hair on his body stood on end. Perhaps it was the fact that he could not see the face of the man waiting with the horse. A shadow covered it, and Nero did not feel right approaching a faceless man when he had Dulcia with him.

'What is the matter?' she asked, looking at the horse, then back at him.

Everything was as it should be. So why was his skin crawling? Shaking his head, he tried to smile. 'Nothing. Let's go.'

They continued towards the horse, but his unease grew with every step. He stopped again. Dulcia did not ask what the matter was that time, just moved closer to him. The man glanced nervously over his shoulder. If there was one emotion Nero had come to recognise in his line of work, it was fear.

They were not alone.

He stepped in front of Dulcia, slipping his hand into the satchel as he did so. His fingers wrapped the hilt of the sword. As he pulled the weapon from the bag, he whispered, 'Run.'

Her eyes widened as she realised what was happening. Staggering back from him, she turned, preparing to flee. But before she had a chance, three men emerged from the shadows, one either side of them and the other directly in front. Nero caught Dulcia by the wrist, pulling her behind him. She would not be able to outrun them.

The men's blades flashed in the moonlight as they closed in.

'Nowhere to run to,' one of them called.

Footsteps sounded behind him, and two more men appeared around the horse. He was foolish enough to fight five armed men, but not with Dulcia huddled against him. They had been so close.

'Hand the girl over, and we might let you keep one arm,' one said.

He tried to think, but before he could make sense of his thoughts, he felt fingertips brush his thigh. He looked down just as Dulcia snatched the dagger strapped to his leg. 'What are you doing?'

She looked around at the men, her breathing shallow and her eyes glassy with fear. 'Fighting. There are too many for you to do it alone.'

*Fighting*? Had she lost her mind? She was not even holding the knife properly. 'Give that to me.' He gestured for the weapon.

She stared back at him as if he had said something outrageous. 'No.'

'Now,' he replied, his voice rising. The thought of her getting hurt was undoing him.

'They will kill you.'

Probably, but not her.

The men continued to close in, watching the exchange with interest. For a moment, he actually considered fighting them, imagined cutting their throats, driving his sword through their stomachs and praying Dulcia would one day forgive him for all she had witnessed. He pictured her swinging that tiny knife at the enormous men, and them disarming her with ease, perhaps breaking her arm in the process. They might even swing their own blades and return her to Manius to be patched up.

He had promised he would not let anything happen to

her. If he handed her over, they would just take her away. No need for weapons and violence. They would deliver her to Manius in one piece so he could have the perfect wife essential to the life he had planned.

'You need to go with them.' The words came out hoarse.

She shook her head and her eyebrows came together, forming a sharp line across her brow. 'What are you talking about?' She glanced cautiously at the approaching men. 'We leave together. That is what we agreed.

'And I told you I wouldn't let you get hurt.'

Her hand went over her heart. 'What is it you think you are doing right now?'

He had to look away. 'They won't hurt you if you just go with them.'

The men stopped five feet away, eyes fixed on them and weapons poised

'If I lose you now,' she said quietly, '*that* will destroy me.'

The words sat between them, stagnating. He kept hold of his weapon.

'Be smart,' one of the men said. 'You're outnumbered five to one. You have a sword and the lady a dagger I'm guessing she has no idea how to use.'

His sword hand wavered.

'Please,' Dulcia whispered. 'Do not hand me over.' She looked around at the men, her face hardening. 'I would rather die here with you than walk back through that gate.'

That image was too much, and he blinked against it. The sword fell from his hand, clanging at his feet. He held his arms up in surrender. 'Don't hurt her. I forced her to come with me. She'll go with you willingly.'

The expression on her face was haunting. Equal parts betrayal and disbelief. But he forced himself to look at her so he would never forget what he had done to her.

'Go with them,' he said. 'Don't fight.'

That seemed to break her. She let go of the dagger and

stared at him like he was a stranger. Two men stepped up and took hold of her arms, gripping so tightly she winced.

'I said don't hurt her!' Nero roared as they dragged her away. He went to go after her but was grabbed by two other men. One of them kicked his knee, and he dropped to the ground. Dulcia cried out as the fifth man walked around to stand in front of him, blocking his view of her. She was all he cared about in that moment. She needed to calm down. The only thing he could do was remain completely calm himself.

'Get off me,' he heard her say. He could hear her struggling.

*Be still.*

The sound of a hand slapping her put an end to that plan. 'Dulcia—'

It was the only word he got out before a foot connected with his stomach, knocking all the air from him and causing him to double over. Another kick, that time to the jaw. The familiar taste of blood filled his mouth.

'Stop it!'

That was Dulcia again, more desperate that time as she struggled against her captors. He did not want her to see.

Something hard came down on his head, the hilt of a sword perhaps. Warmth spread through his hair. His legs gave out beneath him, and he collapsed onto his side. For a moment he considered fighting back, unleashing hell. If only he knew which way was up. If only he could see through the blood running over his eyes.

'Please, stop!'

She had resorted to begging, having likely figured out she could not break free. The anguish in her voice made him lift his head and look for her. Her tear-soaked face came into view, but then she blurred again.

He was regretting his decision. Perhaps he should have fought, trusted that he would never let a blade come near her. He swung a leg out, connecting with a knee. The cry of pain fuelled his ambition. But then another foot landed in his side, accompanied by a jolt of pain that tore through his chest. He bit back the cry that rose in his throat, knowing it would only distress Dulcia.

'Stop it,' she shouted. 'You'll kill him.'

She sounded farther away that time. They were probably taking her back to her father, to her mother, to Manius. What would a man like him do to a woman like her? Shatter all her hopes, suffocate her childish joy, crush her gentle spirit. He would destroy whatever was left of her.

Tearing one arm free from his captors, Nero tried again to get up, ducking the first punch and blocking another kick aimed at his groin. He tried to pull his other arm free, but something hard slammed into the side of his head, and everything went black.

# CHAPTER 29

When Nero opened his eyes and looked around, he recognised the apartment Mila and Remus shared with Felix and Albaus. He tried really hard to remember how he got there, but for the longest time, nothing came. An aching hand reached up to touch a tender part of his head, and the image of men beating him flashed in his mind.

*Dulcia.*

He tried to sit up, but a sharp pain in his chest stopped him.

'I wouldn't do that' came Felix's voice. 'The physician says at least one of your ribs is broken. I would guess more judging by the bruising.'

Nero turned his head to the doorway, where Felix was standing with his arms crossed. 'Where's Dulcia?' His voice came out raw, his mouth impossibly dry.

Felix's mouth pinched with concern. 'No one knows.'

Nero tried to swallow before speaking. 'She better be all right.'

Felix wandered into the room. 'She is doing better than you, I imagine. You are lucky to be alive. The only reason you are not buried somewhere outside of the city is because one of Gallus's men threw you over the back of a mule and brought you here.'

Nero tried again to sit up, ignoring Felix's disapproving stare. Every inch of him ached and throbbed. Mila must have heard them talking, because she appeared in the doorway looking exhausted.

'Thank the gods,' she breathed, then rushed to his bedside. Her gaze moved over him before a scowl settled on her face. 'What in heaven's name were you thinking? You almost died.'

Felix cleared his throat. 'I thought you might get a few moments of pity before this part. It appears I was wrong.'

'You would have bled out if someone had not dropped you on our doorstep,' she continued as if Felix had not spoken. 'Now Remus is running about the city, out for blood. No one even knows where Dulcia is.' She crossed her arms. 'Manius has her locked up gods know where.'

'She's with Manius?'

Mila glared at him. 'Even if I did know, I would not tell you. You cannot be trusted.'

He stared at the blanket covering him, head pulsing. 'We were so close. Someone alerted them.'

'It was probably Gallus himself,' Mila said, throwing her hands up. 'Why on earth did you trust that man to begin with?'

Felix raised his hands in an attempt to calm her. 'Gallus is many things, but I would be very surprised if he would conspire against Nero. He values his life more than coin, and he knows we would come for him.'

Nero winced as he swung his legs over the edge of the bed. 'Well, someone told them.'

Mila's hands went to her hips. 'Where on earth do you think you are going?'

'To Remus. This is my mess. I don't want him cleaning it up.'

She shook her head at him. 'Oh no you do not. You are not moving from this bed until the physician says you can. Be thankful for your injuries or I would beat you myself.'

'I need to find Dulcia.'

'What do you think Albaus is doing right now?' Her retort was abrupt.

Nero hung his head in his hands as a wave of nausea washed over him. 'Great idea. Send a mute man to make enquiries.'

'He might not have a tongue,' Felix said, 'yet somehow he is one of the most well-connected men in Rome.' He made a gesture for Nero to stay put. 'Do not move from that bed unless you want Mila to start breaking things. *I* will go to Remus, tell him you are awake. It might soothe his agitation.'

'How long have been I out?'

'Two days,' Mila said, much louder than was necessary.

It occurred to Nero that they were supposed to be at sea by now. He had watched them leave that morning. 'Why are you still here?'

Mila glanced at Felix before replying. 'We really thought you would come with us. We believed it right up until the moment we were supposed to board.' Her shoulders fell. 'Call it intuition, but we decided to delay a few days, until we could convince you to join us.'

'You made it all the way to Ostia, then turned around?' Another wave of nausea. 'You should have just gone.'

'Thank heavens we did not.' Mila sighed. 'Have you not figured out yet that we love you, that we are your family? We cannot leave you behind any more than we could leave one of the children. At least not now.' She took an unsteady breath. 'The entire way to the port we were watching the road behind us.'

Felix walked over and patted his shoulder. 'For me it was the seasickness. You were just a convenient excuse.'

Nero raised his head, noting the mischievous glint in Felix's eyes.

'We will leave as soon as you are well enough to travel,' Mila continued. 'And this time you will come with us. I will bind and gag you if I have to, but you will come.' She stared at the wall for a moment. 'I am going to send Asha in to watch you, to make sure you do not leave this room.'

'Best lie down for that visit,' Felix said, walking over and picking up Nero's legs, easing them back onto the bed. 'She is almost as mad as her mother.'

Nero winced and lay down again. His eyes met Mila's. 'You will tell me as soon as you hear anything about Dulcia?'

'That depends if my anger subsides.'

'It appears to be still rising,' Felix whispered.

Mila glared at the dwarf. 'The problem is I love you far too much to sit back while you self-destruct.'

A choking noise came from Felix. 'Sorry.' He pounded his chest with his fist. 'Do not let your own past actions get in the way of this memorable speech. Please, continue.'

She turned to him again, a warning in her eyes.

'I should probably go find Remus,' Felix said, giving Mila a wide berth.

Nero closed his eyes and heard Mila calling Asha. Despite his best effort to remain awake, sleep took him once more.

NERO WOKE when he felt the mattress shift beneath him. He opened his eyes slowly, the only speed he was capable of. Remus sat on the end of the bed, his elbows on his knees and his head in his hands. His knuckles were swollen and bruised.

'Who or what did you punch?'

Remus turned, surprised to see him awake. He looked exhausted. 'How are you feeling?'

'You know, you are the first person to ask me that.'

Remus laughed through his nose. 'Well, we know Mila expresses her concern in other ways.' His eyes moved over him. 'They did a good job on your face.'

'Certainly feels that way.' He tried to sit up, the pain no better. Rather than object, Remus moved to help him. 'Any news on Dulcia?'

Remus settled himself on the bed once more. 'No one's talking. Mila's losing her mind.'

'Tertia must know something.'

He shook his head. 'Rufus won't let Mila near the house to ask.'

Nero blinked slowly and stretched out his legs. 'This is all my fault.'

Remus leaned on his knees again. 'No, I think it's my fault. I taught you to fight like a gladiator instead of a man.'

'Gladiators are just men with armour.'

A nod. 'Yes, but Dulcia's not a prize, and real life's not an arena.'

Nero glanced at the door. All was quiet in the house. The light in the room suggested it was late. 'Tell me then, what should I have done?'

'Been honest.' Remus thought for a moment. 'You should've knocked on Rufus Papias's door the moment you realised you loved her. You should've told the senator there is no better man for her.'

'Lied?'

'It's not a lie. If you don't believe it, they never will.'

'To be clear, you think I should've gone to Rufus Papias and explained why I'm a *better* option then Manius Liberia?'

Remus looked at him. 'You must believe it deep down if you were prepared to smuggle her out of the city and away from her family for the rest of her life.'

'I love her.' It was such a bland description of what he felt. 'And I need to know where she is and if she's all right.'

Remus studied him for a moment. 'Then what? Sneak her onto a boat and hope Manius and Rufus forget all about their humiliation? Not much of a plan.'

'I can't do anything. Manius has made sure of that.' He raked a hand through his hair. 'I don't understand him. He has wealthy women forming a line praying the wedding doesn't happen, and he wants the one who's shown the least interest.'

A hum of voices came from the next room, little boys protesting to being put to bed.

'The thing you need to understand about men like Manius,' Remus said, 'is that his interest in Dulcia might've been genuine in the beginning, but now it's about winning. He's rich, he's worshipped as a charioteer, and he's used to getting his way. His pride couldn't take the hit of a woman so beneath him choosing a man with barely a sestertius to his name.' He paused to take in Nero's reaction to his words. 'He's not from our world. He can't fathom it. And he doesn't know you as we do.'

Nero blinked. 'He sees a rodent.'

Remus rubbed the knuckles of his hand. 'I see someone who hasn't reached his full potential, but is still twice the man Manius is.'

'Bet you wish you hadn't labelled me a Latinius.'

Remus's eyebrows rose. 'Why? Because you made a few mistakes? Latinius men are notorious for doing things the hard way. Besides, you're doing better than me at that age. I still had a lot to prove.'

'As do I, it seems.'

Remus patted Nero's leg as he stood. 'Just remember to prove them wrong, not right.'

'Sounds like something Dulcia would say.'

A slow nod from Remus. 'Well, she's a smart girl. That's why she chose you.'

A pang of guilt hit Nero. *I would rather die here with you than walk back through that gate,'* she had told him. He had not listened. She had chosen him, and then he had destroyed her, exactly as she said he would. 'I need to get out of this bed.'

Remus was already walking away. 'Take it up with the physician in the morning. He's coming to check you over. Until then, don't move.'

'Wait,' Nero called. Remus paused in the doorway, one arm resting on the frame. 'Who tipped off Manius's men?'

Remus sniffed. 'Don't know.'

He gestured to his swollen knuckles. 'But you found the men who did it?'

Remus looked down and stretched out his fingers. 'All five of them.' His mouth lifted in a weak smile. 'Get some rest.'

Nero lay back down, an arm draped over his face as his thoughts crashed in on him. There had to be a way to fix everything, to fix Dulcia. If anyone could piece her back together, it was him. And the moment they let him out of that bed, he would figure out a way.

# CHAPTER 30

*T*here was only so much bad poetry one could take, and Junia's poems were very bad.

The pair were sitting in the garden of the house Dulcia would share with Manius for the rest of her life. Instead of listening, Dulcia was reflecting on the past week.

Panic, anger, then suffocating disappointment.

She had thought Nero dead for three entire days before Junia had finally put her out of her misery and brought her news of him. The panic had dissolved into anger. He had handed her over after she begged him not to. He had given up after he swore to fight. And he had let go of her hand after promising to keep hold of it.

Now on day six, she had resigned herself to a permanent state of disappointment. Every hope had to be abandoned. That was what Manius had said the night his men brought her to the house. She had fought them the entire way, thrashing and kicking and crying like a mad woman. When she had collapsed at Manius's feet, he had pulled her up by the arm and shouted so loudly in her face that a spray of spit accompanied the ringing in her ears.

*'How many times must we do this? Why are you so deter-*

*mined to humiliate me and your own family? For some fantasy? I thought you were a smart girl. I thought you understood. A good marriage is built on foundations stronger than love.'*

She had covered her ears at one point, unable to take in what he was saying. It was all just noise competing with the screaming in her mind.

Rufus knew. Her mother knew. Yet no one came to her. They let Manius deal with the situation as he saw fit. After all, she was to be his problem in a few days.

*'Your own father does not even want to see you,'* Manius had said.

Those words had the effect he was hoping for, stinging almost as much as Nero's words, the ones she replayed in her mind.

*'Go with them. Don't fight.'*

She had fought anyway, because she had seen Nero collapse to the ground, blood pouring down his face, while Manius's men kicked him over and over. She could still hear the sickening thud of their feet.

Junia, who had been assigned the role of guard, had eventually taken pity on her. She had her own connections, people Manius was not aware of, and sought information for the purpose of closure.

Nero was alive.

Manius had buried the scandal. Not even his mother knew. Wealthy people could afford to cover their problems with a big pile of money.

'Are you even listening to me?' Junia asked, dropping the parchment on her lap. 'This one was inspired by your heartbreak.'

Thank goodness she had tuned out.

Dulcia poked her needle through the tapestry and set it aside. 'Very touching.'

Junia sank down in her chair and signalled for the slave

by the wall to bring the plate of fruit to her. It seemed leaning to get it herself was too great an effort.

'At least you have known love. Many women do not get to experience it at all.' She crossed her legs, one foot bouncing. 'I was just twelve when I was in your situation, and my husband was not nearly so handsome. While you have made it *abundantly* clear that Manius is not your first choice, you could certainly do a lot worse.'

'I know.' It was all she could manage.

'Beneath his competitive nature is a decent man.'

Dulcia shook her head when the plate of fruit was brought to her. 'I never said he is a bad person.' She just did not love him.

Junia cocked her head. 'Poor Dulcia. She must marry the rich man and live in a big house. I am sure Rome's poor would love to hear all about your woes.'

She was right, of course. It was obscene to be trapped in a house of luxury, feeling sorry for herself. And she had a new problem now. Even if by some miracle Manius released her from her obligations, she had nowhere to go.

'*I won't let go.*'

Her palms pressed her thighs. Before she had a chance to respond, another servant entered the garden and announced that Tertia was at the front door, wishing to see her daughter. Dulcia and Junia looked at one another.

'She knows Dulcia is here?' Junia asked, visibly surprised.

Dulcia held her breath, not daring to speak. Manius had been very clear—no visitors.

'I did not say anything, Era. I told her to wait at the door.'

Exhaling, Junia replied, 'Show her to the atrium. Dulcia will be there momentarily.'

Dulcia released the breath she had been holding and went to stand.

'Just a few minutes,' Junia warned, eyes on her poetry. 'And not a word to Manius.'

'Thank you,' Dulcia said before rushing off.

Her mother waited inside, taking in the beauty and size of the room. Relief broke out on her face the moment she spotted her daughter. Dulcia felt six years old again as she ran into her mother's arms. She could not stop the tears she had been holding back for days.

Tertia held her shaking body as she cried.

'Shh. Pull yourself together.'

Dulcia straightened and wiped her face. 'We only have a few minutes. Is there any news of Nero?' First question off her tongue, despite everything.

Tertia shook her head and took a firm hold of her shoulders. 'Enough.'

Her sharp tone made Dulcia's breath catch.

'There is to be no more mention of that man. No more scheming, no more hoping for a different outcome. It ends now.'

Dulcia tried to step back, but her mother kept hold of her. Yes, the trust was damaged between them, but not the love. She still needed to know that he was all right.

'I do not need to tell you how dangerous your actions were, how impulsive and foolish.' Tertia's voice was low, and her gaze kept flicking to the entryways either side of them. 'Now the work begins. You must fix things with Manius, redeem yourself. You must be the wife you ought to be, because that man has done nothing wrong.'

'Nothing wrong?' She hugged herself.

'Listen, carefully.' Tertia looked around before speaking. 'It was me who went to him with the information about Licinia. That is not on him, it is on me.'

Dulcia's heartbeat slowed, her brain struggling with that piece of information.

'I encouraged him to go forwards, to use it for his own purposes.' She swallowed. 'When you did not come home that night, I panicked.'

'But it was a lie.' Her arms fell to her side. 'You passed on a lie.'

Tertia's face fell. 'I know.'

The silence that followed was uncomfortably long. 'You know?' Dulcia finally asked.

A nod. 'My lie, one I made Manius believe.' She reached out to touch her daughter, but Dulcia stepped back. 'Everything I did, I did for you,' Tertia continued. 'And I am asking you not to throw it all away, because then it will have been for nothing.'

Dulcia opened her mouth, then closed it again. 'They were going to bury her alive.'

Tertia shook her head. 'I knew you would never let that happen. I had every faith you and Manius would figure it out, and you have.'

Dulcia wiped at her face, surprised to find her cheeks wet with tears.

'Everything I have done is so you could have a good life, a happy life, because you deserve that.'

Dulcia did not know where to look. 'Do I look happy?' It came out as a whisper. All the pieces began to fall into place. She was beginning to understand more than she wanted to. 'You said *everything*.' Another piece dropped. 'The night we tried to leave.' The question stuck in her throat. 'The men waiting for us. Was that you too?'

Tertia's shoulders fell a few inches. 'I knew something was wrong. You were not yourself that day. At first I thought it was because Mila was leaving. Then you hugged me, and… I just wanted to ensure you did not do anything foolish.'

Dulcia could barely breathe.

'Gallus Minidius is not a good man. When I learned he was helping you—'

'You went to Manius.'

Tertia hesitated. 'He wanted you safe also.'

'Nero almost died because of you.' Another step back. 'I

254

can still see him lying on the ground while those animals attacked him.'

'I did it to protect *you*.'

Dulcia continued to stare at her mother. 'Is that what you really believe? That you did it for me?'

Her mother's eyes pleaded with her. 'I barely know Nero aside from his violent reputation.'

'You did not care to know anything else about him, even after he carried me through flames.'

'We are not talking about him anymore. You need to fix things with Manius.'

Dulcia covered her face. She did not have it in her to fix anything, not even herself. 'I cannot.'

'Of course you can.' Tertia pulled her hands away from her face. 'If you think you cannot find happiness with Manius, then you are wrong. The happiness will creep in with time, once you let go of all the resentment and regret, and embrace your new life.' She let go of Dulcia's hands. 'I speak from experience.'

She was referring to her life with Rufus. It was true, she seemed happy despite the fact that her father had sold her to the man at a young age.

'I had to let my family go,' Tertia continued. 'I have not seen my brother in over twenty-five years.'

Dulcia was having difficulty feeling anything but anger in that moment. 'So I should turn off my feelings, like you did?'

Tears filled Tertia's eyes. 'It is not one or the other. You can find happiness with Manius and still have room for the pain.'

'Dulcia,' Junia called, stepping into the atrium. 'Say goodbye to your mother.'

Dulcia continued to watch her mother for a moment. 'Goodbye.'

Tertia attempted a smile. 'All will be well. You shall see.'

She reached out, patting her daughter's arm before turning and following the waiting servant from the room.

Dulcia stared after her, resignation like mould on her soul. Perhaps it was easier to just welcome it in, let it cover her until one day she looked in the mirror and saw something else entirely. The alternative was too hard.

'Shall we weave?' Junia asked, her tone upbeat.

Dulcia stared after her mother, one hand on her stomach and the other pressed to her breastbone where Nero's ring still hung from her neck. Tertia had said, *'No more'.* But Nero had said something also.

*'I'll only let go if I have to, and I'll always come back.'*

She turned to Junia, cheeks flushed and eyes red. 'Yes. Let us weave.'

## CHAPTER 31

When Nero showed up on Rufus Papias's doorstep, no one would see him. He asked if he should come back later, to which the servant answered with a very pointed *no*.

'Tomorrow, then?' Nero asked as the door closed in his face. The footsteps faded until he could hear nothing at all.

He went back every day for five days, and on the fifth day, not even the servants opened the door. If Rufus Papias was not going to let him in, he would wait for the man to leave the house.

Crossing the street, Nero took a seat in the shade, eyes never leaving the door. The moment the physician had said he could leave his bed, he fled. Light exercise had been encouraged in order to keep the lungs clear, but he was still in pain.

'It is too far,' Mila had called as he left the apartment.

It had not stopped him. One persistent thought kept him going back: he should have done it long ago. He should have done it the moment he had a wage, when he realised his feelings for Dulcia went far beyond the lust of a young boy. At some point she had become the best part of his day, the

257

reason he left the stables at a jog instead of a walk. Every time she smiled, his own was a reflex, her laughter infectious and her tears his undoing. He should have gone to the man who held all the power—before she was promised to another.

The sun sat low in the west when the front door to the great house finally opened. Rufus and Aquila stepped out together, dressed in their finest, likely heading to a dinner party. Nero pushed himself up onto his feet, ignoring the pain in his chest from moving too fast.

Aquila spotted him first. She caught her husband's arm and gestured tiredly in his direction. Rufus turned to look, his mouth flattening into a thin line at the sight of him.

'We are already running late,' Rufus said, attempting to shut the conversation down before it had even begun.

Nero glanced at the approaching litter. 'Perhaps I can walk with you, so as to not delay you.'

'Do we look like plebeians who walk the streets?' Aquila asked, her dark eyes narrowed on him.

Nero struggled to keep his face neutral, remembering all the times the woman had laid her hands on Dulcia. 'I'll walk alongside your litter, then.'

Aquila waved her hand dismissively. 'My husband is not interested in anything you have to say. In fact, if Manius's men had not done such a good job on you already, he might have sent men of his own.'

Rufus raised a hand to silence his wife. 'I will walk ahead for a few minutes.'

Her mouth pinched. 'In this heat?'

Rufus gave a silent sigh. 'The heat is not so bad.'

Aquila gathered the skirt of her garment and turned in a swoosh of fabric before stepping into the waiting litter. The men walked on ahead while Aquila settled herself.

'You have five minutes,' Rufus said, walking off.

Nero hurried after him, with no intention of wasting one

second of the time. He knew what he wanted to say. 'I have come to ask for Dulcia's hand.'

Rufus laughed, but it was not a happy noise. 'I truly hope you are joking. You have a lot of nerve showing up at my house after the trouble you have caused. The only reason I have not had you exiled is because I have been assured you are leaving the city.'

That was what he had promised Mila. If the wedding went ahead, he would leave with them on the next available ship.

He brought a hand to his aching ribs, trying to match the senator's pace. 'I should've let you know my intentions sooner.'

'To be clear, no one cares about your feelings except Dulcia, and her input on the subject is no longer welcome.'

'Is she with Manius?' He could not help himself.

'That is not your business.'

He thought it best not to disagree. 'Can you at least tell me if she's all right?'

Rufus cast a sideways glance at him. 'If you are fishing for information, you will get nothing from me.'

He was running out of time. 'I know you don't want to hear this, but I love Dulcia.' No reaction. 'And she feels the same. That's why she risked everything to be with me.'

'Dulcia is naive. She has lived a very sheltered life. Of course she would agree to your foolish plan.' He looked over his shoulder, no doubt gauging the distance of the litter. 'You have said your piece.' His eyes returned to Nero. 'This is where we part ways. You leave the city, and I never see you again.'

Yes, his time was most definitely up. 'See, the thing is, I can't move on, because I made a promise to Dulcia.'

'I am guessing it is one you cannot keep.'

'I love her.'

'You mentioned that, but it is not enough.'

Nero's breath was catching as his ribs burned. 'What *would* be enough?'

Rufus laughed and shook his head. 'Perhaps you have not heard the news. I already have a husband for my daughter.'

'I know her better than anyone, and she will be miserable if that marriage goes ahead.'

'Better than her own mother?'

'Yes,' Nero replied without hesitation.

There was amusement in Rufus's eyes. 'I am curious enough to hear your theory on the subject.'

Nero stopped walking, unable to continue at that pace and talk at the same time. Rufus stopped also, turning impatiently. Soon the litter would catch up.

'She shuts down around him.'

'She shuts down around everyone.'

Nero shook his head. 'No, she doesn't. Not with me.'

'I pray that is not the entirety of your argument. There is far more at play here than her shy demeanour.'

Nero's hands rested on his hips as he watched the litter approach. At that point he had nothing to lose. He looked at Rufus. 'I know how to make her laugh, her favourite foods, what frightens her, what it means when her forehead wrinkles in that particular way of hers. I know what she values most in life and how to make her happy.' At least the man was listening. 'But more than that, I know the lengths I would go to in order to give her the life she deserves.' He drew a breath. 'I'm not the wealthiest man, or the most educated. It's possible I don't even deserve her. But I swear before every listening god that there is not a man on this Earth who will love her like I do.'

Another sigh from Rufus. Hope surged in Nero as silence followed.

'That may be true. However, it does not change the facts. You say you should have come to me earlier, but my answer would have been the same.' His expression did not change. 'You are a man without a last name, raised by whores. You fight on the streets, kill men for coin. You are a criminal, and the sort of man who would take another's wife.'

'I'm not without morals—'

'You gamble.'

'A lot of men gamble—'

'You have no ambition, no plan, and no wealth. Shall I go on?'

Nero shifted his weight from one foot to the other. 'I think you've made your point.'

Rufus exhaled. 'Perhaps if you had come to me and offered up something other than feelings, *before* Dulcia was promised to someone else, I might have listened. You stand here with nothing of value to me.'

'If it's coin you want, I can get it.'

'I am not interested in your thug money.'

The litter stopped behind them as the men stared at one another.

'Do not come to the house again,' Rufus said, turning away.

Nero watched as he climbed into the litter. Aquila did not even glance in his direction.

'Good day,' Nero called as the litter pulled away.

NERO FELT at home inside the familiar stables. He wandered past the stalls, whispering greetings to the horses he knew, before coming to a stop in front of Amator's old stall. Inside was a new stallion, large for its breed, its mane reaching past his neck, tail thick and glossy. Exactly the type of horse Nerva would buy.

A groom appeared from behind the horse and did a double take of Nero. A grin spread across his face. 'Didn't think I'd see you back here.' He walked over to the door and offered his arm, and Nero took hold of it.

'I'm looking for Nerva. He's usually here at this time.'

'He'll be by soon.' The groom lifted the latch and pushed the door open. 'You're welcome to come in and wait.' He stepped back to let him through. 'Watch this one though.' He nodded towards the stallion. 'Doesn't like people—even me.'

Nero watched as the wary stallion snorted and side-stepped, his ears flattening. The door closed behind him, and he heard the groom enter the next stall. Nero slowed his breathing, relaxed his shoulders and opened his hands. He had nowhere to rush off to and was keen to see if the horse would settle around him. Nero spoke calmly and quietly, and eventually the stallion's ears came forwards to listen. He extended one hand, and the horse snorted again before stretching his neck to sniff it.

'That was quicker than most.'

Nero turned to see Nerva leaning on the stall door, watching them. He had not seen the general in some time and was unsure how his visit would be received.

Turning back to the horse, he said, 'He's a beauty.'

'He arrived from Spain two weeks ago. We call him Avra.'

'Avra,' Nero repeated. The horse's ears pricked at the familiar word. 'Are you running him on the inside?'

'No. Vita runs the inside now.'

Nero turned in surprise. 'Vita? Really?' She had always done best in the middle.

'Go on, say it,' Nerva said, his expression slightly amused.

'Say what?'

'Whatever is on the tip of your tongue.'

Nero walked around the stallion, keeping enough distance so as to not spook him. 'She wouldn't have been my first choice for the inside is all.'

'Noted.' Nerva opened the stall door and stepped inside. 'Now tell me what you are doing here. I have no idea where

Dulcia is, if you are sniffing about for information.' He closed the door behind him and crossed his arms, waiting.

Nero cleared his throat. 'Who's your new charioteer?'

Nerva studied him for the longest time before replying. 'You want to race, is that it?'

'Yes.'

A slow nod. 'Why?'

'To win.'

Nerva drew a tired breath. 'To beat Manius, you mean.'

'I need the prize money and the recognition that comes with it.' His lips twitched. 'Beating Manius is a bonus.'

Nerva shook his head and watched the stallion for a moment. 'When I took your job from you, I told you that you were too hot-tempered, that you could not be trusted. You never disagreed with me.'

'Would it have made a difference?'

'Perhaps once I had gotten past the image of your hands on my sister.' He smirked. 'We both know you are a better man than the one you have become of late. Mila is an excellent judge of character, and she sees something in you.'

So had Dulcia until he had let them both down.

Nerva gestured towards the stallion. 'Now you want to prove yourself.'

Drawing a breath, Nero considered his words. 'I am your best chance at winning. This one is already beginning to trust me. I race clean, and we both know I can beat Manius.'

Nerva's brow creased with disapproval. 'Yes, I heard about your little races at the Trigarium, despite your best efforts to cover them up.'

'And I've been driving a biga chariot for Gallus. If I can drive while under attack, I can drive anywhere.'

'Four horses is different, as you well know.'

'I'm up to it.'

Nerva looked him up and down. 'Mila told me you broke a rib. Are you even fit to race?'

'It's already healing, and the race is not for another four days.'

Nerva looked to the heavens. 'Ribs take longer than a few days to heal, but I suspect you know that also.'

Avra wandered closer, sniffing Nero's arm. Slowly, he raised his hand and stroked the stallion's long face. 'The physician says some exercise will do me good.'

'Oh, yes.' A laugh from Nerva. 'I bet chariot racing is exactly what he had in mind when he spoke those words.' He wrestled with the decision for a moment. 'My father is not going to suddenly hand Dulcia to you because you beat Manius at one race. His agenda runs much deeper than that.'

Nero nodded. 'I know.'

'She is not for sale.'

'I know that too, but this is the only plan I have. I can't do nothing. I made a promise to your sister.'

Nerva sighed heavily. 'If I give you this opportunity, I want you to promise me something.'

'What's that?'

'When Mila and Remus leave on that ship, you will leave with them. They remain here for *you*.'

He nodded. 'Don't worry. You're not the only one keen to see the back of me.'

'It is not personal. It is just that I am not always able to look out for my sisters. And when Dulcia marries Manius, your interference could bring her to ruin, and I will not let that happen.'

'I wouldn't do that to her.'

'A bold statement given recent events.'

Nero's hand fell away from the horse. 'Everyone's pointing their finger in my direction, talking about how I moved in and tried to steal another man's wife.'

'Do you deny it?'

'Yes.' It was a swift reply. 'Dulcia has belonged to me since we were twelve years old, from the moment I saw her walking down the street towards me, from the first time I made her laugh despite Mila telling me she laughs for no one. It just took us time to realise what we were to each other. But if you look back, you will see it.'

Nerva thought for a moment. 'I remember that day. You told me you were Mila's bodyguard.'

Nero gave a sheepish smile. 'I was, of sorts.'

Nerva regarded him for a moment. 'So you are taking back what is yours, then?'

'I suppose I am.'

Nerva leaned on the wall and let out a noisy sigh. 'I am going to regret this.' He set his hard gaze on Nero. 'I can only give you the race, not my sister.'

'I understand.'

'Assuming you come out alive, you will go straight to that ship when it is over.' He straightened and extended his arm. 'I want your word.'

Nero took a firm hold of it. 'You have it. Thank you.'

Nerva clapped his arm before letting go. 'Get to work, charioteer.'

*I*t was the day before Ludi Apollinares, the games honouring the god Apollo. It also happened to be the day before Dulcia's wedding. She was restless, pacing the house like a caged animal. The July heat was suffocating the entire city, and the absence of a breeze meant no reprieve.

Manius had come by the house to spend time with her. He lay on one of the luxurious lounges in the triclinium, a slave either side, furiously fanning him. If he only knew how spoiled he looked.

'For goodness' sake, Dulcia, sit down. Just watching you wandering about like a lost lamb is making me feel hot.'

She walked over to the spare lounge and sat without a word. When a servant approached, lotus leaf in hand, she shook her head. 'No thank you.' She had fanned Aquila enough times to know how one's arms ached and how quickly thirst grew in such repressive heat.

'I would like to go to the market and select the flowers for your ceremony,' Junia announced.

Manius rolled his head to look at his sister. 'You have plenty of servants to fetch flowers.'

She sighed. 'But none with my sharp eye.'

'Since when do you care about flowers?'

'Since I have been locked up in this house for days on end. Come now, be reasonable. I have played chaperone without complaint and kept your betrothed entertained to the best of my rather limited abilities.'

'Fine, go.' He waved her off.

'Perhaps Dulcia could come with me.'

His eyes remained closed. 'My wife stays here.'

*Wife.*

Dulcia watched him from her seat. While the word was premature, a familiar emptiness filled her. One day she hoped to feel something else. She did not care about going to the market. The city walls were just another, much larger cell. No point in leaving if she was to be forced to return.

Her hand went to the ring hanging from her neck, then fell to her lap. Manius did not notice. That would require looking at her.

'People are going to be wondering where Dulcia has disappeared to. No one has seen her in days.'

'Let them wonder.'

The triclinium was large, comfortable, and beautifully decorated, but despite the high ceilings and open space, she always felt claustrophobic. 'You go,' she said to Junia. 'There is no reason you should suffer for my mistakes.'

Manius opened his eyes and sighed. Placing two fingers either side of his head, he rubbed small circles. 'Go. Perhaps you will return with a smile.'

She tried to remember the last time she had smiled. It was in the back room of the shop where she had waited with Nero for the guards to change. She had been curled up in his arms, wrapped in his scent, imagining their tomorrow. In hindsight, she was naive to believe such happiness could last.

'Excellent,' Junia said, clapping her hands together.

Manius was watching Dulcia, and she stared right back at

him, wondering what he was hoping to see. She was not afraid, because fear required feeling something.

'Can you leave us for a moment?' Manius said to Junia.

His sister looked between them before standing and sauntering from the room. Once they were alone, Manius got up and went to crouch beside Dulcia. He took her hand, his own damp and uncomfortably warm.

'We have both done things we are not proud of, but we have a chance to begin our marriage how we mean to go on. It has all gone too far now for either of us to back out, and believe me, I have thought about it.' He cleared his throat, searching her blank face. 'How do you feel about starting again?'

What was she supposed to say to that? Nothing. When she did not answer, he continued.

'I suppose I am asking something I should have at the very beginning. Will you marry me?'

She almost laughed aloud at the ridiculous question. He had asked it like she suddenly had a choice. If she told him no, it would change nothing. That said, it was the first time he had admitted doing anything wrong. Her thoughts went to Licinia, a victim of their struggles. She could not walk away now. Everyone had made sure of that.

'Your silence is unsettling,' Manius said, letting go of her hand.

She drew a breath, having forgotten to breathe. 'Now you ask what I want? You and Rufus made plans long ago, then told me my part. My answer will change nothing.'

'You are probably the only unwed plebeian in Rome who would say no to me. I still cannot fathom it.'

She folded her hands in her lap. 'Well, no was never an option for a woman like me—you told me that yourself.'

He drew a long, slow breath before speaking. 'So perhaps I asked the wrong question. The choice is really whether you want to marry against your will, resent the role and me, or, embrace it.'

'And thank the gods for my good fortune?'

He took her hand once more. 'I truly believe we could be happy if you would just give us a chance.' He searched her eyes. 'Still you hesitate. Still you hold on to that man.'

Yes, still. Her feelings would die with her one day. 'I am not sure I can ever love you.'

His jaw tensed. 'I do not need you to love me. I need you to perform your role, and to do it well.' His expression hardened. 'Can you just agree to that?'

Could she? Probably.

'It is time for you to choose this life for yourself.' He let go of her hand and stood.

She opened her mouth to respond, and Nero's face flashed in her mind. 'I can promise to try.'

*Gods, let that be enough.*

He nodded, stepped aside, and gestured to the door. 'Go on, then. Select your flowers. Do whatever it is you women normally do the day before you are wed. Just do it with a smile. The last thing we need is gossip.'

She stood, her tunic clinging to her back. 'Do you have a colour preference?'

He pinched the top of his nose, and then his hand fell to his side. 'Something happy.'

She stopped next to him, touching a hand to his arm. She had promised to try. 'I will not be long.'

THEY WENT to the nundinae where the flowers were freshest, two servants and a bodyguard in tow. Junia seemed oblivious to their presence, acknowledging them only when she handed them something else to carry. Roses, irises, violets, poppies, as well as some wildflowers and fragrant herbs. She smelled each before passing them off.

When they were done, Junia bought some dried apricots and pears to eat on the way back to the house. She smiled playfully at the merchant as she handed him the coin, then turned, threading her arm through Dulcia's.

'Very handsome,' she whispered.

'And married,' Dulcia pointed out.

Junia rolled her eyes. 'The handsome ones always are. It does not matter anyway. Can you see my father handing me over to a fruit merchant?'

She offered some to Dulcia, who took a piece and nibbled at it.

'I suppose not.'

Junia stopped to purchase some nuts. 'It is nice to be out of the house.'

'Is my company that bad?'

Junia's lips turned up in a smile. She paid the man generously and walked on. 'You are not the only one who wishes things were different. The key is to be discreet.' She leaned in conspiratorially. 'You do not honestly think I have not been with a man since my husband's passing, do you?'

They rounded the corner, ignoring the merchants who called out to them. Before Dulcia could answer the question, she spotted Felix and Nero standing on the other side of the street. They were deep in conversation, Felix gesturing with his hands and Nero listening. Her heart began to drum at twice its normal speed. She had been unprepared to see him. Yet there he stood, handsome as ever, the lazy slant of his body and deep frown so familiar. She had hoped it would be different, hoped that when she finally laid eyes on him, the feeling would not be all consuming like it had been in the past. She should have known better.

'What is it?' Junia asked, turning to see why she had stopped. 'Oh.'

Dulcia should have kept walking, but then Felix glanced in her direction. She saw him curse. Nero followed his gaze, and his eyes locked on Dulcia's. She could tell by his expression he was as surprised by the encounter as she was. They stared at one another for a moment, her earlier conversation with Manius replaying in her mind. She had promised to try.

Bruises coloured Nero's face. She felt sick as she recalled that night. She had been certain the beating would kill him. Her hands went to her stomach, and the nuts she had been holding fell to the ground. It drew the attention of the bodyguard, his eyes narrowing on her. Nothing good would come of crossing the street.

When Nero went to move in her direction, Felix caught his elbow and said something. He stayed where he was, no doubt waiting to see what she would do. The most sensible thing was to go straight to the litter waiting around the corner. It was time to be smart about these things. There was no need for Nero to be beaten a second time. Yet when she turned away, every muscle in her body seemed to object to the action.

*One foot in front of the other.*

'Dulcia!'

He was calling her, a voice she would recognise anywhere. Footsteps approached at a jog, and she closed her eyes when she heard their bodyguard stop walking.

'Let us get you out of here,' Junia said, threading her arm through Dulcia's once more.

'Dulcia!'

He was so close now. If she reached back, she could probably touch him if it were not for the enormous man parked between them.

'Just keep walking,' Junia said, her face showing no signs of distress. She was experienced at remaining composed in difficult situations. It was a basic life skill for the wealthy. Dulcia, on the other hand, was trembling uncontrollably.

'I'm racing tomorrow,' Nero called to her back. 'I'm going to win—'

He was cut off as he was shoved back by her guard.

She turned to look at him. 'Go home.'

He raised his hands and took a step back to show the guard he was no threat.

'Winning one race will not change our fates. Do not get yourself killed on my account.' She was surprised by her cold tone.

Felix finally caught up to them, slightly breathless. He cast an apologetic look in her direction. He understood their predicament better than most, because he had come from that world.

'I hope you told him he is mad,' Dulcia said to the dwarf. 'It is too late.' She looked at Nero. 'The time for heroics has passed.'

Felix glanced between them. 'That was the general theme of the conversation, yes. I might have used some stronger language.'

Close up, she could see small cuts all over Nero's face. Her fingers pressed harder into her stomach, and she swallowed down the nausea. Manius had been right, she could not keep doing this to herself and everyone around her. 'Race if you want to race, but do not do it for me. You told me to go back to Manius, so I did.' The words tasted bitter in her mouth.

He looked at her as though she were a stranger, then went towards her again, but a large hand landed on his shoulder.

'That's far enough,' the guard said.

Nero did not even look up at him. 'I promised to come back for you. Did you think I would just give up?'

She shook her head, face contorting as tears came to the surface. 'Stop doing this to me.'

'What?'

'All of it. You cannot win this fight.'

'You want me to stop trying?'

The guard shoved him back, and she flinched.

'You are feeding me these breadcrumbs of hope, destroying any chance I have of moving past you.' A few merchants and shoppers looked in their direction. 'I am stuck in this pit of... of *you*. I need to get out, but you keep pulling me back.' When she inhaled, it sounded like a gasp.

Junia tugged gently on her arm. 'Let us save it for our poems,' she whispered. 'Time to go.'

Nero linked his hands on top of his head, his broken expression mirroring her own. 'I don't know how to stop. I don't know how to give up on you. So I'm going to race tomorrow, and I'm going to win.' He dragged one hand down his face. 'Then I'm going to offer your father whatever I have, anything he wants, and when he says no, at least I'll know I've exhausted every possibility of us being together.' He took a step back. 'Only then will I board that ship.'

Dulcia covered her face with her hands, feeling the crowd's eyes on her.

'Let us go,' Junia said a final time.

Dulcia gained control of her breathing before looking up. 'Please board that ship.' She was pleading. 'You have always deserved better than what this city can offer you.' She turned away, her feet like lead. Every step away from him felt like another piece of flesh torn from her bones.

'Leave it,' she heard Felix say behind her.

Drawing a breath, she raised her chin. People moved out of their way as they passed.

'I truly hope he does not race tomorrow,' Junia said, tutting. 'Manius is going to paint the wheels of his chariot with him.'

Dulcia's eyelids sank shut.

# CHAPTER 33

*M*anius must have heard about the encounter at the market, the details no doubt relayed to him by the guard. He was in a good mood, so much so that he invited her mother and sister to the house to prepare for the day—her wedding day.

It was tradition for the bride to soak in a luxurious scented bath, to wash away her previous life, her sins, her indiscretions, so that she arrived at her wedding clean in every sense of the word.

It would have to be a long bath.

The problem was the scalding water could not wash Nero away. As shameful as it was, he was the one person she needed most at that moment. She would have given anything to hold his hand, feel the weight of his much too heavy arm draped across her shoulders. He would press his lips to her ear. '*I have a plan,*' he would whisper. '*I just need time. Trust me.*' And she was foolish enough to do it. Just thinking about him brought that familiar excitement, the one that began in her belly, expanding until it filled her chest and changed the rhythm of her heart.

'*I'll only let go if I have to, and I'll always come back.*'

Hope was a disease. And she could not afford to catch it on her wedding day. It was better not to mention him at all.

Her mother did not mention him.

Her sister did not mention him.

Junia did not mention him.

Dulcia was submerged in steaming water while the other women talked around her, thinking back to the day Nero had risked his life trying to save his beloved Amator. It was the first time she had faced the possibility of losing him, and it had turned her bones to ice. On the day of her wedding, she found herself with that same feeling.

Mila crouched down next to the tub, combing Dulcia's wet hair with her fingers. 'He will be all right,' she whispered, reading her mind. 'You both will.' She was a much better liar than Dulcia.

'I can live with him gone, but not with him dead.' She kept her voice low so the others would not hear.

Mila went to fetch a towel.

'First, we dress you for the festival,' Tertia said. 'I have laid out your wedding robe for later.'

Her mother looked so happy.

Fixing the towel around herself, Dulcia walked over to the bed, running her gaze over the pure white robe. The colour felt like another betrayal to Nero, as though she were erasing their history. If only she could bring herself to regret it. But the truth was she had never felt so alive, so hungry for another person. So *good*. She had imagined many times what it would feel like to lie beside him with her bare skin on his, her cheek pressed into the nooks of his body, to wake up with his arms around her. The reality had not disappointed.

Her eyes went to the woollen belt which would be tied in a knot called *Nodus Herculaneus*, symbolising the virility of Hercules, who fathered seventy children. The knot could only be untied by her husband. As she imagined Manius's hands tugging on the belt, a lump formed in her throat.

'Your hair will be divided into six sections and fastened with *vittae* atop your head in a *tutulus*,' Junia said, running her fingers over the fabric. 'We will crown you with flowers and finish with a yellow veil.'

Almost there. Soon she would be lady of the house, travel by litter, host dinner parties, bear Manius's children. She leaned her knee on the bed for balance.

'But first we must stroke my brother's ego by watching him win,' Junia added with a smile.

Yes, first into the belly of Rome to applaud the violence, danger and cruelty. She would eat the food offered, drink the expensive wine. She would clap for her soon-to-be husband, while praying to every listening god to keep Nero alive so he might leave Rome in one piece. He would build a life without her, fall in love again. It did not need to be her hand he held at night or her fruit tarts he ate. Perhaps his wife would make them with extra butter—just the way he liked.

'I still cannot believe you are soon to be lady of this house,' her mother said, looking around the room.

Dulcia glanced around at the rich tapestries, colourful paintings, then down at the luxurious bed linen. The room opened up to immaculately kept gardens, maintained by slaves. She had trouble remembering their names. So many, all moving about the house with their eyes down, as she had done her entire life.

'It is like a dream,' Tertia went on. She reached down and smoothed out the robe.

Dulcia glanced at Mila, who was staring out at the garden. Perhaps not such a great liar after all. 'Yes, I am very fortunate.'

'Bet you never imagined such a thing,' Junia said.

'Never,' Dulcia agreed, her tone flat. Though she had imagined being married to Nero so many times it was embarrassing. In that version of herself, she was free to race hoops along the Tiber, without it being a topic of conversation at some tedious dinner party.

'I should go,' Mila said. 'We leave this afternoon. The ship sails in the morning whether we are on it or not.'

There was that lump in Dulcia's throat again. But her sister deserved to return to her paradise—as did Nero.

'Sorry I cannot make the wedding, despite Manius's generous last minute offer.' She winked at Dulcia. 'Remus will be at the circus with Felix and Albaus, though not anywhere near you, I imagine.'

Dulcia would be sitting on a balcony, like a fraud.

'We did not think it was a good idea for the children to attend in case anything should... go wrong.'

What she meant was in case Nero died a horrendous death on the track, like so many novices before him. The children would never get over it—nor would she.

At Aquila's request, her mother was also not attending either of the events.

'Do not worry,' Junia said, picking up on the tension. 'I will be there to ensure all goes smoothly. But first, I must get ready myself. Manius will not forgive us if we miss his big win.' She turned to Mila. 'Safe travels to you and your family.' Then she strode elegantly from the room.

Mila's departure was not drawn out. She was not one for big emotional displays, unless it was anger, then she could put on quite the show. Pulling Dulcia into her arms, she whispered, 'Be brave and smart.'

Dulcia held on for a moment longer. She would not cry, would not risk her sister feeling guilty for leaving. Mila deserved to be happy and safe, and Dulcia's new life threatened that.

A few more words, a kiss from her mother, a tense smile from her sister, and then she was alone in the enormous room. She stared down at her wedding attire and sniffed. She had to paint her face for the event, and that was the sort of thing she was supposed to prioritise over a broken heart.

Staring at the door her sister had disappeared through, she wondered how many years it would be until they saw each other again. She would probably be an entirely different person by then. Her hands went over her face, and a sob escaped her.

*Vesta, give me strength.*

# CHAPTER 34

*N*ero had only had a handful of days with the horses. He had worked with them one on one, then all four together, playing with their positions until he found the optimum order. As predicted, Avra thrived on the inside, and Nerva approved the last-minute changes.

Nero had managed to avoid Manius right up until the morning of the race—Dulcia's wedding day. He had pulled up next to Nero, face hard and eyes narrowed.

'Nerva must be falling on hard times if he is letting you near his horses again.'

It was tempting to step up to the overdecorated chariot, drag him from it, and lay into his pretty face. Nero's gaze fell to the protruding whip. So many ideas, but he was not about to do anything that might put Dulcia in danger or jeopardise his chance to race. He turned away.

'Do not fret,' Manius said. 'She is in safe hands now.'

Nero straightened and looked at him. 'You better go practise. You're going to need it today.'

Manius's expression did not change. 'Why is that?'

'Because you're racing me.'

There was no hiding his surprise. 'I had heard rumours,

but dismissed them as such. Do not tell me Nerva is actually letting you race.'

Nero lifted his shoulders in a cocky shrug. 'Guess you'll find out later.' He turned back to the horses.

'You are going to embarrass Nerva, your team, and yourself.' Manius flicked the reins and his chariot lurched forwards. 'This might just be the best wedding gift of the day.'

Nero glanced over his shoulder at the scowling charioteer. 'See you at the starting gate.'

Dulcia arrived late to the games and was surprised to find her father seated next to Claudius Liberia. She froze at the edge of the balcony, trying to figure out why the sight was so unsettling. Then it came to her. She only ever saw him at the house. It was the only thing that connected them—aside from blood, of course. Outside of those walls they lived separate lives: Rufus as a key player in the senate, with his important friends and fancy dinner parties, and Dulcia with her trips to the market, temples, visits with her sister, and walks along the Tiber.

*The Tiber.*

'Are we just going to stand here watching everyone else drink the wine?' Junia whispered.

Dulcia swallowed, coming out of her trance-like state. She was about to reply when Rufus spotted her. He looked her up and down, then nodded towards the vacant chair beside him. It was an invitation. For the first time in her life, he was inviting her into his world, to sit by his side like the daughter she would have been if Aquila had been her mother instead of a slave who served in their house.

Her entire body warmed. For a moment, she forgot about her fear, her disappointment, her shattered heart. She forgot about her sister leaving, the children who would grow up without her, Remus whom she loved like a brother, and the two men with enormous hearts who shared their house.

The sound of a throat clearing pulled her from her thoughts.

'Shall we?' Junia asked.

Dulcia swallowed. 'Yes.' Walking over to Rufus, she bowed her head, then greeted Claudius and the surrounding guests, who watched her with interest. She lowered herself onto the seat next to her father, the one he had reserved for her, the one that announced to the world that he had a daughter who no longer lingered in the shadows.

For just a short time, she even forgot about Nero. It was a brief reprieve, a fleeting moment of feeling whole.

Rufus nodded to one of the slaves, a signal to tend to her, feed her, fill her cup, fan her if she felt the slightest bit hot. That was what a simple nod meant to a slave. She knew, because not that long ago, she had been that slave.

Junia spoke briefly with her mother, then walked over to join Dulcia. Before taking her seat, she bowed her head at a man on the next balcony. It was Caracalla. His eyes met Dulcia's before facing forwards again. Even the emperor's son saw her that day.

'Is he looking?' Junia whispered as she took her seat.

'Who?'

Junia gave her a look like she should know better. 'Caracalla, of course.'

Dulcia glanced at him. 'No, sorry.'

Junia let out a disappointed sigh and settled in to watch the comedic re-enactment below. Dulcia tried to focus, but her mind wandered. What if her mother and Manius had been right? What if she could make peace with her new life, even learn to enjoy it? Time could heal old wounds, open new possibilities.

The crowd applauded, marking the end of the performance. The laughter evaporated, and the people grew restless. A trumpet sounded, signalling a race would soon begin. And just like that, all the fear and anxiety poured back in, returning in a wave so forceful she had to hold the edge of her seat to stop from falling out of it.

'Something the matter?' Rufus asked.

She had not realised he was watching her. 'No.' She let go of the chair, blinking away the stars dancing in front of her eyes.

Junia leaned forwards until she could see Rufus. 'Wedding day jitters,' she offered with a smile.

Rufus nodded and turned back to the track.

'Breathe,' Junia whispered. 'It will all be over soon.'

THE NEXT TIME Nero ran into Manius was at the starting gate at the Circus Maximus. The eager crowd had already watched several gladiator battles; a play inspired by the Gallic war; a two-horse chariot race, where by some miracle no one had died, despite multiple crashes; and a comedic play that had the spectators in fits of laughter.

But it was the four-horse chariot race that drew the crowd. This was reflected in the sizeable prize pool. Four teams, twelve chariots, and only one victor.

Manius cast a sideways glance at him. They were positioned in the middle, one chariot separating them. 'Should have backed out when you had the chance.'

The driver in the middle looked between them before facing forwards again. Nero just shook his head. His nerves were starting to get the better of him, and the last thing he needed was to be heckled at the starting gate. It did not help that Avra was unsettled. His front hooves left the ground, clipping the gate.

'Easy,' Nero said.

It did not go unnoticed by Manius. 'They can sense fear.'

Nero looked at him. 'I've nothing to lose, so nothing to fear. Can you say the same?'

Manius's expression darkened. He looped the reins around his body and adjusted his grip. 'It seems I have much to celebrate today, including your departure from Rome.' He faced forwards again. 'Keep out of my way, Rat. I would hate to see you miss the boat.'

The crowd grew more excited, cheering, applauding and whistling. The noise rang around them as they waited for the gates to open.

'Easy,' Nero soothed when Avra began pounding the ground with his hoof. The horse swung sideways into Vita, who laid her ears back in warning.

The drivers braced, and finally the gates were flung open to deafening cheers. The noise hit hard, and Nero blinked against it. 'Ha!' he shouted, leather slapping rump as he spurred the horses forwards.

The thunder of hooves helped balance the noise that echoed around the open space. Chariots formed a line across the track, but before they had even reached the spina, a wheel flew across Nero's vision, hitting the driver to his left and knocking him from his chariot. Nero glanced in the direction the wheel had come from and saw an empty chariot being dragged on its side. Already the race was down to ten. In that short time, two chariots had blocked him in. Nero eased the horses back to prevent a collision of his own. He could not afford to get distracted.

The chariots made it safely around the metae, much to the disappointment of the crowd gathered at that end for prime viewing of collisions. He tried to block out the noise, tried not to think about Dulcia holding her breath the entire race. There was no room for her with everything else he had to think about for the next six laps. Yet she seeped in. He wished he was there to remind her to breathe.

283

*Bang.*

He was thrown sideways when his wheel clipped the stone edge of the spina. One rein fell from his hand as he grabbed the edge of the chariot to steady himself. Pain jolted through his side. The injured ribs had not had enough time to heal. Thankfully the slack of the reins was around his waist, ensuring he did not lose them completely. If he was thrown from his chariot, and survived the fall, he would have only a small window of time to cut himself free and roll to safety. He had seen men dragged and trampled to their deaths enough times to know how small that window was.

He collected the reins and regained control of the horses, just as Manius moved in.

DULCIA DID the only thing she could do in that moment—prayed like a lunatic. She remained in her seat, hands clasped so tightly in her lap that her knuckles turned white. Her father's gaze drifted regularly in her direction. She might not have known much about racing, but she knew that being pressed against the inside was not a good thing. Manius was moving closer and closer, his inside horse now in front of Nero's outside one.

*Pull back.*

As if he could hear her, Nero checked behind him, then slowed his horses. Dulcia released the breath she had been holding, drawing the attention of those either side of her.

'Manius is a very experienced driver,' Junia said for Rufus's benefit. 'Do not fret.'

They both knew it was not Manius she was fretting over. 'I can see that.' She had watched Nero enough times to know he could make up the lost distance at the turns, but she did not need him to win—she needed him to live.

A second dolphin went down.

Five laps to go.

◇

During the third lap, the pain grew in Nero's chest. The knock had undone what little healing had taken place, and now he was paying the price of his early mistake. There was nothing to be done but to continue racing.

The air was thick with dust, and he almost did not see the accident ahead where four chestnut horses lay in a twisted mess of leather straps, the chariot nowhere in sight. He leaned right and pulled hard on the rein, narrowly missing both the fallen horses and the ones he had cut off behind. A string of curses chased him.

Nero went wide at the metae, clearing the corner without incident and avoiding the cluster of chariots that fought for prime positions. He searched for Manius among them, then realised he was not there. Across the spina, he saw a flash of blue and realised Manius was far ahead, just a few lengths behind the Spanish favourite.

Four laps to go. Nine chariots still in the race. Five of those in front of him. Soon he would need to make a move to stand a chance.

As he neared the next metae, three chariots swept sideways in a tight cluster. They were too close, and two of them locked wheels. By some miracle, they made it out of the turn, but as the driver behind tried to ease back, his outside horse went down. Nero veered left, knowing it was his only chance at making it past the wreckage that would follow. Before he had a chance to think, the turn was upon him, and he had no option but to take it sharply and pray he did not hit the chariot to his right. His wheel lifted off the ground, and he thrust the weight of his body to that side to prevent it tipping all the way. The chariot returned to the ground with a thud, sending a shot of pain through his chest. He gritted his teeth and waited for it to ease. In a few more strides, he would be clear to make up some of the distance. Through a veil of dust, he could see Manius at the far end, preparing to turn. Two chariots remained between them.

'Ha! Ha!' Nero shouted, urging the horses faster.

Three laps to go.

At the metae, Nero took a chance and moved to the inside once more, slipping through a gap barely wide enough for the animals. He thanked the gods when he made it through, the heavy breaths of more horses so close behind him. He focused on the chariot in front, the only one remaining between him and Manius.

Increasing speed once more, he closed the gap between them, then tried the same manoeuvre at the next turn. That time, his chariot slid right, almost hitting a horse. The driver moved out of the way to avoid a collision, and Nero could feel the man's eyes burning holes in the back of his head as he shouted a string of curses. Muttering a quick prayer, Nero went after Manius.

'Ha!'

He knew the charioteer would crush him if he tried for the inside, so he went wide, maintaining the same pace. Another dolphin nose-dived.

Two laps to go.

The horses heaved, froth flying from their open mouths and sweat gathering beneath the harnesses. They seemed to be absorbing the charged energy inside the stadium.

Manius glanced over his shoulder and yanked his right rein. His horses swung towards Nero's. A wheel narrowly missed Avro's leg and would have ended his race if Nero had not been ready for Manius's dirty tactics. Sparks flew as his right wheel smashed into the stone wall. There was a collective intake of breath from the spectators.

Nero leaned left, holding the reins steady. When the wheel separated from the stone edge, he lifted his gaze to the enthralled crowd and saw something that made the noise fade and time slow. On the balcony above him was Dulcia, sitting at her father's side. She was draped in blue with a crown of flowers on her head. Her lips were painted the colour of ripe peaches, her grey eyes burning in his direction. She looked every bit a daughter of Rome.

In that moment she belonged with the elite, at the side of a powerful senator, on a throne of cushions, surrounded by slaves. She glanced sideways at her father, and he felt the loss of her. When her eyes returned to him, there was panic in them.

Noise crashed in on him once more, and time sped up. His head snapped forwards just in time to swerve clear of a bloodied grey horse lying in his path. Its front leg was tangled in the harness, its head restricted. It struggled fiercely as Nero swept past, barely missing it. His relief was short-lived as he noticed the remaining three grey horses galloping in all directions over the track. Men rode out, trying to secure them, but their trauma made them run.

The Spanish favourite was out of the race.

Nero steered left, then right, narrowly missing the panicked horses running at him. Manius was pressed against the outside, somehow making it all the way to the metae without incident. Nero glanced over his shoulder at the remaining chariots, a moving wall behind him. One wrong move and he would be crushed under hoof.

Swinging left, Nero aimed for the narrowing space between Manius and the spina. If he made it through, he would take the lead. But Manius was one step ahead and closed the gap completely. On instinct, Nero shifted right, going wide instead. He would make up the loss on the straight. The crowd cheered as they moved around the bend. But neither of them was prepared for the wreckage on the other side.

Two men were carrying a broken chariot off the track.

They had no choice but to drop it and dive for safety. Nero was able to swerve around it, but Manius was on the inside and had nowhere to go but over it. The horses leapt in unison, clearing the broken pile of wicker and leather. But Manius's chariot could not jump. He was propelled high into the air, with no time to react. His body hit the ground so close to Nero that he heard the air leave the charioteer's lungs. Behind him were the remaining chariots, gaining, waiting for their opportunity to pass him.

One more lap.

Manius was dragged along the ground, his skin torn and bloodied as he tried to reach for his knife to cut himself free. Just as he got hold of it, he was flipped onto his back. The blade flitted across the dirt, vanishing into the dust.

All Nero had to do was signal to his horses one more time. One final push and they would move ahead, win, and take the prize, along with all the riches fans would bestow on the novice charioteer.

Manius's horses slowed without the presence of a whip on their backs. He would likely be trampled by the approaching horses, or if by some miracle he made it to the end of the straight, he would hit the stone wall through the turn.

Manius's death was imminent, and Nero was about to win. So why on earth was he hesitating?

*Dulcia.* The answer was always Dulcia.

Peach-coloured lips, a crown befitting an empress, grey eyes pleading. She would carry Manius's death like a cross on her back for the rest of her life. She would blame him, or worse, herself. The man's death on their wedding day would tarnish her. Sure, she did not love him, but she would never wish him dead.

Pulling back on the reins, Nero's chariot slowed to match the pace of the runaway horses. He veered left, getting as close to Manius as he could without running him over, then bent to retrieve his dagger from the sheath strapped to his leg. A chariot swept past him on the outside, and the crowd went crazy as the red team took the lead. Nero tugged the outside rein and the chariot skidded in the opposite direction, close enough to Manius to reach the leather straps in which he was tangled.

'Get ready to roll!' he shouted, glancing behind at the approaching chariots.

With one mighty swing of his dagger, Nero cut through both reins. Manius tumbled a few times, then went still. For a moment, it looked like he might be trampled. But he managed to roll himself towards the edge of the spina, where he was snatched up by two men and dragged to safety.

Nero rounded the bend on the outside. Two more chariots overtook him, and on the straight, he could not catch them. He crossed the finish line in fourth place, his chest burning and hands raw.

*What have I done?*

# CHAPTER 35

*D*ulcia stood at the foot of the bed while the physician tended Manius. Whenever he flinched or cried out through gritted teeth, she placed a hand on his ankle. The aim was both to soothe him and balance herself. She was trying very hard not to faint.

His mother was on the other side of Manius, mute with shock. The skin from hand to elbow was missing, along with patches on his shoulders and thighs. The leather vest covering his tunic had protected his torso to an extent, but the bruising suggested multiple broken ribs.

'You are very lucky,' the physician said, packing up his supplies while his assistant gathered the soiled items. 'Aside from some scarring to the arms, you should make a full recovery.'

Manius said nothing. He was staring at the far wall and had barely said two words since he was brought into the small room. They could hear the crowd leaving the venue, their footsteps a constant rumble of noise above them.

'Never seen anything like it,' the physician continued. 'A charioteer from an opposing team sparing the life of his competition. The gods must favour you this day.' He closed

290

his bag and looked down at Manius. 'Is he a friend of yours?'

Manius turned to him, eyes dead. 'He is no friend of mine.'

Dulcia pressed her leg against the cot to steady herself, and the physician's bushy brows rose in surprise.

'Well, I imagine he will be a friend for life now.'

Dulcia stared at the floor while the physician gave post-care instructions to Livia. She nodded absently, looking close to tears.

'I shall come by the house tomorrow,' he finished.

Another nod from Livia. 'I will see you out.'

A few moments later, Dulcia was alone with Manius. Needing something to do, she stepped forwards to adjust the pillows behind him. She could feel him staring at her.

'Go on, say it.' His words were a growl.

Dulcia took a step back so she could see him properly. 'Say what?'

'Nero is a better man than me.'

She exhaled. 'Stop.'

His nostrils flared. 'You have believed it from the beginning. This is the proof you have been waiting for.'

She had never needed proof. 'He did not do it for you. He did it for me.'

A nod. 'Then I suppose I should be thankful you did not secretly wish me dead, or your lover would have ploughed right over the top of me.'

She could not stop the disapproving frown. 'Perhaps I should leave you to rest.'

He laughed. 'I was supposed to win today. In every sense of the word, I was supposed to win. Now look at me.' He raised both bandaged arms. 'Even if I could stand in front of guests to speak the words, I could not even have you in my bed.'

She swallowed. 'We can have the wedding when you are

feeling better.'

He stared at her for the longest time, all that resentment and anger directed at her. She almost felt sorry for him in that moment. He was not used to losing, and she could tell it was eating him up.

'You will marry me out of pity, is that it?'

'I will marry you because that is what was agreed.' She looked down at his arms. 'I am really trying here. In return, I would appreciate it if you did not act like the heavens are falling. You lost one race. Your body is wounded, and your pride, but they will both heal.' She drew a breath before continuing. 'Nero is leaving Rome empty-handed. He lost everything today.' Her heart was breaking at the thought. 'Yet I stand by *your* bedside while the people I love are driven out of the city.' She struggled to keep calm. 'You dare speak to me of loss.'

His gaze drifted to the wall at the far side of the room. 'Your bedside manner needs work.'

She could not stay there without crying or shouting at him. 'Rest.'

As she walked away, he called to her.

'I would have let him die, you know.'

She knew he was talking about Nero. Her hand sat limp on the door handle.

'I would not have let him live for your sake. I would have run my horses over him without a second thought. What does that say about me?'

It said everything, but nothing she did not already know. Nero had always put her above all else, and she had never felt so unworthy of his devotion.

'I will send your mother in.' With that, she fled the room.

'WHEN DOES YOUR SHIP LEAVE?' Nerva asked.

They were standing outside a tavern across the street from the Circus Maximus, the road hot beneath their feet.

Nero kept glancing across the street, knowing she was still inside. 'High tide, just after sunrise.' He offered his arm. 'I'm sorry I lost.'

Nerva took hold of it, his other hand going to the charioteer's shoulder. 'So am I. Though my horses are in one piece, so I will not complain too much.' He gestured to the coin pouch tucked away in Nero's tunic. 'I have never seen coin thrown down to fourth place before. You might have lost the race, but you won plenty of hearts with your gallant display.'

Nero had left the coins on the sand. Rufus Papias had no time for men who placed fourth. The moment he had seen Dulcia seated beside her father, he had realised that no amount of denarii could buy her away from that life. He had been foolish to think otherwise—foolish and desperate. It was Nerva who had organised collection of the coin and delivered it to him in person.

'It will fund your adventures south,' Nerva said. 'Mila will accept coin from you. I get tutted and shooed away when I try to give her anything.'

Nero smiled down at his feet. 'There's a lot of pride in our crazy household, if you hadn't noticed.'

'Hard not to.' Nerva's mouth lifted in a smile. 'But there is also a lot of love.' Another clap on his shoulder. 'Take care of Mila for me. I gave the same instruction to Remus, Felix, Albaus, and the twins. Hoping between the six of you it will be enough to keep her out of trouble.'

Nero laughed, eyes across the street once more. 'Unlikely.'

'Safe travels.' Nerva turned into the harsh western sun and headed off down the road.

Nero ran the toe of his sandal across the stone, working up the courage to leave also. One more glance across the street, and there she was—a broken goddess, her shoulders rounded, hair loose. Her crown was missing. That was not what he wanted to see. How was he supposed to leave her when she looked that way?

Looking both ways, he crossed the street, stepping between people and loaded mules. Then he was in front of her, feeling the immediate shift in the air that always happened when she was close. His hands hung empty, unable to touch her. She felt completely out of reach.

'Are you all right?' he asked.

Her eyes were immediately glassy. 'Not really. You?'

He had to take a step back or he might be tempted to pull her into his arms, fit her against the nook of his chest the gods had gifted him for just that purpose. There were so many things he could not give her, but his comfort was endless. She could bury her face in him forever.

Her lip trembled, and she bit down on it. 'It just about winds me when you move away from me like that.'

'I can't be close to you right now.' It would require a group of men to pry him off.

They were silent a moment, watching the passers-by, looking everywhere but at each other.

'How is he?' He could not say his name.

'Some scarring, otherwise fine, thanks to you.' Her gaze flicked to him. 'What you did…'

'I didn't do it for him.'

'I know.'

He brushed a finger down his nose, one hand resting on his hip. 'Tell me I did the right thing, because it doesn't feel like it right now.'

She looked at him properly then, her expression so tender. 'I was sitting next to his sister, behind his father and mother. His death would have hurt a lot of people.' She stepped closer, reached out and brushed her fingers over his before her hand fell away. 'You did the right thing. You get to leave with your head high, unmarked by his death.'

He nodded. 'And what do you get?'

She thought. 'I get all the unwed women from wealthy families glaring at me.' A smile flickered.

'They must really hate you.'

'Oh, they do.'

Nero drank in the sight of her, conscious of the time. He needed to leave soon or risk missing the boat. 'I'm sorry I failed.'

'You did not fail.' She clasped her hands in front of her. 'You were a true Roman hero today.'

'But it wasn't enough.'

She glanced cautiously over her shoulder at the waiting guard. 'I better go.'

There was always someone watching, waiting. 'Before you do, there's something I want to say.'

She wrapped her arms around herself as if she were suddenly cold.

'When I saw you at your father's side today, it was as though you had been sitting there your entire life. Despite what you might believe about yourself, you fit in that world. The slave is gone, replaced with this'—he gestured towards her—'magnificent thing. Now I struggle to imagine any other life for you.'

She looked down, and he could tell she was fighting back tears.

'I do not want you to go.' Her words were barely audible.

'I can't stay.'

She drew a shaky breath. 'I know. I just…' She took a moment to compose herself. 'I truly hope you find happiness away from this place.' With her head down, she rushed off down the street, her blue stola catching the breeze.

Nero knew it was the last time he would see her that way. The pain in his ribs grew unbearable. He stared at the spot where she had disappeared, as though expecting her to re-emerge at any moment. When she did not come back, he turned and walked in the opposite direction.

## CHAPTER 36

*D*ulcia was halfway home when Nerva found her. Rufus wanted a word.

'Now?' she asked, her mind so tired.

Nerva smiled. 'Is there any other time with him?'

He was right, of course. When Rufus Papias summoned, one generally came at a run.

She felt sick entering the great house, despite the familiar surroundings. Even knowing her mother was nearby no longer brought the comfort it once had.

Nerva led her through the atrium, the only sound their sandals on the marble floor. When they arrived at the tablinum, he knocked. Dread pooled inside her. She was craving solace and space, a moment to think and grieve. Prayer. Prayer might help. As soon as she was done, she would go to every temple in the city and throw herself at the mercy of the gods. She closed her eyes as she realised that nothing could stifle the loss of him.

'Come in.'

Dulcia opened her eyes as Nerva pushed the door open, He stepped aside to let her pass. She was surprised to see her mother standing by the wall, looking pale and tired. Perhaps guilt was taking its toll.

Rufus was seated behind the table. Aquila must have been out of the house, or she would have been knocking the door down trying to break up their little meeting. Dulcia entered, and Nerva followed close behind her.

'How is Manius?' Rufus asked, standing and walking around the table.

Was it wrong that the charioteer had not entered her thoughts since leaving the Circus Maximus? 'The physician says he will recover. Some scarring though.'

'Scars add character.'

If that were true, then she was going to be displaying a lot of "character" moving forwards.

Rufus sat on the edge of the table. 'And how are you?'

It was the first time in her life he had ever asked her that question. Whenever she was brought before him, she was given a set of instructions, a lecture, or disciplined, then sent on her way. 'I am… fine, thank you.'

Nerva crossed his arms, one finger tapping. 'No wedding celebrations today, then?'

She glanced sideways at him. 'No.'

'I have reports that Nero has left the city,' Rufus said. 'True to his word, he is on his way to Ostia.'

Just the mention of his name was like a punch to the stomach. 'Yes. I saw him briefly before he left.'

Rufus and Tertia exchanged a look, then Rufus said, 'He surprised me today.'

'I think he surprised a lot of people.'

'But not you?'

She blinked. 'I know who he is.'

Rufus nodded, then considered his next words. 'I enjoyed your company today, the novelty of a daughter by my side.'

Her throat thickened. *Daughter*. Even feeling the way she

did, she could not stop the flutter of joy at hearing that word. 'Me too.'

They looked at one another for a long moment.

'Your marriage to Manius will open new doors. The Liberia connection is an opportunity for you and me to have a more... public relationship.' Rufus cleared his throat, and if Dulcia did not know any better, she might have guessed he was as nervous as she was. 'I would think you would like that.'

Even as he approached fifty years, he was still the handsome man she had idolised as a little girl. Straight back, white teeth, broad chest. His hair might have greyed, but it still matched Nerva's in thickness. 'Yes,' she breathed. But the moment the word left her, she felt an emptiness in her chest. Tears rose, threatening to humiliate her. 'But there is something I want more.'

Rufus shifted on the table. 'And what is that?'

'Nero.' She knew what the confession might cost her, but the relief she felt at admitting it aloud was immense. 'I am sorry.' She pressed her palms over her eyes, as though trying to push the tears back in.

'It is the name that affords you a place at my side,' Rufus replied, watching her reaction to his words. 'The Latinius name affords you nothing. It is a name recognised only by gladiator fans.'

Dulcia's hands fell away. 'And that is a shame.' She tried to slow her breathing. 'Because he is so much more than a name handed down to him.'

Rufus's expression changed to one bordering on troubled. 'He came to me, you know, desperate for your hand.' He was not looking directly at her, but at the wall behind. 'I told him plainly he was not good enough, that he had nothing to offer.'

Dulcia blinked, imagining the damage those words would have done. 'He has always had a lot to offer. It is just that some things cannot be measured in coin.'

His gaze returned to her. 'You might be right. He sacrificed the race, the prize money, the glory. He spared Manius's life. It took me some time to figure out why.'

'For Dulcia,' Tertia said. It was the first time she had spoken.

Dulcia swallowed and looked at her mother. 'Yes, for me.'

'It might have solved a lot of problems if he had just let Manius die,' Nerva said.

She turned to him. 'A lot of *his* problems, but Nero is not that selfish or short-sighted. He did not make the decision for himself.'

Rufus was studying her intently. 'I see that.' He paused. 'But Manius remains a far more sensible match.'

She should have nodded, agreed, stayed silent. 'And by law, I must do as you say.'

'I sense some defiance.'

Her hands were sweating, her ears burning. Whatever was building inside her, she could no longer contain it. 'I do not want to marry him.' She dropped to her knees, tears streaming down her cheeks and hands splayed on the floor. 'So I am at your feet, begging. Please, let me go.'

No one moved. No one spoke. The only noise was the sound of her mother sniffing.

After a long silence, Rufus straightened, reached down, and pulled her up off the floor. He kept hold of her, and her heart pounded in her throat as she looked up at him. It was the most fatherly thing he had ever done for her, his grip firm but gentle—exactly as she had imagined. Dulcia felt a strong urge to fall forwards into his arms, to see what that would feel like. Instead, she planted her feet and waited.

'Earlier, Nerva pointed something out.' He kept hold of her arms as he spoke. 'He reminded me that your sister chose her own husband, and has made a success of it by all accounts.'

She blinked away the dizziness threatening to take her legs out from under her. 'Yes.'

'So I asked you here to see what you would do with that same freedom. Perhaps you deserve the same choice.'

She stared at him like a fool. 'Choice?' Her voice did not sound like it belonged to her. 'You... What about Manius? All your plans?'

'I can handle Manius. He wants a place in the senate, a foot up. We can still help each other.' He cleared his throat. 'Of course, if you choose not to marry the man, you would need to leave the city for a while, give things time to settle.'

That explained the state of her mother. She had known this was coming.

Dulcia's hands went to her chest. She could feel the outline of Nero's ring through the fabric. 'And you will just let me leave?' She was really struggling to comprehend what was happening.

'To be clear, I hope you will stay here, with your family.' He glanced at Tertia.

*'Be brave and smart.'*

Her sister's mantra came back to her. Drawing a calming breath, Dulcia considered her next words carefully. 'If it is really my choice, then I choose friendship and laughter. I choose respect and love.' He let go of her, and somehow, her legs held up. 'It has always been Nero, and I will choose him every time.'

Rufus nodded, walked around to the other side of the table and sank down onto the stool. 'That is exactly what your mother said you would say.'

Tertia wiped away the tears on her cheeks. 'I also said that, if you choose to leave, this time it will be with my blessing.'

Dulcia's expression collapsed, and she covered her face with her hands. Her mother went to her, hugging her shaking body tightly as she had done Dulcia's entire life.

'I am sorry,' Tertia whispered. 'For everything.'

Dulcia's arms went around her, teeth gritted to stop the tears. Such an emotional display was too much for a man like Rufus. 'Thank you.'

Her father rested his elbows on the table and looked at Nerva. 'Perhaps you can take your sister to Ostia. Pay her passage, and see that she boards safely.'

Tertia released her, stepped back, and pulled herself together for the sake of their audience. Rufus leaned back on his stool, eyes meeting Dulcia's across the table.

'I truly hope you made the right choice.'

*A* small boat carried them out to the ship. Then, one at a time, they climbed the ladder to the deck. Nero had sailed many times, but now he had the twins to worry about. They were already fighting over who would board the ship first. Remus took hold of Atilius, and Nero pulled Caius onto his lap.

'I need you here to help guard your sister,' he whispered into the boy's ear.

Caius stilled in his arms and looked out at the water. 'Guard her from what?'

'Pirates.'

Caius's eyes widened slightly, and he gripped Nero's arm. 'Real ones?'

Nero nodded and winked at Asha, who smiled back at him.

The journey to Alexandria would take around six days if the weather held up. From there, they would travel to Cana, then board another ship to Muziris.

'I'll take Atilius up,' Remus said. 'You sure you're all right?'

It was said like he might fall apart at any moment. 'Fine.'

'His heart is broken,' Asha said to her father, so much

sadness in her eyes that anyone would think the heartbreak was her own. That was how it was with people you loved.

Nero looked up at Felix, who had almost reached the top of the ladder. He had been complaining the entire climb about the distance between the rungs. Short legs were problematic at times.

'Almost there,' Nero called.

Felix let go of the ladder to make a crude gesture with his hand. Asha giggled, and Remus shook his head. Nero smiled to himself, glancing back at the bustling dock. All he had to do was get on the ship and let it carry him away from her. He could do that.

Once everyone was settled on board, the twins running laps of the deck and getting underfoot of the crew, Nero wandered to the stern of the ship. His gaze drifted to the men carrying crates and sealed pots along the dock, mules led back and forth, boats coming and going. Leaning on the taffrail, he watched, knowing soon enough the only scenery would be the open sea.

'You only have yourself to blame,' Felix said, joining him.

Nero watched as the dwarf pushed a crate of iron bars closer to the rail and climbed up. They both stared out at the port for a moment.

'If you had just let him die—'

'Dulcia would've found a way to blame herself.'

'She would have gotten over it eventually.'

'She feels those things deeper than the rest of us.'

Felix snorted. 'Might have toughened her up.'

'She's tougher than you think.' He watched another boat depart below.

Straightening, Felix drew a deep breath. 'I can already feel the change in my stomach.'

'We're still anchored.'

The dwarf rolled his eyes. 'I am perfectly capable of getting seasick while the ship is docked.'

A smile flickered on Nero's face. 'Six days is not so long.'

Felix punched him in the arm. 'Careful. If I throw myself overboard, I might be tempted to take you with me.' He leaned forwards again. 'I must focus on the horizon if I stand any chance of surviving…' He trailed off, eyes narrowing on the dock.

'What's the matter?'

Felix leaned farther over the taffrail. 'If my eyesight was not deteriorating with age, I would swear that is Nerva.'

Nero followed his gaze and found the man he was referring to. It did look like Nerva. But what caught his attention was the woman at his side. It was Dulcia—unmistakably Dulcia. Even at that distance he recognised her.

'What is she doing here?' Panic surged when he heard the anchor being raised below. He turned in search of a crew member, almost knocking Felix off his perch in the process. He grabbed hold of the first person he saw. 'You need to lower the anchor. I'm going ashore.'

The man pushed him off. 'We leave with the tide. The only way you're getting ashore now is if you swim there.'

Felix winced. 'You just had to say it.' He looked at Nero. 'I swear to the gods, if you—'

'Don't let them leave.' Nero grabbed hold of the taffrail, swung his legs over the top, and dropped down. He had forgotten about his ribs until the moment he hit the water. He cursed into the sea, bubbles rising from his mouth. When he surfaced, he heard Felix shouting at him from above.

'If you think I am going to have you rescued, you are wrong!' There was silence for a moment as Nero swam away from the boat. 'And what am I supposed to tell the captain? What reason shall I give for the delay? Love?' He made an exasperated noise. 'I am going to enjoy watching you drown!'

Nero treaded water for a moment, clutching his chest where the pain came in nauseating waves, then resumed swimming.

Dulcia must have seen him jump, because she was on her knees at the edge of the dock when he got there. She reached a hand out for him.

'Are you mad?' she asked, panic in her voice.

He took her hand but did all the work climbing out for fear of pulling her into the water. When he emerged, dripping and panting, people stopped what they were doing to stare at him. He looked around for Nerva, finding him at the far end of the dock, chatting with someone. When the general glanced in their direction, he stopped talking, looked Nero up and down, and shook his head.

'What are you doing here?' Nero asked, focusing on Dulcia again. 'What happened? Did he hurt you?' His eyes moved over her. She was wearing a simple belted tunic, reminding him of the Dulcia of his youth.

'Did who hurt me?' She was still holding his hand, unfazed by the water running down her arm and pooling at her feet.

'Anyone,' he breathed, realising how ridiculous that sounded. His eyes moved over her again. 'What are you doing here?'

She turned and looked at Nerva. Done with his conversation, he now stood watching them, giving what appeared to be a nod of encouragement to his sister.

She faced forwards. 'I came to tell you that you are wrong.'

He frowned. 'You came all the way to Ostia to tell me I was wrong?'

She nodded as people resumed work around them.

'All right. What was I wrong about?'

She focused on his chest while she worked up the courage to say whatever she had travelled twenty miles to say. 'You said I belong at my father's side, that I belong in that world.'

He tried to think back to their conversation. 'You do

305

belong in that world.' His hands went to her arms, and she shivered as water ran down her skin.

'No.' She shook her head. 'I belong with you. I have always belonged with you.'

Nero let go and took a step back. His gaze drifted to Nerva, wondering if he could hear what his sister was saying. 'Why did he bring you here?'

She drew a breath, visibly nervous. 'I am coming with you.'

Five words that nearly knocked him into the water. 'Where?'

She glanced at the ship behind him. 'Wherever you are going. Anywhere. As long it is with you.'

His hands went to his hips, trying to remain calm. 'What about Manius?'

'There are probably a line of suitors at his door as we speak.' She stepped closer, tentatively reaching for him. 'My father is going to deal with Manius.'

Nero's eyebrows were drawn so tightly that Dulcia apparently felt the need to run a finger between them. Her other hand held his wet tunic, as though he might dive back into the water and swim away.

'What about your mother?' He knew he was in shock because all he could manage were more questions.

She gave an exasperated laugh. 'What are you doing? Trying to talk me out of coming with you?'

There was pure light in her eyes, a light he had not seen in some time. His hands went to her face, cold fingers spanning her jaw and neck. 'This is exactly what I didn't want to happen.' His eyes moved over her. 'Now I won't be able to let you go when you tell me it's all a cruel joke.'

She tilted her head, eyes glassy. 'Promise?' Her expression turned serious. 'This time you do not let go. I don't care if Severus sends his army after us. You hold your sword in one hand and keep the other firmly wrapped around mine.'

It still did not feel real. 'Should I be expecting Severus's army?'

She smiled up at him. 'You are not afraid of one emperor and a few thousand men, are you?'

He studied her face intently for a moment. 'No.' It felt real then, and his body hummed with the realisation that she was going with him.

Reaching for the neck of her tunic, Dulcia pulled out a leather thread with a ring hanging from it. It was the one he had given her. She untied it at the back and slipped the band onto her finger. 'Finally. Everything is as it should be.'

He bent to kiss her, but she pulled abruptly away, a hand going over her mouth.

'What's the matter?' he asked, fearing she had changed her mind. He kept hold of her just in case.

'You taste so salty.'

His shoulders fell in relief. She had never tasted the ocean before. 'Is that all?' His mouth was on her again, and that time her hands slid up his neck, allowing him to draw her closer. The instant heat of her was spectacular.

'All right you two,' Nerva called. 'That ship is not going to wait forever.'

He felt Dulcia smile against his lips before her heels returned to the ground. She wrapped her arms around his middle, pressing her cheek against his soggy clothes. 'Do not let go.'

His arms tightened around her. 'Not a chance.'

'That poor man over there has agreed to take you out to the ship—again,' Nerva said, his words aimed at Nero.

In the water bobbed the man who had rowed him out the first time, looking less than pleased.

Dulcia slipped her hand into Nero's as she looked over at the small boat. 'Gods, help me.'

Nero smiled and squeezed her hand. 'First chance we get, I'm going to teach you how to swim.'

They walked over to Nerva. He bent and kissed his sister's cheek, then clapped Nero on the back. 'Take care of *both* my sisters.'

Nero nodded. 'I will. Thank you.'

He led Dulcia down to the waiting boat and stepped in first, ignoring the man's look of disapproval as water dripped at his feet. Turning, he lifted Dulcia down. She gripped him tightly, unsure. The boat rocked beneath her as they settled themselves on a seat. He put his arm around her as they pulled away.

Nerva watched them leave. Once they had reached the ship, he gave a final wave and returned to his horse.

'Are you all right?' Nero asked as a rope ladder was thrown down to them by a disgruntled crew member.

'I think so.'

'Because you are going to need both hands to get up that thing.'

She smiled and let go of him. 'I know.'

'It's high, but I'll be right behind you.'

She glanced over her shoulder at him. 'I have climbed trees twice this height.'

His lips twitched. 'All right, clever girl. But let's see how you go when the branches wobble.'

She waited as the oarsman secured the bottom before taking hold of the ladder. 'But you will catch me if I fall?'

He brought his lips to her ear. 'Yes, I'll catch you.'

Dulcia looked up to where the rest of their family had gathered along the rail to watch, then turned to him a final time, her grey eyes bright. 'Am I really going to see the pyramids?'

Her smile was contagious, and he could not help but grin back at her. 'Let's see if you make it to the top of the ladder first.'

He placed a hand beneath her elbow, and she began to climb.

# EPILOGUE

*D*ulcia fell in love with Giza. It was not just the twenty-five-hundred-year-old pyramids, as tall as they were wide, but the people, landscapes and colours. It was the land of kings, and she felt it in the atmosphere. It was enough to make her want to stay a while.

Nero and Dulcia rented a mud-brick house close to the river with two rooms and plenty of light. From their front door, they could see the water; from their window, the pyramids in the distance. Their neighbours were an older couple who fussed over Dulcia as though she were an abandoned child, even though she explained to Rana and Lateef that they had family waiting for them in India. For now, they needed time to rebuild their lives—together.

As well as helping with the spice business, Nero found a job tending horses for some of the local wealthy families. It paid for everything they needed.

Dulcia filled her days cooking, helping Rana care for her grandchildren, and tending her garden. She would carry water from the river, despite Nero's objections. She had to gently remind him that she had carried water her entire life, and she was no lady of Rome—nor did she want to be.

Most evenings they ate dinner with their neighbours, enjoying the easy company, the food, and the sound of children laughing, crying and occasionally fighting. At the end of the night, they would catch each other's gaze across the room and say their goodbyes.

She never tired of holding his hand on those walks home, never tired of going to sleep tucked against him, or waking up to find him watching her.

'At some point we are going to have to leave this place,' Dulcia said one morning. 'I am certain Rana thinks we are in hiding.'

They had been in Giza six months and had only planned to stay for two.

Nero pushed her hair back from her face. 'Are you happy here?'

'Very.'

'Then we stay.'

She turned her head to kiss the arm wrapping her. 'I can be happy anywhere with you.'

He drew her closer. 'There are no pyramids outside your window in India.'

A content sigh passed her lips. 'Maybe a little while longer.'

Two months later, a letter arrived from Nerva, with three smaller letters tucked inside. The first was from her mother asking after her health and updating her on household news. The second was from Junia, who wrote occasionally for the sole purpose of sharing gossip.

'Manius got married,' Dulcia said aloud.

She was leaning against the bench while Nero fiddled with one of the stools. A leg had come loose. He looked up at her announcement and was silent a moment.

'That's good news, isn't it?'

She smiled down at him, and the moment she did, he

grinned back. That was how it was between them, their happiness contagious. 'Wonderful news.'

Nero's smile faded. 'Last letter from Nerva for a while?'

She nodded. 'He would have sailed by now.'

'Can't imagine we'll hear much once he's north of the Antonine wall.' Seeing her expression, he added, 'He'll be fine.'

She attempted another smile. 'I know.'

He nodded towards the final letter. 'Who's that one from?'

Dulcia frowned down at it. She had been wondering that herself. Most of the people she had grown up with were servants in the Papias household, none of whom could read or write.

Unrolling it, her eyes went straight to the name at the bottom, and her hand flew over her mouth.

Nero put the stool down and went to her. 'Who's it from?'

She looked up at him, tears already falling down her cheeks. 'Licinia.'

He looked down at the paper. 'Everything all right?'

Dulcia scanned the letter. 'Yes, I think so. She is living with a cousin in Segni. She seems... happy.'

He leaned in and kissed the top of her head, then left her alone to read.

A month later, Dulcia got sick. Nero returned home one day to find her lying on the floor with a basin tucked against her. Despite assuring him that it would pass, she could see the worry on his face. He stayed awake that night, watching over her.

In the morning, she forced down some food just so he would go to work and leave her to be sick in peace.

'I'm staying home,' he insisted.

'Do not do that. I will be absolutely fine. Off you go.'

Nero asked Rana to check in on her, then reluctantly went to work. By the time Rana came past around noon,

Dulcia had relapsed. She struggled just to keep down water. Rana insisted on staying with her until Nero got home.

'I'm going to get the physician,' he said immediately, hands raking his hair the way they always did when he was not in control of a situation.

Dulcia placed a clammy hand on his arm. 'There is really no need. It is probably something I ate.'

The next morning, Dulcia rose first and prepared breakfast. She hummed the songs from her youth, as she always did when she cooked.

'Tell me you're better,' Nero said from the doorway.

Dulcia looked up, taking in the sight of him naked from the waist up. Her gaze travelled slowly up to meet his. 'Much better.'

A knowing smile spread across his face. 'I don't have to go to work, you know.'

Her cheeks coloured. 'Yes you do.'

He winked at her before leaving to get ready.

When it was time for him to leave, he lingered by the front door. 'You're certain you're better?'

'I know you already asked Rana to check in on me.' She gave him a weak smile from her chair, the small amount of energy she had mustered already spent. 'Please do not worry. Go.'

By the afternoon, Dulcia had taken to her bed again. Rana sat perched on the end, a wide smile on her face.

'How are you smiling right now?' Dulcia asked, pushing the basin away.

Rana clicked her tongue. 'The physician is coming past. I thought it best he take a look at you.'

Dulcia closed her eyes. 'Thank you.'

When Nero arrived home in a panic, having heard that the physician had been by, Dulcia was seated at the table looking like death. Rana met him at the door, her beaming smile probably more unsettling than anything else.

'She's going to be just fine,' Rana said, stepping past him and leaving them alone.

Nero went straight to Dulcia and sank down in the chair beside her. 'You look awful.'

She tried to smile. 'Thank you.'

'But still beautiful.'

'Much too late.'

He put a hand on her leg, the action cautious. 'I was thinking. The fish we ate a few days ago came from a different vendor. It didn't taste as fresh as usual.' He shook his head. 'I know where he lives. I'm tempted to go to his house, drag him from his bed—'

'Please do not do that.' She almost laughed. 'It is not the fish. I am pregnant.'

He stared at her as though she had spoken another language entirely. 'Pregnant?'

She shifted nervously. 'Yes, I am going to have a baby. *We* are going to have a baby.'

'Pregnant?'

She nodded, trying to read him.

'Are you sure?'

She would have laughed if she did not feel so ill. 'The physician seemed fairly sure, yes.' Apparently he had not considered that possibility. 'Please say something. I feel as though you are about to run out the door and never return.'

His hand went over her belly. 'I don't know what to say.'

'Because you are surprised?'

He leaned forwards, touching his forehead to hers. 'Because it's amazing.'

'This is a happy reaction, then?"

He drew a shaky breath. 'Of course I'm happy. Look at everything I have.'

She closed her eyes, her overwhelming affection for the man momentarily distracting her from the nausea. 'I think it is time to go to India, be with family.'

He did not reply straight away. 'Rana is going to be devastated.'

Dulcia could not hold in the laughter. 'She really is.' Pulling away to look at him, her hand went over his. 'I know it is hard for you to believe sometimes, but you deserve this. Me, the baby, to be unapologetically happy—you deserve all of it.'

He swallowed, his free hand going up to stroke her pale cheek. 'I keep waiting for it to be taken away.'

Her head returned to his. 'That is never going to happen.'

'I hate seeing you sick.'

She leaned into his touch. 'Forget today. Focus on tomorrow, next week, a year from now.'

He brought her hand to his mouth, a lazy smile on his lips. 'I'll never forget this day.' He pulled her into his lap, and she curled up against him. Strong arms went around her, gentle fingers stroking her arm. 'What do you need?' He whispered the question into her hair.

Her answer was always the same. 'I have everything I need.'

# AUTHOR'S NOTE

There are a few things I wanted to mention about the writing of this book, the first being that all the characters are fictional, with the exception of Emperor Septimius Severus and his son Caracalla.

I thought long and hard about the type of story I wanted to tell next in book two. After bringing the colosseum to life in *A Gladiator's Oath*, I decided it would be fun to introduce readers to chariot racing at the Circus Maximus—in all its glory and brutality. My mind is blown wide open by a sport where basically the only rule is that the first charioteer to cross the finish line wins.

There were some other aspects of Roman life that I wanted to explore in this book, one being the city's most relentless enemy: fire. Fires were frequent in the city, spreading fast due to highly flammable constructions built in close proximity. In July 64 AD, a fire erupted in shops near the Circus Maximus. Flames raged for six days, spreading to the slums and destroying over 60 percent of the city. We can only imagine the devastation.

The Vestal Virgins are also worth mentioning. After extensive research, I finished with more questions than when

I started. I assume they would have formed close friendships with one another, but what about friendships outside of the house? Sometimes an educated guess is all we have, and I feel such relationships would have been frowned upon. That doesn't mean they didn't exist, only that the priestesses would have been very discreet. As Mila points out in the beginning, they may have been independent, but they were at the mercy of the very men who granted them that *independence*.

Finally, I have used some modern phrases in instances where I felt the reader would not understand some words in a particular context. The last thing I wanted was readers coming out of the story to google terminology. You might also have noticed that the dialogue is not a true representation of that period, and that's intentional. I wanted the story to be accessible to a wide audience.

I truly hope you enjoyed this blend of history, action and romance.

# ACKNOWLEDGMENTS

I would like to express my gratitude to the many people who contributed to this book. My biggest thanks always goes to my readers. Without you guys, I wouldn't get to do what I love. Next, a huge thank you to my rock star husband who supports and encourages me even though my writing takes time away from him. I love you to bits. A big thank you to Joanna Walsh for your ongoing feedback and support. A shout-out to my beta readers, who each brought a unique perspective. Your comments were so helpful. Thank you to Kristin and the team at Hot Tree Editing for polishing the manuscript into something beautiful, and to my proofreader Rebecca Fletcher for catching everything I missed. A round of applause for my cover designer, Domi, from Inspired Cover Designs, for this *gorgeous* cover. And finally, a huge thank you to my Launch Team for your encouragement, honest reviews, and being the final set of eyes on my work. You guys are amazing.

## ALSO BY TANYA BIRD

You can find a complete list of published works at
tanyabird.com/books